DATE DUE		
MAR 1 3 2018		
APR 1 0 2018		

THE MAN ON THE WASHING MACHINE

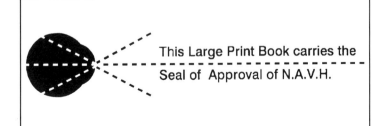

This Large Print Book carries the
Seal of Approval of N.A.V.H.

A THEO BOGART MYSTERY

THE MAN ON THE WASHING MACHINE

SUSAN COX

THORNDIKE PRESS
A part of Gale, Cengage Learning

GALE
CENGAGE Learning

Farmington Hills, Mich • San Francisco • New York • Waterville, Maine
Meriden, Conn • Mason, Ohio • Chicago

GALE
CENGAGE Learning·

LIBRARY OF CONGRESS CATALOGING-IN-PUBLICATION DATA

Names: Cox, Susan R., author.
Title: The man on the washing machine / by Susan Cox.
Description: Large print edition. | Waterville, Maine : Thorndike Press, 2016. |
  Series: A Theo Bogart mystery | Series: Thorndike Press large print mystery
Identifiers: LCCN 2016015582 | ISBN 9781410491701 (hardcover) | ISBN 1410491706 (hardcover)
Subjects: LCSH: Large type books. | GSAFD: Mystery fiction.
Classification: LCC PS3603.O927 M36 2016 | DDC 813/.6—dc23
LC record available at https://lccn.loc.gov/2016015582

Published in 2016 by arrangement with St. Martin's Press, LLC

Printed in Mexico
1 2 3 4 5 6 7 20 19 18 17 16

To Frank,
who never lost the faith
and who saved the bubbly until
the Fates were no longer tempted

ACKNOWLEDGMENTS

Thanks to Helen Norris for allowing me to borrow her San Francisco shop for Aromas; to Susan Dunlap, Judy Greber, Louise Ure, Linda Williams, and Gloria White for being the role models a writer needs, and for their unflagging encouragement; to the Mystery Writers of America and to Minotaur Books who jointly had a wonderful idea for a writing competition; to Kelley Ragland and Elizabeth Lacks of Minotaur for knowing their way around a blue pencil and for making me feel welcome at the Flatiron; to Melody Chasen for not being surprised and to Gabriella Kennaston Schuermann for sharing the ups and downs. And special thanks to my mum, Jean "Cis" (Gibney) Cox, who has taught me by example how to triumph over tragedy and paddle my own canoe.

CHAPTER ONE

Nothing was different about the Wednesday morning Tim Callahan died. Tim was a petty thief and a bully. I can't think of anyone who'll miss him, but being thrown out of a three-story window seems like more punishment than he deserved.

When I woke up, fog was obscuring my slice of Golden Gate Bridge view but sun was expected later, which is fairly typical. I pulled on jeans after a quick shower, and gathered my emotional resources to face another day of lying to every single person I knew. The effort took a toll I hadn't considered when I moved here eighteen months ago. All the same, for no particular reason I was feeling more hopeful that morning than I'd been for a long time. The dim sum aroma from Hang Chow's down the block was more appealing; the air a little crisper; colors a little brighter. If I'd been less absorbed with how my friends would react if they found out the truth, I might have wondered what the hell was wrong with me.

I walked down to Helga's coffee shop and strolled back with my morning tea. The climbing rose was doing its best to obscure the front window of my fancy little bath and body shop, and I made a mental note to have Davie trim it back. He'd turned a corner since he tried to rob me the first week we were in business and, somehow, he never left. We gave him a fifteenth birthday party last month. The rose needed attention, but the planter had been repaired and the whole building painted just after I bought it so it looked good on the outside, even if my top-floor flat was still in the throes of an endless renovation. My tenant in the middle apartment was good at handyman stuff, so his place was nicer than mine at the moment. A friend of a friend was about to move into the ground-floor studio apartment and then I'd have a full house.

Like the British Royals I live over the shop, and I climbed the two flights of stairs to my flat, still thinking about the rose because it was easier than facing other things. Lucy, a burdensome representative of her short, bad-tempered canine gene pool, lumbered out from the bedroom to welcome me back. She realized I was carry-

10

ing a muffin instead of Milk-Bones, gave me a disillusioned look, and went back to the bed we shared. Until a couple of days ago we'd slept on the Murphy bed in the studio behind the garage rather than risk brain damage upstairs from the fumes of paint and glue. Finding the new tenant meant I'd have to risk it, and besides, I was fed up with sleeping downstairs and commuting up here to my small selection of identical jeans and T-shirts. A couple of days before I'd had a mattress delivered and dropped on the floor of my bedroom. Lucy and I were both more comfortable and I could stop worrying that the Murphy bed mechanism in the studio would fail somehow and stuff us, still sleeping, into the wall cavity. I know — never going to happen. But irrational fears are irrational by nature, right? In any event, I hoped my new tenant had no Murphy bed issues. I liked the view much better from up here, and if I kept the windows open the fumes weren't too bad.

I wandered back through the mostly unfurnished flat, picking my way through the jungle of timber propped against the walls and the coils of electrical cable littering the floor. The building trembled as it does every now and again. Minor earthquakes can be shrugged off after you've lived here for a while. The first few raise your heartbeat a little. The ever-present threat of a big killer shake had added to the renovation costs because shear walls and foundation bolts don't come cheap. Even so, the result was a priceless refuge from my former life. So far, no one from my Maserati and Bollinger days had come looking for me behind the counter of a small neighborhood store five thousand miles from home.

I could hear Davie shuffling around in the tiny yard behind the shop and the vigorous swishing of a broom. I leaned out of the window and saw the top of his closely cropped head balanced on his thick body like a basketball. By some instinct he looked up and caught sight of me. "Hey, Theo," he called in his foghorn voice, "you need me up there?"

I shook my head and he went back to his sweeping. I'm not particularly maternal (that's English understatement right there), but I make sure he does his homework and try to feed him a healthy meal occasionally. Some of his pals have done time in juvie; I'm reasonably sure Davie hasn't.

I finished my muffin and sipped my tea looking down from my bedroom window at the leafy pocket park that occupies the combined property behind all the buildings on our block and reminds me of my home in England. San Francisco is great in a lot of ways, but I still get homesick sometimes. The way the residents tell it, the landscape has survived nearly a century of volunteer caretaker-gardeners with different and often opposing views of how the space should be used. Pine-needle pathways meander in random directions. Benches and strategic clusters of Adirondack chairs provide places to relax, read, or doze. There are several areas of lawn, a koi pond, some lush perennial borders, and a ruthlessly disciplined knot garden the kids use as a maze and the adults use as a meditation labyrinth. A large compost pile and a toolshed share the blue-collar end of the garden with the ragged abundance of a raised-bed vegetable garden. One of the swings in the cedarwood jungle gym was still rocking gently from the effect of the earthquake.

I was turning away when a flash of movement caught my eye in one of the third-floor windows opposite and very quickly something landed with an abrupt and repulsive thud on the lawn near the children's swings. I squeezed my eyes shut for a second, certain I must have imagined it. But when I opened them he was still there — a man dressed entirely in white, crumpled on the neatly shaved green lawn with his arms and legs arranged around him like a swastika.

CHAPTER TWO

I called 911 while I was tripping and stumbling down the back stairs and across the garden. Others were running toward the same awful rendezvous. A few of us arrived more or less together, breathless and stunned into silence.

It was hard to look at. With his painter's overalls gradually soaking up epaulets of deep red, Tim Callahan's crumpled corpse glowed like graffiti on the green velvet lawn. As usual his chin bristled with a three-day stubble, his truculent expression replaced by a slack-jawed, wide-eyed stare. Given his crushed skull — I looked away quickly — I didn't expect him to be breathing, but the absence of the life signal that gently raises and lowers the chest in a living being was deeply unnerving. The only things moving in the lifeless tableau that had been Tim Callahan were the tufts of wood shavings stuck to his hands and the front of his overalls. They quivered in the breeze.

Davie stood next to Tim's body like a postmodernist Colossus, still holding the broom in one huge hand, looking as if his face might crumple into tears at any moment.

"Davie, you should go inside," I said.

"You might need me." Then he reached out a big hand and patted my arm. He's built like a UPS truck and wears an earring in his nose, but he's still only a kid and he was asking for reassurance, not giving it. I rubbed his hand gently.

I didn't know what to do. Should I be feeling Tim's neck for a pulse? There didn't seem much point given the unnatural angle of his neck. I was saved from having to touch Tim's broken body when Kurt Talbot — *Doctor* Kurt Talbot — pushed Davie aside with an irritable shove. He eased the knees of his Armani slacks before crouching to touch those sensitive fingers of his under Tim's jawbone. After half a minute or so he leaned back on his heels and shook his head. He glanced over at me with an expression I refused to recognize as concern, but neither of us said anything. I don't remember noticing during our brief affair that Kurt's winter-cloud eyes are a bit too close together. Maybe I'd forgotten. He's good-

16

looking if you like the Nordic Snow Prince look, and unattached surgeons are thin on the ground so he doesn't usually lack for company. Unfortunately he has a lump of ice instead of a heart and no woman has been brave enough yet to risk frostbite on a permanent basis. I think shrinks call that transference: remembering how little Kurt and I meant to each other stopped me thinking too much about the awful sight in front of my eyes. Or maybe it's called something else. Either way, that's what I was doing.

Helga, who owned the bakery coffee shop a few doors down from me, came up to us and covered Tim's body with an afghan of brightly colored squares before anyone could stop her. It immediately started soaking up blood, which made things worse somehow.

"What happened?" she whispered.

Helga was a big woman — a voluptuous, curvy goddess in bakery whites — with golden hair and a fondness for bright pink and leopard-print Crocs. She was looking a little shaky, so I took her hand and squeezed her fingers gently as I shrugged the universal I-have-no-clue shrug. We weren't close friends, but we'd spent some early morning hours together in the past couple of weeks.

Her father had recently died and I was one of a handful of neighbors who'd taken turns playing baker's helper to give her a bit of a break. She and her dad had been close and his death had hit hard. It had taken me a while to get used to it, but people looked after one another here, and a few hours of shifting bakery trays and kneading dough before sunrise was the way we did it for Helga.

"Looks like he fell out of number twenty-three. That quake — he must have lost his balance," Kurt said. After another silent moment had passed, he pulled his phone out of his pocket and began to check his e-mails.

"Seriously?" I said. He slid it back into his pocket without a word. Doctor or no, the man was a tool.

"The earthquake had finished before he fell," I said. Kurt looked annoyed and, since Helga has a crush on him and tends to follow his lead — more English understatement — she withdrew her hand and looked annoyed at me, too.

Someone opened the padlocked gate to the street and gradually the garden filled with police cruisers, an ambulance, and a huge fire truck, complete with firefighters, police officers, and EMTs. The firefighters and EMTs were okay — sort of cute in fact

— but I had a bad experience once with police and I don't like them. Well, it's more that they scare the hell out of me. An English policeman broke my nose — they're not all as polite as everyone thinks — and American police are armed. With guns. My muscles tensed and my weight shifted as my subconscious clicked into flight mode and prepared me to back away. I ignored my very sensible subconscious, took a deep breath instead, stayed still, and faced them all down, feeling valiant. They didn't appear to notice.

We were kept isolated as the bustle and activity level grew, and our little group grew more talkative in a disjointed sort of way, but the conversation was no more illuminating. I was the only one who'd seen any part of Tim's fall; everyone else had only heard his scream. Helga muttered, "Poor Tim, huh?" at Kurt, who put on his sympathetic doctor face and nodded. I thought he might put a comforting arm around her but he didn't.

I knew something about Tim — he had put up drywall in my garage and stolen a pair of my mother's earrings, and he'd once struck Davie in the face and drawn blood. So not feeling too sorry, no. Shocked, but not particularly sorry.

Sabina D'Allessio bit her bottom lip and put an arm around Helga's shoulder. Sabina was a messenger — she rode a poison-green Kawasaki and hid her mane of springy red curls under a matching motorcycle helmet. I could see she was choking down a giggle and I was afraid to catch her eye since the situation was so dire. She tends to react to pressure that way. She was famous for giggling through her cousin's funeral and it didn't take much to set her off. I couldn't imagine anyone would appreciate it.

Paramedics bundled the afghan out of the way and were working over Tim. The five of us moved away a few yards, keeping together like a school of minnows.

"I hope the homeowners association isn't liable," Kurt said abruptly. He pays huge malpractice premiums and tends to worry about things that never occur to anyone else. "If it was the earthquake, it's an act of God and we're not responsible."

"The earthquake was over by then," I said again.

Kurt frowned and then his expression cleared. "Are you feeling okay? It must have been a shock." He reached out a hand toward my cheek and I saw Helga's scowl out of the corner of my eye.

"I didn't see much of anything." I jerked

my head a couple of inches so his fingers brushed the side of my hair. That had nothing to do with Helga.

"Good. You don't need more nightmares," he muttered, and dropped his hand. He was making nice and I felt a little bad for being a bitch. He used to hold me when I woke up from my nightmares. I was starting to get used to it when he ended things. He said I was emotionally unavailable, which was almost funny coming from him, but he didn't know the half of it.

"I'm fine," I said, and tried to unclench my jaw and smile at the same time. I was successful enough that Helga scowled at me again.

"Does Tim have a paintbrush?" Davie said. He looked worried, as he often does, but it was the most intelligent remark I'd heard so far. Where *was* Tim's paintbrush? His white overalls were smeared with blue and yellow paint and so were his hands — it was fresh, because the wood shavings were sticking to it. If he'd fallen while he was painting a window frame or something, the paintbrush would be somewhere near him on the ground. Wouldn't it?

"What the hell does that matter?" That was more like the Kurt I knew. Davie looked hurt and I tucked his arm under mine. I'm

21

only eleven or so years older than he is but I swear sometimes I feel like a hen with one enormous chick.

The knot of uniforms nearest to us parted in a lazy wave around a new arrival, a woman with deep, depressed-looking lines from her nose to the corners of her mouth. I guessed she was in her late forties, although she might have been younger and aged by what she'd seen on the job. Her round shoulders were hunched inside a red wool jacket and one was supporting a heavy Coach shoulder bag. She had nut-brown hair cut, apparently, with hedge shears and her expensive-looking glasses were faintly shaded. As she approached us, some instinct made the hairs on my arms ripple like the fur of a defensive dog.

She showed us a badge and introduced herself as Inspector Lichlyter, pronouncing it "lick-lighter," which struck Davie as funny for some reason. He sniggered and she gave him a look sharp enough to bore a hole in plate steel. See? I was right about the giggling. Davie's fingers closed more tightly around my arm and he took a half step closer to me.

She rummaged in her shoulder bag for a few minutes and came up with a notebook crammed with folded pieces of paper and used envelopes. She glanced at a couple of the folded notes, found a pen after another rummage, and finally looked up at us. Her shaded glasses reflected the light and prevented me from seeing her eyes.

"Did anyone see him fall?" she said.

No one answered her. I hesitated and watched everyone's eyes drift to the two paramedics kneeling next to Tim, the urgency gone from their movements. Inspector Lichlyter sighed heavily and shifted her shoulder bag.

"Pay attention, people," she said more sharply. "Did anyone see him fall?"

"I did," I said after another moment. She prodded the bridge of her glasses and turned in my direction. She made me uneasy. More uneasy. An inspector in San Francisco is the same rank as a detective in other cities — in other words not someone you would expect to be gathering initial information at an accident scene.

"And your name?" she said.

"Theo Bogart." Which was half true.

"Ah. The owner of the soap store."

"Yes," I said, and didn't ask how she knew.

"Did he seem to jump?"

I thought back to the little I had seen before Tim landed. "He fell facing backwards. On his back," I added when she raised an eyebrow.

"Are you sure?"

"Yes," I said.

She scribbled in her notebook.

"Where were you when it happened?"

I turned to point at my bedroom window. "Up there. On the third floor."

"Did you see anyone else with him before he fell?"

"No."

"Did anyone see you up there?"

That was an odd question. Wasn't it?

"I called down to Davie."

She looked at Davie. "So you spoke to Ms. Bogart?" He nodded, his eyes wide, and she returned her attention to me. "Your store opens at ten, doesn't it? I'd expect you to be there."

"I don't open up every morning. What does this have to do with the accident?"

She didn't answer. She stared up at my bedroom and then at the tall old-fashioned windows of number twenty-three opposite. She scribbled in her notebook again. A few of the envelopes and folded papers fell to the floor and a uniformed officer came over to pick them up. She took them from him absently before continuing: "Do you know the dead man, Ms. uh, Bogart?"

"His name is Tim Callahan. He lives in

one of the studio apartments and does odd jobs for anyone who can't get a proper workman to do the job." He also made up for his low bids by petty pilfering. I was surprised that anyone who knew him would employ him to do anything. I'd hired him, sight unseen, because my business partner Nicole recommended him. Lichlyter gave me a sharp look and I wondered confusedly if I'd said any of that aloud. She asked for my address.

"You know my store opens at ten, but you don't know my address?" She waited, pencil poised, eyes on me with the kind of resolution that could wear away mountains. I gave her my address.

She raised her voice slightly. "Did anyone else see anything at all?" She passed an eye over our dispirited group and apparently found us wanting.

"I heard him scream, looked out, and there he was," Helga said. She glanced over at Kurt and then down at her pink Crocs. Kurt and Sabina said much the same thing. Lichlyter wrote it all down.

Davie shifted his grip on the broom in his hand and gave me a worried look. Lichlyter frowned slightly at the broom, closed her battered notebook, thanked us all with a touch of irony, and went to confer with her colleagues. They stood back respectfully as she joined them. They had everything necessary to record the scene, from iPads and tiny video cameras to laptops, and I wondered why she bothered with the notebook.

They let us leave eventually. Sabina suggested we all go to Helga's for coffee. I gave her big eyes and she looked away quickly, hiding a smirk with a splutter and a cough. Inviting us all to coffee as if we were some new book club she'd organized earned her some shit later on and she knew it. Kurt left without responding. He smiled absentmindedly at Helga, who watched him walk away. She pulled herself together and she and Sabina headed in the direction of her coffee shop.

Davie had to go to school and I went to Aromas, where Haruto pumped me for details of what he insisted on calling our police grilling. Haruto looked like a hippie Mikado and lived in my middle-floor apartment. He'd been working for me a couple of days a week in the store. Before I went inside I heard Lichlyter's harsh voice tell a uniformed officer to arrange a search for Tim Callahan's missing paintbrush.

Within hours — gossip traveling at twice the speed of light — we all knew Tim had been hired by a new tenant to paint the inside of number twenty-three. Tim's paint-brush wasn't found, although the yellow paint in the attic room had been wet.

Inspector Lichlyter telephoned. She asked me odd questions, as if she was hoping to surprise me into saying something new. I told my bald little story twice more, but it didn't seem to discourage her. Without knowing why I felt anxious about it, I reminded her that Davie had seen me up on the third floor a couple of minutes before Tim's accident.

She said: "Ah?" but that was all the re-action I got.

She asked me about Davie, and whether I had definitely seen him in the yard at the time Tim Callahan fell. I insisted, with more emphasis each time she asked, that I had, although in truth there were several minutes between when I saw him and when Tim fell to his death. That's the horrible thing about police investigations — and believe me, I know. Everything suddenly has grave signif-icance and the difference between "now" and "a few moments ago" feels like an hour. By the time she hung up I was covered in sweat. I couldn't decide if I should be more worried about Davie or about myself. Before I had time to decide, he climbed heavily up my back stairs.

"Hey, Theo," he said.

I knew he was nervous about going home, where by this time of night his father would be drinking and waiting to pick a fight.

He sat on the kitchen floor picking at his thumbnails while I heated a couple of cans of chili. Canned chili is Davie's favorite food. He says his mother used to fix it for him. I sometimes wonder how he grew so big and strong on a childhood diet of canned chili and Dr Pepper. I usually try to feed him some vegetables, but I couldn't summon the energy to steam broccoli. We ate the stuff with corn tortillas torn into pieces with our fingers. Davie sat on the floor and I perched uncomfortably on an upturned spackle bucket.

"Did she ask you anything else?" Lichlyter had called him, too.

"Sure. She asked if I'd ever argued with Tim. But don't worry," he said. "I told her the truth."

That gave me a jolt on several levels. I thought she would only ask him about what he'd witnessed; she hadn't asked me much more than that. "You told her you worked for Tim?"

"Yeah. And I told her Tim cheated me and wouldn't pay me, the asshole."

My fault — I asked Tim to hire Davie

before I noticed the missing earrings. "I remember. Did you — did she ask anything else?"

"I told her Tim and I had a fight and Tim hit me."

My fault again — Davie got my mother's earrings back for me. "Did you tell her you didn't hit him back?"

"Sure. Don't worry. If I hit him, he wouldn't get up again." He grinned.

"Don't say things like that to her, okay?"

I told him everything would be fine and hoped I wasn't lying. He hung around helping me shift lumber and drop cloths out of my bedroom until nearly eleven, by which time his father was usually unconscious and Davie could get into their apartment unnoticed. I went to bed and, as usual, didn't sleep.

So nothing much was different about the day Tim Callahan died. He was a petty thief and a bully, and I couldn't think of anyone who would miss him. But it was pretty clear Lichlyter thought he'd been shoved from that third-story window, which meant intense police scrutiny for all of us, which meant our secrets might no longer be our own, which meant my life was going to be even more complicated than it was already.

CHAPTER THREE

A friend of mine says she becomes a different person every few years. I think she means it literally — she lives in a Northern California ashram — but I've noticed the same thing about myself. University flunkout, society bubblehead, celebrity photographer — I'd worn a series of personalities. But I'd never literally become a different person until I survived the worst time of my life.

The day after my father somehow managed to hang himself in his temporary cell at the Old Bailey during his murder trial, I fled my home in London with a swarm of paparazzi on my trail, willing to pay anything for a ticket on the first plane flying anywhere English was spoken. On a different day, I might have ended up in Australia or East Africa. Instead, nearly staggering with jet lag and emotional overload, I registered at the San Francisco Ritz-Carlton under an assumed name and didn't stir from my room for three days. When I felt the trail was cold, that photographers weren't going to be jumping out of the lobby palm trees (and believe me, the irony was not lost on me), I began to walk the hilly city streets. For three more days I walked, falling into bed late at night, exhausted and aching and mentally blank. On the fourth day I raised my head sometime before dark and saw a For Sale sign on an empty storefront.

I had no idea where I was — it turned out to be the nicer end of Polk Street, away from the rent boys and SRO hotels farther south — but it didn't matter anyway. I don't know why the building interested me. It was in terrible shape; most of the wood was bare where the paint had simply cracked and fallen away. Window boxes full of dead grass hung at each of the four upstairs windows and a rambling rose with no blooms but plenty of thorns smothered most of the street level. The rose was flourishing somehow in a broken brick planter full of old coffee cups and evidence that the neighborhood was home to at least a couple of dogs. The jewelry store on one side and the gourmet chocolate store on the other looked busy and prosperous; same for the produce place and the dry cleaner opposite. This ugly, derelict building was the neighborhood blight.

I rubbed a peephole in the dirty front window and saw an empty retail space with shelves around the sides and a counter at the back. I remembered something my grandfather once said, when he was urging me to buy a highly charged Thoroughbred he approved of: "It might be a risk, Theophania, but impulsive isn't necessarily the same as imprudent." I wasn't exactly feeling impulsive, but mildly curious and grateful to be feeling anything, I called the number on the For Sale sign and the Realtor hotfooted it over there to meet me within ten minutes. Her eagerness was understandable once she led me inside; it clearly hadn't been occupied in a very long time. She described it as being in "original" condition.

"Probate," she said. "The heirs were split on whether to sell and then couldn't decide on an asking price. It's been empty for seven years. If you decide to open a business here, the neighborhood will welcome you with open arms."

When I didn't respond she glanced down at my Christian Louboutins and smoothly changed gears. "And it's a great investment property. A few improvements and you'd have a real jewel. Rents here are sky high." She walked me through the pair of full-floor flats, the garage with its entrance on a side street, and the studio apartment behind the retail shop on the ground floor. She clearly thought the cracked, sooty fireplaces and the pitted claw-foot tubs were desirable features instead of expensive renovations waiting to happen. I opened a small door high on one wall and shut it hastily on a jumble of fabric-covered wires and round glass fuses.

Ten minutes into the tour it was time to shut things down. I had no idea what I was doing anyway. Before I could get the words out, she seemed to sense I was done. She led me down the outside back stairs into a small, dirty paved yard and through a tangle of head-high shrubs blocking a narrow pathway. I assumed it led to an access alley behind the buildings and that we would soon be back on the street where I intended to thank her for her time and get back to the Ritz-Carlton. Instead I sidled through a broken gate into a different world. Blooming flower beds, trees, a pond with floating lilies, a neat vegetable garden, a set of children's swings — it was unexpected peace and order, a haven, a sanctuary.

In a change of heart that should have given me whiplash, the city block of small apartment buildings and retail stores with their faces to the busy street and their backs to a hidden park was suddenly and urgently irresistible. That same evening I e-mailed my grandfather in England. He sent me a chunk of my mother's estate and a letter full of admonitions and reservations, all of which I ignored and later wished I hadn't. His solicitor made a connection for me with an American lawyer with the unlikely name of Adolphus Pratt who practiced in a large law firm in the city's Financial District. He was expensive, efficient, and discreet and handled the purchase through a corporation he set up for me to avoid revealing my name or my identity to the sellers. Before the end of the month Safe Haven Enterprises and "Theophania Bogart" owned a ramshackle building in Fabian Gardens. I hired a local architect who got the entire building re-wired, set up with Wi-Fi, and largely re-plumbed before I left the Ritz-Carlton six weeks later. I paid for quick results and I got them. There was still a lot to do in the way of surface repairs, built-ins, and some painting, and the kitchens and bathrooms needed gutting, but at least I could take a hot shower, use my laptop, and even cook a meal without setting the place on fire.

Aromas came about almost by accident while I was still wandering around like a shadow in my new neighborhood. I was camping in the building, making life bearable if not luxurious with an Arctic sleeping bag and some backpackers' supplies from the big sporting goods store down the hill. It wasn't the Ritz, but that was okay with me. The one suitcase of clothes I'd brought with me from England didn't suit my new life. I bought the first of my new jeans wardrobe and seven long-sleeved T-shirts at a neighborhood store and gave my other clothes, along with three pairs of Christian Louboutin heels and two Chanel handbags, to the Salvation Army thrift store in the Mission District. I didn't have any particular plans; I was fine being anonymous.

I was mostly eating in cafés and coffee shops and the regulars were starting to look vaguely familiar and exchange fleeting eye contact when Nicole collided with me one morning and sent my tea flying. After she replaced it, with a stream of breathless, laughing apologies, we were somehow sitting at the same table.

She was thin and vivacious and her face was bright with curiosity as I clumsily deflected her questions about my family,

job, interests, and preferred movies. Nightmares and night terrors were still making
sleep difficult; I wasn't sharp enough for
the machine-gun questions and random factoids that she kept shooting at me without
letup. She told me the best place for organic
produce was three doors down; that the
antique store on the corner was run by two
lesbians from Texas whose Limoges box
selection was the best in the city; and that
the variety store two blocks up was where
to buy anything from plastic Slinkys to case-
hardened steel wrenches. Nicole confided
another tidbit of insider information:
"Whenever anyone says they're 'from the
neighborhood' around here, it means they
live in Fabian Gardens," she whispered.
"These folks are all from the neighborhood." She seemed to know everyone and
introduced me casually to several people
sitting at nearby tables and the large blond
woman who was filling the countertop
display cases with muffins and scones.

"Everyone, this is Theo Bogart," she said.
"She's English and just moved into the
neighborhood. I go way back with a few of
these guys," she added to me as people
waved or smiled vaguely from various
tables. "San Francisco's kind of like that.
People you thought were out of your life

keep popping back up."

The Japanese-American man with the raffia-wrapped, silver-streaked ponytail was Haruto Miazaki, garden designer (and, I learned later, a sort of freelance security consultant who was paid to hack computer systems to test their firewalls). He looked up from his laptop and waved cheerfully as Nicole said his name. His coarse, powerful hands made the keyboard look several sizes too small.

"You bought the vacant place down the block on Polk, right?" So much for the anonymity of my new corporation. It was my first experience of the neighborhood bush telegraph. It hadn't occurred to me to swear the architect to secrecy. Haruto kept talking over my internal muttering. "Place was empty forever. Lemme know if you need help with the back. Man, those shrubs." He shook his head. "Way gnarly. Do you have a tenant for the middle apart-ment yet?" He hardly waited for me to shake my head. "I'm looking for a new place. Here's my number." He leaned over and handed me a business card. "Call me when you're ready. Save you advertising. It's me and my cat and the occasional overnight visitor. No one permanent yet. May be too late for me." He didn't seem unhappy about that; he grinned and turned back to his laptop.

A movie-star handsome, multiracial god in a pale yellow cashmere sweater came over to take my hand. "Welcome, and don't worry; you'll get to know everyone. You're the newest member of the neighborhood association and we have regular meetin's. Nearly everyone shows up." His mouth twitched as if he was suppressing laughter, and his intelligent eyes smiled, too. "I'm Nat. My lover and I have a jewelry showroom above Union Square. He trained at Tiffany, and if you ever want to commission a piece —" He handed me a business card, winked at me, and went back to his iPad. I was still staring at his profile when I realized Nicole was moving on with her introductions. Seriously, he was the best-looking man I'd ever seen. And he had a beautiful, syrupy Southern accent of some kind. And gay. Damn.

Sabina D'Allessio was a sultry-eyed twentysomething in black leather with fiery hair like young snakes and leather gauntlets flung over one shoulder. She stood and brushed a gentle hand against the cheek of the man she was sharing a table with. He was good-looking, with Nordic, white-blond hair and pale gray eyes. "Welcome. Us redheads have to stick together, right?" she said with a grin. Except her red hair was probably genuine while mine was an expensively maintained disguise for my natural blond. She raised a hand in farewell to the room generally before striding out to the green Kawasaki parked at the curb. At nearly six feet tall, the girl moved like an athlete and looked like hell on wheels astride that motorcycle. She roared off down the street and the light in the coffee shop was dimmer somehow after she left.

Her table companion was Kurt Talbot, a surgeon at SF General. His eyes stayed aimed in her direction and didn't drop to his phone until she'd been out of sight for a full minute.

The stern-faced elderly man with a double espresso was Damiano D'Alessio, Sabina's grandfather, "one of my favorite professors back in the day," Nicole added. She gave him a dazzling smile and he made an irritable little fanning motion with one hand in front of his face as if to brush away the compliment.

Helga Lindstrom was the thirty-ish buxom blonde behind the counter who I learned was the coffee shop's owner. "Bring in a mug and we'll keep it here for you — saves using the paper ones. I bake everything fresh every day — the best muffins and scones in the city. Right, guys?" she added loudly to the room. A ragged chorus of "Right, Helga!" came from the tables all around and she laughed. Her eyes flickered to the pale and beautiful Kurt Talbot, but his eyes were still on his phone.

"You have a nice place here," I said to her, looking around at the artwork on the walls.

"Local artists," she said with a wink at Nicole. "Those paintings are Nicole's, and the skateboard collages are by a guy I went to school with. They're kind of large for the space, but I like 'em," she said with a shrug. "The photography is mine."

"You're a photographer?" I perked up a little. A kindred soul, perhaps. Not that I could tell her.

"Not anymore," she said. "I'm all about muffins and lattes now. You look as if you could put on a few pounds." She clearly thought it was fine to make personal remarks. Good to know. I shook my head, a little embarrassed.

"Don't listen to her," Nat said without looking up from his iPad — seriously he looked *really* good. "You look great the way you are." But Helga wasn't wrong; I was underweight and hollow eyed and my T-shirts and jeans were two sizes too big because I'd bought them without realizing I'd dropped twenty pounds. Nat told me later, when we were each other's best friend and he had saved my life, that I looked so fragile the day we met he thought I'd been seriously ill.

I needed to get the hell out of there. I didn't expect to need a cover story so soon and I was telling lies at random, making things up on the fly and hoping to God I remembered everything. Before I could make my excuses to Nicole and flee, she started on a funny story about organizing a busload of Berkeley professors and multicolored, pot-smoking students to picket the whites-only Adelphi Club's golf course. Chaos had ensued and the color bar had come down. But that was in the past, she said; now she was an artist with an entrepreneurial, creative spirit and a hunger for success. As she chattered I felt myself relax. Being near her was like warming my cold hands by a campfire.

She told me the idea she'd had for a luxury bath and body shop. A chemist friend of hers made creams and lotions and vitamin face masks. I got the impression he was transitioning from a less acceptable line of chemical products and Nicole was anxious to support him in his new, legal endeavor. We tossed ideas for a store name back and forth as a joke and within minutes had agreed on Aromas. When she showed up a few days later with a business plan, we sealed the deal and within weeks we were open for business.

Haruto moved into my middle flat with his Siamese cat, Gar Wood (don't ask). Haruto tamed my overgrown shrubs, refinished the hardwood floors in both flats, installed new light fixtures, and offered to maintain the window boxes on the front of the building in exchange for a break on the rent. So with a series of what-the-hell impulses I became property owner, landlord, and shopkeeper in one dramatic month. Oh, and dog owner. Lucy showed up at the back door and soon shredded my $400 sleeping bag. No one claimed her at the city pound — big surprise — and I felt sorry for her.

Things hadn't always been perfect in the last year and a half (that's more English understatement there), but nowadays I had a quiet life and I was willing to do a lot to preserve it. I selfishly — and fervently — hoped that witnessing Tim Callahan's death wouldn't change that.

CHAPTER FOUR

The second shoe dropped on Friday, two days after Tim died, although at the time it felt inconsequential. Nicole had asked a month before if a friend of a friend could stay in the studio for a few weeks without paying an arm and a leg in rent. He worked for a nonprofit, he was in the city temporarily, nonsmoker, no pets. I vaguely wondered which of her discarded lovers this was. Sure, I said. I've got to stop doing that.

A few minutes before ten o'clock I walked up the hill from the bank and Helga's with my morning mug of tea in one hand and my phone in the other. My new tenant was Bramwell Turlough — great name — and he wanted to move into the studio behind Aromas at the end of the week. And that was the other shoe. Doesn't seem all that dramatic, right? That's what I thought at the time, too.

I stuffed my phone in the back pocket of

my jeans as I got to the front door of Aromas and watched my reflection in the glass door tweak a couple of dead leaves off the rose. I looked pretty much the same as usual, which is to say unremarkable. I'd gained a few pounds in the last year but I was still pretty lean. I always wear jeans and a long-sleeved T-shirt. The long sleeves cover some scar tissue. I'm self-conscious about my nose, which isn't so easy to hide; one of these days I should get it fixed. It's not hideous, just a little off-kilter from the time it was broken.

I tugged at another leaf, stabbed myself on a thorn, and irritably sucked the small spot of blood. Resting my tea on the planter wall, I unlocked the door and sidled past a carton of new stock from an English supplier in the middle of the floor. Scent is evocative and their soaps and lotions were my mother's favorites. Nicole must have dropped them off earlier that morning or the evening before. She was still occasionally conscientious, just not reliably so.

It hadn't taken me long to learn that Nicole's enthusiasms tended to be short-lived as she leaped to the next bright, shiny thing, which is why both my apartment renovations and Aromas were currently in my less-than-competent hands. When she'd learned

I was living with eighty-year-old bathroom fixtures and a stove from the 1970s, Nicole had taken the lead on my renovation. She found out I had money to spend and she spent it with the energy and enthusiasm I conspicuously lacked. She was a good artist with a knack for design; she and my architect were soul mates. But she gradually lost interest.

I'd also realized that Nicole's hectic, 24-7 life relied on artificial stimulants. Her triple espresso grande latte phase had passed, and lately she was relying on occasional cocaine. I had secrets of my own; I didn't feel justified, or qualified, to poke around in her life. But in the past few weeks she had simply dropped out for days at a time, and I was keeping Aromas afloat by myself. I could have let it wither on the vine — I hadn't intended it to be my life's work — but I was proud of it and didn't want to let it go yet. It was making a small profit, Davie and Haruto relied on us, I was making friends in the neighborhood, and most of all, Aromas gave me a comfortable place to hide in my Potemkin life.

The shop was small, but packed tight. Unguents, lotions, creams, shampoos — we carried every beauty and bath aid we could find a customer for. Much of our merchan-

45

dise was in plastic gallon jugs sent to us by Nicole's chemist friend, whose name was Alex. Nicole called him Smart Alex. We kept the jugs in a dedicated alcove, so the open shelf space could be devoted to the more attractive jars, bottles, and boxes.

High on the walls above the top shelves were some of my sepia-tone photographs of wildflowers, hand-colored and embellished by Nicole. She won an art show prize with a series of them. There was the faintest scent of turpentine on her hands the day we met, and I wondered later whether I had been attracted to her because of the pleasant memories it raised. My father had been an artist.

I tied bunches of dried flowers and herbs to the rafters when we opened up — more to hide the exposed pipes than anything — but we added to them over the months so that now the "ceiling" is a patchwork of lavender, basil, dried roses, statice, straw flowers, hydrangeas, and others so jammed together that it's a game with our regular customers to identify them. They bring us sage and Indian paintbrush and other flowers from their vacations; every now and again someone brings in a herb or wildflower book and points out what they've discovered in the ceiling. It was fun for a while.

Nicole and I were on the schedule together, which meant I was almost sure to be alone all morning. Remembering that Davie wouldn't be in until noon gave me a sudden pang of anxiety for him. I didn't like the way Lichlyter had harped on his relationship with Tim Callahan.

I counted out $150 in various denominations to place in the cash drawer and broke open four fresh rolls of quarters — people often came into the store to ask us for change for the parking meters — wondering what the hell I was going to do about Nicole. It wasn't only the cocaine; we were disagreeing about every little thing.

I was only half paying attention as I served my first customer of the day. I hadn't seen or heard anything new about my high-profile English family for months. I was beginning to think I might be yesterday's news at last. Which meant that I could maybe come out of hiding — if I could find a way to explain a change of name and appearance and personal history to everyone who had befriended me since I moved to San Francisco. For the time being I was stuck with my lies — a classic case of being, not only hoist on, but crushed under the weight of my own petard.

"Thanks so much. Hope you enjoy the herbal bath salts," I said with a friendly shopkeeper's smile in my carefully cultivated trans-Atlantic accent. The woman's expression changed to thoughtful speculation as I handed over the turquoise-and-white-striped bag and I braced myself.

"Has anyone ever said you look like that girl — what was her name? You know, the photographer, the daughter of that artist who murdered his wife — remember? Except she was blond, wasn't she?"

"Hmm. Doesn't sound familiar."

"It was a huge deal a couple of years ago. He used the one name, Theopold. He painted all those London street scenes with rock stars and actors in them — you've seen them. There was a PBS special. He did a famous portrait of the Queen, too. The one she didn't like and then Paul McCartney bought it." She looked at me inquiringly.

"Oh, right," I said. "Now I remember." Because it was ridiculous to keep denying I knew about one of the most notorious murder trials since O.J.

"Anyway, his wife was a cousin to the Duke of, I forget where, and he shot her and hanged himself during the trial. There were articles in *People* and *Us* and *Vanity*

Fair and one of the books made the best-seller list." I listened as if she was telling me something mildly interesting instead of something that tore my life to pieces.

"Are you talking about that artist who murdered his wife?" Another customer joined us and came to the counter with four large jars of shea butter. Seriously, what do people do with it all? Is there some new kink I don't know about? "What an ordeal for the family." He shook his head sympathetically.

"I was saying to this gal I thought she looked like the daughter."

He tipped his head, considering. "Well, a little. But wasn't she a blonde? And a hot-shit photographer or something? Always jumping into fountains and getting arrested. A real airhead with more money than good sense. Not like this lady here." He smiled kindly. I rang up his purchases. "Have a good day, you guys," I said, emphasizing the American part of trans-Atlantic.

I felt partly responsible for my mother's death — she and I had both known my father was emotionally unstable and getting worse. After their separation she often said that if anything happened, I was to try to help him. She thought he might try to hurt himself; neither of us expected his rages and madness to result in murder.

My broken nose was a legacy of the moment of his arrest when I'd tried to intervene. The police apologized afterward.

Except for conversations like this one, I mostly managed to keep from thinking about it too much. All the same, I felt my stomach clench and made it to the bathroom in time to empty it of my morning muffin.

Okay, so maybe I wasn't quite as ready to come out from hiding as I thought.

When I came back into the shop I saw Inspector Lichlyter approaching outside. She raised a hand in salute and I waved her inside, reflecting that even a bad day can always get worse.

"Good morning. I happened to be passing," she said. Unlikely. She took off her shaded glasses to clean them on a crumpled tissue and before replacing them she looked directly at me. For the first time, I saw that one of her eyes was blue and the other was brown. The disparity gave her expression a built-in skepticism, like a permanently raised eyebrow. She settled the glasses on her nose and the anomaly disappeared; both eyes looked brown.

I expected her to ask me more questions about Tim Callahan, so her opening was a surprise.

"I'm looking for a gift for a friend," she said. She stirred the contents of that Coach shoulder bag and came up with several notebooks and a pile of used envelopes held together with a rubber band. She spread them out on the counter and read aloud from one of them.

"She's into alternative treatments and natural vitamins. Can you think of something?"

I tried to settle my stomach by force of will. "We have a line of natural lotions and cosmetics without preservatives. They have to be refrigerated, otherwise they spoil, but they're very popular."

A middle-aged couple wandered in and started to browse; I gave them a friendly smile.

"She doesn't have a refrigerator." She picked up a small muslin bag from a basket on the counter. "What's this?"

A man came in alone and started to read lip balm labels. He was wearing purple running shorts and nothing else, not even shoes. I gave him a quick once-over, but he was absorbed by the lip balm labels so I left him to it.

"You can fill the bag with your choice of

herbs from those tubs next to the window," I said.

"Like what?"

The tubs were labeled, but I launched into my act anyway. "There's chamomile to use in a rinse after you shampoo to bring out blond highlights in your hair; or rosemary for brunettes. Or a combination of several herbs that you can use as a sort of *bouquet garni* in the tub. Lavender, lemon verbena, rose petals. Pennyroyal if you have fleas. Just kidding," I added as her eyelids flickered.

She didn't smile. "She doesn't have a tub. Showers. What about face treatments?"

"Avocado? Strawberry? Lemon astringent?" I pulled an assortment off the shelves and lined them up on the counter.

"Sounds like a supermarket produce department," she said, and sighed heavily. I tried to imagine what her friend could be like — a frothy, bubbly type or another depressive like herself?

A regular customer came in and picked up products on her way to the cash register, chatting to me as she went. She handed me one of our reusable bottles and I filled it with aloe shampoo from a plastic gallon jug. I rang up her purchases, wrapped everything, and handed her the shopping bag. She was in and out of the shop in less than five minutes leaving nearly sixty dollars behind. I gave her a cheerful wave as she left.

"What did you put in that bottle?" Lichlyter said. She was chewing the lipstick from her bottom lip.

"We have an in-house line of lotions, creams, shampoos, cream rinses, that kind of thing. If you have your own container we can fill it with any one of about a dozen different products. Or we'll start you off with one of our bottles; your friend can bring it in to have it refilled when it's all used up."

"She doesn't get out." Her expression sharpened. "You make your own products? Do you have a lab?"

Somehow I didn't want to mention Smart Alex. "We buy them in bulk and put our own labels on them." She appeared to lose interest. I looked around for inspiration. The sooner her shopping was done, presumably, the sooner she'd leave. "Is your friend allergic to animal products?"

"I don't know."

"There's a lanolin-based hand and body lotion made by Gibney Brothers; but some people are allergic to lanolin. And it's expensive."

My other two customers were beginning

to look seriously at some Gibney Brothers lotions.

"We're the only outlet in the city for those products besides Gump's," I said to them with another professional smile. "I think I have a couple of samples here. . . ." I pulled out two minuscule plastic pillow packs from under the counter and held them out. The woman made up her mind and carried a couple of the ribbed glass bottles over to the counter.

"I'll take these. They're so beautiful," she said. People often say that, as if good-looking bottles with red and gold labels are a guarantee of quality inside. For some reason I thought briefly of Kurt.

I tossed the samples into the bag, wrapped and rang up the purchases, and then watched in dismay as they left and four teenage girls, pushing and shoving and giggling, fell into the shop. They were a typically San Francisco quartet — one pink-lipped blonde; one African-American with neat cornrows; one stocky Asian girl with a ponytail; one Latina with an elaborate chignon and heavy makeup — and I knew them of old.

"No school today, ladies?" I said.

They ignored me and went on clowning, one of them splitting off from her crew while the other three knocked over a display of sea sponges.

"I'd like you to meet Inspector Lichlyter of the San Francisco Police Department," I said, somehow keeping an eye on all four at once.

Still giggling, but empty-handed, they sidled out of the door. Lichlyter turned to me. "That looked like an incomplete pass."

I picked up the scattered sponges. "They were in here a month ago and after they left we realized they'd lifted forty or fifty dollars' worth of small items. It's like a game for some people. Once they succeed, they come back and try again."

"I've noticed a similar pattern in my line of work," she said heavily. "What were we talking about?"

"Lanolin, I think."

The man in the purple shorts left without buying anything. I went over to check on the lip balms, but there were no gaps indicating a missing tube. Not that he'd had anywhere to conceal it.

"Lanolin. It's from an animal?"

"From sheep. In its natural form it looks like something to grease an axle with — it's the stuff that makes wool water repellent." I reached over and took a bottle of the lotion off a nearby shelf.

"Wool isn't water repellent."

"While the sheep is wearing it, it is," I assured her. "Modern wool processing removes a lot of it, but that's why the original Aran sweaters were so popular with Irish fishermen — they were as good as a raincoat. Warm, too."

For some reason she looked wary. "You know some pretty obscure things."

I felt suddenly cautious myself. Wariness so often leads to mistrust. And in this case it went both ways. "You probably know some pretty obscure things yourself," I said. She pursed her lips in acknowledgment. I went on chatting as if nothing had changed, using my shopkeeper's cordiality as a shield: "I have to know these things. You know what it's like in this city — everyone wants to know if your products are organically grown, hypoallergenic, and politically correct. Is that handwoven Guatemalan scrub mitt from an Indian craft cooperative? Are those sponges harvested responsibly? Is this shampoo tested on rabbits?"

She looked at the colorful jars and bottles in front of her and up at me. "You sound — amused?" She said it tentatively, as if the emotion was unknown to her. I thought of Tim Callahan's body and decided that a sense of humor was probably something she didn't need too often.

"You need an appreciation of the ridiculous in a small business."

"Do you ever get asked for, well, politically incorrect items?"

Odd question. "Like what?"

"Nothing in particular," she said. "I'll take that strawberry face mask for my friend."

I rolled it in our trademark turquoise tissue. "I can put it in a box and gift wrap it for you. Would you like a white ribbon or a gold one?"

"Um. No gift wrap."

"There's no extra charge," I assured her, but she shook her head. I slid the package into a bag. "Anything else?"

"Did you take off the price?"

I raised an index finger decorated with the sticky label I'd pulled off the bottom of the jar. You'd be surprised how many people want proof you've done that. Like it's something anyone would lie about.

She looked around, apparently not yet ready to leave. "The store is pretty small. Where do you keep your extra stock?"

"We keep supplies in the garage; there's plenty of room. I don't own a car."

She dug around in her shoulder bag and took out another notebook and laid it on the counter. She gave me two ten-dollar bills, which she found crumpled loose in the bag. "Nowhere else?"

"If we're jammed up, Nicole has one or two places she juggles things around in. That happened around the holidays, but otherwise we don't order too far ahead. We need to move merchandise through quickly."

I rang up the sale and handed over her change. "Is your friend in jail?"

Her eyebrows went up.

"She doesn't get out. No refrigerator. No tub. No gift wrap — as if the contents of a gift have to be checked before she gets it. She could be a nun. But what would a nun do with a strawberry face mask?"

"She has six years to serve on a sentence for armed robbery," she said, eyeing me thoughtfully. "She was eighteen and drove the getaway car. She says I saved her from a life of crime and helped her find the Lord. It's her birthday in a few days."

I looked noncommittal.

She said: "Have you always been in retail business?"

"I used to be a photographer." A lifetime ago, I thought.

She raised an encouraging eyebrow.

"A sometime paparazzo," I went on, hoping I wasn't giving away too much. "Chasing down reluctant celebs and their lovers.

Great fun."

"Why did you give it up?"

"I developed too much sympathy for my prey to be a good hunter," I said aridly.

"Not a problem I'm familiar with."

"No, I suppose not."

"Is your partner here today?"

"She probably dropped off some merchandise earlier, but — no."

"Maybe I'll catch her at home." Her glance sharpened. "By the way, we've taken the seal off the attic rooms at the building where Mr. Callahan fell."

"Oh," I said. And then, because she seemed to expect more, I added: "Good."

"There are new people moving in; some sort of shelter or halfway house, I'm told."

"Already?" That was an unpleasant surprise. I'd been lobbying neighborhood association members for a couple of months, trying to calm the panic about a harmless group home in the Gardens, but they were still twitchy. I thought I had a little more time to bring them around.

"The attic rooms contain some storage boxes and furniture. The shelter people say it's nothing to do with them," she said, still watching me closely.

"The property manager has been renting out storage space. I guess I'd better men-

59

tion it at the association meeting tonight. I know some of us have stuff at number twenty-three. The new people will want it out of there. We didn't expect them to move in so soon."

"I'd like a list of the people who have their belongings stored in the building. Can you get that for me?"

"I'll do my best."

She nodded and surprised me by glancing around the store and adding: "Do you have somewhere private we can talk?"

"I'm here alone. This is as private as it gets. What do you need?"

She hesitated. "This is something I'd prefer to discuss without customers coming in."

I didn't feel too good about that, but I walked to the door, locked it, and flipped the Open sign to Back in Ten Minutes. I led her back into our tiny office and waved her into the only chair.

"I can stand, Ms. Bogart. Why don't you take a seat?" She waited while I sat down, and cleared her throat. "We do a surface investigation of everyone who witnesses something like Mr. Callahan's death," she began. I felt the color drop out of my face. "In your case of course we learned about the robbery and attack on you last year."

"Of course you did," I said, and tried to keep the relief out of my voice. Could my life tolerate any more irony? I was relieved she was digging into my terrifying run-in with a knife-wielding robber instead of my family history.

"The man was never caught."

"No. No, he wasn't. He covered his face. I wasn't able to identify him."

"I'm sorry to bring it all up again." She paused briefly. "We've been told Mr. Callahan was a petty thief. Is that true?"

I nodded. "He called it hand jive, and thought people were fools to leave their stuff where it could be stolen," I said.

"And yet people hired him?"

"He was a fixture around here. Mostly he worked where there was nothing to steal. Attics. Garages. Places like that."

"I see. You're our only witness to Mr. Callahan's death, but even you didn't see the start of his fall and, according to you, Davie Rillera —"

I stood convulsively and ran both hands through my hair. "I saw him sweeping downstairs and I spoke to him!"

While my heart rate had about doubled in the past sixty seconds, she looked unfazed. "A weapon isn't always designed for violence. Sometimes ordinary household items can kill. Think of that broom, Ms. Bogart." She pantomimed a waist-high lunge with both fists around an imaginary broom handle. "Mr. Callahan had a deep bruise on his midsection, which the M.E. tells me would have occurred immediately before his death."

The image of a broom being shoved at Tim Callahan as he stood on a windowsill painting the window frame was all too clear.

"I'm told your young helper would do anything for you." God, she was relentless.

"Not absolutely anything," I said anxiously, falling back into my chair. "Besides, why would I want him dead? It's not as if Tim was the one who robbed me. I don't think." God, that was something I'd never even considered. "And Davie was —"

"I know, Ms. Bogart. He was in the backyard sweeping." She nodded coolly and let herself out of the front door.

CHAPTER FIVE

By the time I recovered, the Ten Minutes was closer to half an hour and I found several customers waiting patiently on the sidewalk when I reopened. They kept me busy, so it was some time before I noticed Lichlyter had forgotten her notebook. I couldn't resist the impulse to leaf through it but it was almost new. One page had been used for the kind of doodles people make while they're talking on the telephone: several circled words, the most unusual of which were "Rhino" and "Chinese" surrounded by lines, arrows, and squiggles. There was a rough sketch of the Gardens and a list of names — mine, Nicole's, and Davie's among them. Vaguely sinister perhaps. I wrote her name on a Post-it note, stuck it on the notebook in case she wanted to retrieve it, and tucked it at the side of the cash register. It only occurred to me much later that she might use the notebooks so she could "accidentally" leave them behind somewhere.

To settle my nerves I began to unpack some new merchandise, including a lidded Waterford crystal jar I filled with small lemon soaps. I planned to leave it on the counter as a sort of showpiece to see if our customers were interested in more high-end, gift-type items. We add them to inventory slowly, partly because it doesn't make sense to tie up money in unsold stock, but also because our customers are conservative about change. In a town famous for its flexible attitudes toward love, race, marriage, and politics, San Franciscans can be curiously hidebound in small things. They react immediately (and not always positively) if we move things around in the shop or if their favorite face cream suddenly appears in a newly designed box. I wasn't sure the Waterford jar would fly, but the price point was worth the experiment.

I gave the jar pride of place on the counter and took a handful of Gibney Brothers soaps out of the carton on the floor to mark them. I began with my favorite white gardenia. We've had none in stock for weeks and I'm the only one who's cared. Still, what's the point of being in charge if you can't have a few things you like? I took some comfort in the familiar routine. Nicole had designed a new price label for us, and this was the first time I'd used it. God, and profits, are in the details.

Almost before I started, a customer came in — all muscles and a blond crew cut. He asked for help deciding between a kimono or loofah gloves as a birthday gift for his lover. It's funny how people here are so comfortable with using that word. Part of the American habit of revealing everything about themselves — "lover" being so much more descriptive than "girlfriend." I often wonder if people are bragging, or simply clueless that no one cares about their sex lives. Especially those of us who have no sex life of our own. He went on to tell me more than I needed to know about her, including that she was a city firefighter and he found the smoky smell of her skin and hair after she'd fought a fire so sexy he could hardly control himself. I urged him to pick the kimono.

"No buttons," I said neutrally. And five times the price of the loofah gloves.

His expression brightened. "Right. So which do you think, the blue to match her eyes or —" His voice faded as he considered the possibilities and I left him to it, dreamily holding up various kimonos against his reflection in our long mirror.

The bell over the door jangled and Haruto stuck his head in, ponytail swinging, his arms full of garden tools. In between his days at Aromas he was installing a Japanese garden on the next block. I didn't know when he did his computer hacking and I was careful never to ask.

"Hi, Theo. Do you know anything about this ecumenical shelter or whatever going in at number twenty-three?"

"It's an ecological center attached to a halfway house."

"Our favorite surgeon says the shelter is for drug addicts," Haruto said. "They've started moving in, did you know?"

"Kurt is a pain. He's so worried about his damn property values —" I took a breath. "It's for a handful of women and children," I said firmly.

"They didn't waste any time moving in," he grumbled.

I laughed unkindly as he dropped a rake and a couple of machete-like choppers. "What are you up to, anyway?"

He stood everything against the open doorway and wiped his brow with his jacket sleeve. "I'm supposed to install moon bridges and waterfalls in a yard the size of a Kleenex with old shrubs taking all the space. I've borrowed every tool in the toolshed. If axes and machetes don't do it, I'll hire a backhoe."

I helped him rearrange his load until it made a neat pile across both of his arms. "You're sure about this shelter thing?" he said. "Homeless drug addicts won't be pissing in the flower beds and sleeping on the benches back in the garden?"

"Trust me," I said, and waved him on his way. He staggered down the block with his precarious burden, looking like a cartoon character.

His half-assed concerns about the shelter had me worried. I hoped it wasn't going to raise its ugly head at the association meeting that night. I didn't want Haruto — or anyone — stirring things up again, even a little.

I heard a clatter and banging from outside that could only be hoes and rakes and machetes hitting the ground. "Haruto!" I said aloud.

"Huh?" said my kimono customer, following me out the door. I was in time to see Nicole sail past Haruto without looking at him. He grabbed her by the arm and spun her around to face him. After a brief exchange of not-very-friendly words, she twisted away from him, and after a frustrated moment he gathered up his ungainly burden and stalked away.

Nicole came toward us, rubbing her upper arm. Her curly brown hair was wild around her shoulders. She was wearing jeans, a flashy gold-and-blue-sequined bustier, and last night's makeup. She brushed her hair back from her forehead with a would-be casual gesture. But her face was pale.

"You okay?" the kimono guy said gruffly to Nicole.

She smiled at him automatically. "Sure, sweetie. Boyfriend trouble."

Nicole followed me inside. The man went back to the kimonos, looking dissatisfied.

"What the hell was that about?" I whispered.

She chose not to hear. "Did you find the Gibney Brothers stuff?" she said.

I waved a hand at the carton, still open on the floor.

"Great. Look, I've got to pay my rent, can you lend me fifty?" The scene with Haruto was apparently forgotten.

"You're not staying?" I said.

She gave her sequins an ironic downward glance. "Does it look like it?" I must have visibly bitten my tongue because she held up a hand. I jerked my head toward the office and she went there ahead of me, tossing her curls and impatiently snapping her fingers.

"All I need is fifty," she said as soon as I closed the door. "You'd already done the bank drop when I got here last night, or I wouldn't —" She stopped short at my expression. "Dammit, it's my money, too. Come on, Theo. I've got the rest of what I need. And my money troubles are over. I'm owed big money — I am! But if I don't pay the rent right this minute I'll be out on the street."

This was Nicole's strength in recent weeks — fifteen seconds of indignation, irritation, wheedling smiles, and pathos.

"You've been saying someone owes you money for two weeks," I began.

"Big money, sweetie. Honest."

"You sold a painting?" Nicole's work had developed a good, local reputation.

"Not exactly." She smiled a secretive little smile, which did nothing to ease my mind.

"We should talk —"

She flushed and waved away whatever else I might be planning to say with an impatient gesture. "By this time next week I'll be straightened out and we can sort out how much I owe the store. I'd have it now except for *goddamn* Tim Callahan. My bloodsucking landlord wants his money now, this instant, and I'm short fifty. I ran into him in the street and he's waiting, if you can believe it!"

"What does Tim Callahan have to do with —"

"Dammit, Theo! I need the money now!"

I thought of how this rapidly developing drama would play with the customer outside and calculated whether I could get through the morning with fifty dollars less in the till.

"For God's sake, Nicole, this can't go on. Where have you been? You're never here; you're not home — Haruto said he had to open up yesterday."

"I came by last night to deliver the Gibney Brothers stuff," she said sulkily. And to rifle the cash drawer, I thought but didn't say. She patted my cheek and fingered her lips nervously.

I glanced through the two-way mirror into the shop as I heard the old-style spring bell jangle. A woman came in. Two people was at least one too many to leave in the shop alone.

I went back outside and with a small inner struggle, took two twenties and a ten out of the cash drawer.

"I'll write an I.O.U." she said, picking up the inspector's notebook and glancing at the doodles.

"No need," I said.

She dropped the notebook as if it were red hot and unexpectedly clasped me in a fierce hug. "It'll all work out," she whispered.

"I'm worried about you," I said, returning the hug. She had been my first friend in the city and the past few weeks hadn't changed my affection for her. Even if she was driving me crazy.

"I know, sweetie. I know. I'll pay back the store in a few days. I've been feeling like shit for the mess in your apartment; I'll take care of that, too. Pretty soon everything will be back to normal, okay? So stop worrying!" She laughed and patted my cheek.

As she passed the counter, she picked up the two bars of newly priced soap knowing I wouldn't say anything. At nine dollars each, retail, it was probably a halfpenny worth of bread to this intolerable deal of sack, but it still grated. Don't you love how Shakespeare has a phrase for everything?

"The new labels look great," she said. "Anyone bought any of this damn gardenia soap?"

"I've only had time to label those two," I said with a reluctant grin.

"Put out some of the rose; we're low and

it sells." She hesitated a moment and made for the door.

"Take care of yourself," I said, meaning it, and trying not to sound as worried as I felt.

She glanced back at me with a mocking smile. "I said 'don't worry,' sweetie. Bye." She waggled the soaps at me. "White gardenia, eh?" She winked and scrunched up her nose, then waggled them at me again as she left.

I saw her shove the bills at a stolid-looking man on the sidewalk and take off down the street. Sure enough, I recognized her landlord, who carefully counted out the money. At least she hadn't lied about that, although I detected a certain number of uneasy ad-libs in the story of money coming in.

My new customer was carefully inspecting lavender sachets. She was sniffing every little lace bag as if she was going to find one that smelled different from the rest. As she looked about to make up her mind, the last of the red-hot lovers decided on the white kimono with the splashy red hibiscus print.

"Red's her color," he explained as he handed me his credit card. "She loves San Francisco's red fire trucks. Most places use that safety yellow or green. Hershey, Pennsylvania, uses red now but she says they used to use brown. Chocolate brown. See?"

He smiled happily.

I sheathed the ninety-seven-dollar Egyptian cotton kimono tenderly in tissue. The kimonos had been Nicole's idea and they were moving nicely. She was a clever merchandiser. Her only recent failure had been novelty soaps shaped like pistols. I told her I refused to sell them; she dug in her heels and refused to return them. Before now we had always been able to settle disagreements amicably, but the gun-shaped soaps were gathering dust in a box under the cash register, solid evidence of our recent lack of accord.

"Did you remove the price?" the firefighter's lover asked anxiously. I held up the price tag to assure him that I had, but he still didn't believe me, so I unwrapped it to show him, wrapped it again, and put it in one of our striped shopping bags.

"I hope your friend is okay," he said. Which was nice of him. I'm in favor of people looking out for each other.

"Thanks. I'm sure she'll be fine."

A motorcycle roared to a stop outside as he was leaving and a familiar leather-clad figure came in, lifting off her helmet as she came through the door. Sabina shook her head and her fiery red curls sprang sideways like springs. She had a bruise under one eye, but otherwise she was as effortlessly gorgeous as usual.

"Hey, Theo," she said. She removed the huge leather gloves that came nearly to her elbows and flopped them over one shoulder. She began casually looking around the store, waiting while I rang up the sachet lady's choice, picking up hand mirrors and pretending to inspect the display of massage oils.

"Get a cappuccino and stay for a bit?" I said. "What happened to your face?"

She shrugged. "I fell on a skateboard some kid left on my steps. I was in a hurry, trying to get my helmet on, stepped on the damn skateboard, fell face-first into the handrail, the helmet went flying and landed in some dog shit." She scowled. "I don't know who the board belongs to, but if I find him — does Davie have one?" I shook my head. "Helga says there's one missing from one of those hideous collage things in the coffee shop, which is stupid because who would do that? Anyway, I'm off coffee. It's keeping me up nights." She made a comic grimace.

"I've got a couple of Perriers in the office," I said in the same tone I might offer one of Helga's cupcakes or a dish of double chocolate fudge sauce. She giggled, put down a mirror, and squeezed past me to get to the office. The sachet lady closed the door as she left.

"D'you want one?" Sabina said, her voice muffled, and then she came to the office door and leaned against the counter.

"I'll get tea later."

"Busy morning?" She was looking around the store.

"Not too bad," I said. "One of Nicole's kimonos sold. Um, is everything okay?" I said tentatively as she rolled her eyes and took a big swallow from the bottle.

"Nicole being Nicole." They didn't get along and there was usually some minor thing going on between them. "She's been bitching about my music again." Sabina lived in the apartment above Nicole's ground-floor studio. Their last argument was about the smell of Nicole's turpentine seeping through the air vents into Sabina's apartment. Nicole's complaints about Sabina's music were probably payback. Although classic heavy metal can't really be played softly and I was inclined (silently) to sympathize with Nicole on this one.

She played with the label on her bottle and started to tear it into tiny pieces. "Kurt and I have been dating," she said abruptly.

"Wow," I said, making an effort, "that's big news." The last I heard, she was still dating someone who occasionally sent a limo for her late at night, sending the local gossips into a swoon. She'd told me he was married.

"Kurt wore me down. He said you wouldn't like it and not to say anything. I thought he meant you had PTSD from your breakup or something and I didn't want to trigger anything for you." She ran a hand through her hair. "I think he mesmerized me; I knew you were way over him, but —"

"It's okay with me, honey. Truly," I added for emphasis. Now I knew why so many of my friends thought I was still pining for Kurt. The jackass. Sabina is way too good for him. Not the kind of thing to say at this particular moment. But true, all the same. "I'm fine with it. Er . . . you know you're too good for him, right?"

She grinned. "You say that about everyone I date."

"Yeah, well in this case, it's especially true. Sure you don't want to keep seeing the married mystery man instead?"

She snorted and then grinned. "Only you, Theo . . ." She squared her shoulders, tugged the zipper in her leather jacket, massaged on the gauntlets, and left, looking jauntier than when she arrived. At least one of us felt better.

I sighed as I watched her bump into my grandfather on his way into the shop. He was wearing his weekday uniform — gray flannel trousers with a knife-edge crease and an elderly but immaculate navy blue cashmere jacket. The Aquascutum raincoat folded over his arm was more a matter of lifelong habit than any expectation of rain during our summer dry season. Although, fair enough, the summer fogs are often drippy enough to require not only a raincoat but an umbrella, too.

He courteously stepped aside and held the door open for Sabina. His manner would have been exactly the same if she had been a linen-clad debutante, although he seldom leaves me in any doubt how he feels about things. In this case, as Sabina extinguished her red curls under the green helmet, hopped aboard the Kawasaki, and roared off down the street, the waves of disapproval nearly knocked me down.

"An interesting mode of travel for a young woman," he said.

"She's really very nice," I said, answering the thought.

"Indeed, Theophania?" he said neutrally. "You mentioned that you have a badger-hair shaving brush. May I see it?"

I showed him the brush that I'd special-ordered for him. We don't have many customers interested in $150 shaving brushes.

Several new customers came in, asked me questions about bath oil and natural sponges, paid for their purchases, and left. I served them automatically and watched my grandfather inspecting the shaving brush minutely in the light from the front window, his long face showing only polite interest. He moved to the city a year ago at the age of seventy because, he says, he needed a change. He never accepts my invitations to visit me in my flat. ("I don't wish to intrude, Theophania." "It's no intrusion, Grandfather." Maybe he knows I'm lying.) I visit him at his Telegraph Hill house once every two weeks and we sit mostly in silence while his housekeeper serves us a tea worthy of the Ritz. Sometimes he plays Mozart on the Bechstein grand he purchased when he arrived here. He has a long nose, gun-metal gray hair and eyebrows, and an erect bearing left over from his military career. Whenever I see him I itch to have a camera in my hands. I suspect he was a spy of some sort. I don't know where my blond hair came from — both my parents were brunettes — but my blue eyes stare at me from my grandfather's face. I sometimes wonder what he'd say if I suggested he could make a comfortable living as a fashion model. Probably that he was already quite comfortable, thank you, Theophania. Which is true.

He cleared his throat, and I snapped, mentally speaking, to attention. "I read a small item in the newspaper about a man falling to his death." The reproach was a silken whisper in his otherwise neutral tone.

"I didn't want you to worry," I said.

"That was kind of you, Theophania." He looked around the shop. "I hope business is good?" He'd never said anything else about Aromas. I was sure he wondered what I could possibly be doing behind a counter in a shop. He hadn't approved of my career as a member of the paparazzi tribe, but at least it was a larger life than the one I was living now. He was generally in favor of living on a wide stage. He'd accepted my use of a phony name with hardly a raised eyebrow. It probably reminded him of his days at Checkpoint Charlie.

"Very good, Grandfather. Thank you." Nothing is lamer than my schoolgirl manners when I'm with him. We used to be able to talk when I was younger, but now I can't find the words to break through, and I worry that he doesn't want me to. Grandfather used to breed racehorses, so he's a believer in bloodlines, and my mother —

his daughter — was murdered by my father. I assumed he maintained the connection with me from a sense of duty; being near me had to be hard to tolerate.

He paid cash for the shaving brush, refusing, as always, to consider a gift or even a discount. He allowed me to kiss his cheek in farewell and I watched him leave with a tightness in my chest.

I was exhausted and it was barely lunchtime.

CHAPTER SIX

"Oh, hell," I said aloud, and rested my head in my hands.

"Hey, English. Good day so far, huh?" I looked up and saw Nat, half in and half out of the front door, grinning at me.

I waved him inside with a smile and a slight lifting of the heart. He was beautiful. If the one-worlders get it right, one day we'll all have Nat's almond-shaped eyes and skin the color of milky cocoa. If we're also as thoughtful and funny, the world will be a much better place. This morning he was wearing one of his apparently endless collection of cashmere sweaters and looked, as always, perfect. He was my closest friend, and lying to him was getting harder and harder.

"Hi, gorgeous," I said. "No better or worse than usual, I guess. Did Derek get back from Hong Kong?"

"Last night. He picked up some new

herbal medicine to make his hair grow. The man is obsessed." This was an old story, but I snickered anyway. "Don't dare say a word when you see him; he'll cripple me if he knows I told you."

"You can trust me."

"Why don't I believe you? You haven't said anythin'," he added in a different tone. "Don't you think it looks pretty on the lavender sweater?"

He waved the pendant under my nose. Interlocking double rings of gold were hung with fine gold rods set with tiny semiprecious stones. It sparkled and made a light, clear, metallic tinkle like a tiny wind chime dangling from his fingers. It was a gift from Nat's lover, Derek Linton. I had seen the pendant every day for two weeks.

"Do I have to compliment it every time I see you?" I grumbled.

"What are friends for?" He leaned over the counter and leafed idly through Lichlyter's notebook.

Derek is a Tiffany-trained jeweler and Nat could sell sand to the Saudis. Their Jewelry Studio, a couple of expensively decorated rooms with discreet and gleaming showcases, was on the second floor of a building on ritzy Union Square. Most of Derek's work is commissioned, but they also present

the work of a few avant-garde young designers. I lifted the pendant from his fingers and
rested it in my own. "How does it make that
pretty sound, anyway?"

"The gold tubes are hollow," Derek said
from the doorway. He came over and
squeezed Nat's shoulder. "Knew I'd find
you here," he said good-naturedly to Nat.
"Anyone want another coffee? Tea, Theo?"

I shook my head and Nat waved his half-
full mug. "I'm fine," he said.

One of the kids in the neighborhood
insists on calling them Beauty and the
Beast, which is pretty astute. When he's not
smiling, Derek looks like a giant version of
the frog footman in Alice, and he makes
Nat, who tops six feet, look delicate. He's a
fairly high-maintenance kind of guy in some
ways; touchy about certain subjects and,
once he gets an idea in his head, stubborn
as a mule. But he's generous and talented
and Nat loves him, which is enough for me.

He was hollow-eyed from lack of sleep this
morning. His jaws stretched in a cavernous
yawn. "Sleeping on planes doesn't do it for
me anymore."

"How was Hong Kong?" I asked him.

"Full of pretty sailors in white shorts."

Nat, who had wandered away to run his
fingers through some potpourri, looked

83

mock-indignant. "In Texas, them's fightin' words," he growled.

"I've heard about those Texas boys and their cattle," Derek said. Nat chuckled.

"Any good buys?" I asked Derek.

Derek smiled like a gourmet about to devour a particularly juicy morsel. "A couple of pieces of carved imperial jade — dark, dark green. Beautiful. I'm going to mount them as earrings. There was some ivory —"

"— but he was pure-minded and turned it down," Nat interjected from over by the kimonos.

Derek sighed. "You can't bring it into the country anyway. Besides, my ladies would kill me. They all belong to the World Wildlife Fund."

"I guess politically correct is good for business," I said. "Which is the second time today I've had this conversation." I grabbed a handful of the Gibney Brothers soaps — the rose scent because Nicole was right; the stuff sells — and busied myself with price labels.

"How's Helga doing?" Derek said, leaning back on his elbows at the counter, following Nat with his eyes. "She looked better today, I thought."

"She's still on autopilot," Nat said. "I took

her another casserole yesterday. She said you went over at zero dark thirty on Tuesday to make croissants for hours, Theo."

"She's exaggerating. I was only a pair of hands. Her day starts practically in the middle of the night and she usually does the whole thing by herself. Swear to God, a couple of hours lifting those heavy baking trays and I was ready to go back to bed. She lent me her heatproof gloves and I still managed to burn myself." I twisted my arm to expose the angry red welt on my inner arm and frowned down at it.

Nat made a sympathetic face. "Poor baby," he crooned. I snorted.

"I guess they were close, her and her father, but even if not, it must be hard to lose a parent," Derek said.

As usual, when I received a casual reminder of my own history, I felt it to my bones and didn't have much to say.

He picked up a hand mirror and ran a hand over the silken smoothness of the wooden back. "This is nice work. New supplier?"

"Uh-huh. Turn it over. The mirror is beveled."

"Better not. I might crack it," he said with a wry grimace. "By the way, I want some natural sponges for my display cases — I've done some coral pieces — have any unusual ones?"

"I thought coral was endangered. What about the World Wildlife Fund ladies?"

"These are old carved pieces out of Mainland China, nothing new. One of them is a red coral chrysanthemum — probably a century old. I've mounted it as a brooch in a diamond and gold setting. Fabulous."

"Don't you love the way he admires his own work?" Nat said slyly.

I picked out three large sea sponges from the display. "Take them," I said, tossing them into one of our bags. "Bring 'em back when you're done. Those irregular ones don't sell as well as the simpler shapes." Which is weird, right? I mean why pay the extra for something natural that looks artificial?

Derek thanked me with a grin that transformed his ugly face. "I wanted to pick some up in Hong Kong, but a two-day trip wasn't enough time to check out the wholesalers and get other shopping done."

"I thought maybe you took the chance to pick up some herb medicines," I said innocently. Nat gave me big eyes and a head-shaking grimace from behind Derek's back.

"Who told you about that?" Derek said with a scowl.

I hesitated, mostly because he looked so incensed. "Um, well, everyone takes herb medicines nowadays, and I thought —"

"I told her," Nat sighed. "You know I tell Theo everythin'. Just because your hair's a little thin — and whose isn't?" he added hastily as Derek's heavy eyebrows drew even closer together. He deliberately caressed Derek's new crew cut. "Stylish," he drawled. "And every little hair standin' right up on end."

Derek finally smiled slowly and shook his head. "You bastard," he said, pretending to shake Nat's hand off his shoulder, but holding it there with his own. "I said to keep it private. Have you told anyone else?" We both solemnly shook our heads.

"No, come on, you two. I'm embarrassed enough as it is." And he looked it; his cheeks were even a little pink. Funny.

"Fine." Nat raised his hand in a mock pledge. "I promise I won't tell anyone else except Theo that you are obsessed with findin' a cure for your thinnin' hair. Not that it's thinnin'!"

"And no mention of Chinese medicines! Theo?" Derek growled.

"I promise, too, mardy arse. What about Rogaine?"

Derek said: "What in hell is a mardy arse?"

At the same time Nat said: "He has an allergy to one of the ingredients so —"

Derek rolled his eyes. "Does no one know the meaning of the word 'private'? Has there been anything new about the poor guy who took a nosedive off number twenty-three?" he added firmly to me. "What was his name; did we know him at all?"

Deciding he really was embarrassed, I went with the change of direction. "It was Tim Callahan; you knew him, right?"

"Huh. We went to school together. He was pretty much always a stoner. He and Nicole were married for about five minutes back in the day. Does she know?"

I was taken aback. "I had no idea. She said something about him, but never mentioned they were married! Honestly, she sounded pissed off at him. I thought her husband was a lawyer or CPA or something."

"Husband number two. That didn't last long either," Nat said waspishly. I looked at him in surprise. He wasn't often catty. He rolled his eyes at me.

"Maybe she didn't tell you about Tim because it's not a happy memory." Derek looked at my expression and grinned. "Don't get weirded out, Theo. This is a small town in some ways. Half my eighth-grade class works in the Financial District and the other half belongs to my gym. I bump into guys I went to school with all the time. It's like kids who went to SI for high school —"

"— that's St. Ignatius," Nat said helpfully.

"— they practically all go to USF for college and stay local. Seems like even the ones who go to the East Coast for school come back. Anyway, Nicole and I are going for a drink this evening. I'll take her pulse. My guess, she won't be too cut up about it."

Nat frowned, started to say something, and closed his mouth.

"Okay then," I said into the slightly awkward silence, feeling as if I should send Nicole flowers or bake her a pie or something. "By the way, the police have said we can have access to the attic again. People are supposed to be getting their stuff out."

Derek frowned. "They closed it off? Did they treat it like a crime scene? I thought it was an accident."

"So did everyone. You two coming to the meeting tonight?" I said after a pause during which I served three customers and managed to get a few more price labels stuck on some bottles of Gibney Brothers talc, and they held hands and sipped their coffees.

Derek snorted. "Those meetings make me nervous. Besides, everyone else goes; they don't need me. Nat's going. Right, big guy?"

"Wouldn't miss it." Nat was telling the literal truth. He thoroughly enjoyed them.

"Tonight's meeting is making me nervous, too," I said. "I know Haruto is planning to complain about dogs in the compost pile again —"

"That boy needs a hobby," Nat interjected.

"— he's got a hobby, that's the trouble," I said.

"And everyone wonders why I'm not going!" Derek said. "Compost. Ugh."

"Apparently it's black gold. I also heard this morning that the group home is already moving into number twenty-three —"

A small crash came from the floor at Derek's feet. "Damn!" Derek said. "I'm sorry, Theo." There was a small gash in his hand from the broken mirror and blood welled in it. "It broke in my hands," he said. "Hell —"

"Cover it, quick!" I said hastily to Derek, who tried to hide his bleeding hand, but not quickly enough.

"Urgh," Nat said. I looked over at him anxiously. His eyes rolled back in his head in slow-motion and he dropped like a stone into the rack of kimonos.

"Nat!" Derek yelped.

"Cover the blood!"

Derek patted Nat urgently on the cheek. Nat moaned faintly.

"Great," Derek said as he wrapped the paper towels I handed him around his damaged hand. "Maybe you should call an ambulance to have us both hauled away." There was an edge of fright in his voice.

I tried to reassure him, but I understood. All six feet of Nat in a dead faint was something I'd never forgotten since the first time I saw it happen. "All he needs is some rest. The kimonos broke his fall." I looked at the tangled mess. "Take him home. He'll be fine."

"Are you sure? He told me about the blood thing, but he never said it was so bad he fainted — he doesn't need a doctor or anything?" He tried to wrap his undamaged arm around Nat's shoulders as Nat slowly sat up and gave a convincing, if sheepish, portrait of recovery. I patched up Derek's hand in the office, out of Nat's sight, and they left holding hands. It all reminded me how long it had been since someone cared when I was hurting.

It was midday by then, and fog was starting to fly overhead and block out the sun.

Davie came in to work and we were busy all day, but I still had time to wonder whether broken mirrors meant bad luck for seven years — and for which one of us?

CHAPTER SEVEN

The neighborhood association meeting was controlled chaos. No, check that; it was just chaos.

We meet monthly at the president's home, which is decorated with some of her family antiques — carved tables; silk rugs and rosewood chairs with no cushions; and souvenirs of her husband's African travels — Masai warrior spears, vicious-looking clubs carved to look like fists, and odd little stools. It's difficult to find somewhere comfortable to sit. If it weren't Fabian Gardens tradition to meet in the home of the president, I think we'd all welcome a change.

After the meetings, the secretary — me this year — sends notes to people telling them when they've been assigned in absentia to a committee. For that reason alone, I've always felt, the meetings are pretty well attended. It's easier to fight off the nominations in person. Anyone who lives or works in Fabian Gardens is a de facto member of the association, so we're an interesting mix of well-to-do property owners, professional people, merchants, and the waifs and strays who tend to inhabit the tiny studio apartments.

I arrived as we were called to order, so I had no chance to talk to anyone before things got lively. Nat was perched on an African milking stool in the bay window with his arms clasped around one knee, watching everyone with an engaged and interested expression. He winked at me and I rolled my eyes. Part of the meeting's entertainment value was the bare-knuckle jockeying between the president and her vice president. Both women were forced to make polite noises to each other in public while bitterly complaining later, and in deepest confidence, to their cronies who of course spread it all over the place. Nat loved every moment of every meeting and forwarded the latest e-mails to me with vulgar comments appended.

The first item on the agenda was Sunday's Open Garden, our annual show for the neighborhood. People bring their mothers in from Benicia and Concord to see the little townie miracle as if they didn't have gardens out in the country. I allowed myself to hope that it would occupy us all evening.

Someone meekly proposed that we delay the Open Garden this year because of Tim Callahan's death.

"Why?" Kurt snapped. "He had nothing to do with us."

Maybe doctors develop a shell to protect themselves from emotional involvement, but Kurt was overdoing it. Several people agreed with him and two or three others lined up on the side of a postponement. They were voted down and we determined that the Open Garden would go ahead. However, in a sop to our finer feelings, we decided to print the information about Tim's funeral in our e-newsletter so anyone who wanted to could go to pay their respects. Haruto, resident compost fanatic, made a hot-tempered remark about dogs digging up the compost pile. A dog-owning resident took exception and they nearly came to blows. Haruto and his champions threw out random remarks about leash laws, while the pet owners muttered darkly about Nazis.

I swallowed hard and told them that the women's group home was a fait accompli. Suddenly the factions united — Fabian Gardens was Poland and the shelter was a

Panzer Division. I'm surprised a single soul in the room had any vocal cords left at the end of an exhausting and ultimately pointless shouting match. Our vice president tossed her stiff blond ponytail and said we should hire her cousin the attorney to put the fear of God into the owner of the building and the shelter people. Somebody mentioned that the Catholic Church was backing the shelter. "Screw the Catholic Church," she snarled. "We need to do something; if it isn't already too late," she added with a toothy smile. Her cousin charged $600 an hour, she said, but he was worth every penny.

It was clear from the immediate lack of eye contact around the room that, while no one wanted to admit to putting their personal finances ahead of the association's best interests, no one was rushing to pick up that particular torch, either. In the pause that followed, Kurt suddenly said: "I have some records stored in that attic and the police have been preventing me from retrieving them."

I wondered what kind of records he could be storing in an unsecured attic. Not medical records, surely? Everyone supported his complaint with enormous relief. "I've got stuff in the building, too," someone said.

"No one told me the place was leased for this shelter. The property manager said my mother's furniture would be safe."

The grumbling and yelling went on until it sounded as if everyone at Fabian Gardens had junk stored at number twenty-three.

I told them the police had freed up the attic and they had to move their belongings by Saturday. Then I started a sign-up sheet for Inspector Lichlyter. That gave them all something else to get steamed up about. I felt as if I were drowning. I looked over at Nat. His lips were twitching and he avoided catching my eye.

I opened a note addressed to the association which I hadn't had time to read earlier. As secretary I get a lot of random mail and it's usually uncontroversial. I hoped it would give everyone a breather and calm them down a little. Thank God I glanced at it first. It was from the director of the new group home. At first it sounded harmless enough. It said polite things about hoping to be a credit to the neighborhood he'd heard so much about. I read the signature and realized for the first time that my nonsmoker, no-pets, works-for-a-nonprofit, moving-in-today, old friend-of-a-friend of Nicole's, new tenant Bramwell Turlough was also the shelter director. Telling them

I'd allowed the Trojan horse within the gates would have been like dropping an ice cube into boiling oil — it would have frothed up and covered me before I could catch a breath. I cravenly stuffed his note back in its envelope, grabbed my jacket, and fled as soon as the meeting broke up.

If I'd gone straight home, three indignant people would have overtaken me before I got there, so I avoided my usual route across the darkened garden and took the street route, ducking into Coconut Harry's to give the meeting attendees time to drift away. Harry's is the kind of neighborhood bar strangers aren't inclined to walk into but we all use it pretty much as our personal clubhouse. It has red Christmas tree lights hanging from the ceiling and a general air of having been last painted in 1947. The strong smell of very old cigarette smoke and beer is tinged with the faint aroma of disinfectant. No one is permitted to smoke in San Francisco bars nowadays, but that doesn't stop a few of Harry's older patrons. I sat at the bar, nodded to Joe the bartender, and ordered a gin and tonic. Each booth has a bamboo-and-rattan sign with the name of a tropical island. I sipped my drink and mindlessly read them backward in the gold-veined mirror behind the bar, and accidentally caught the eye of the man in Haiti. What a choice, when there was Bora Bora, not to mention Fiji. I looked away, but not without noticing powerful shoulders in a black leather jacket, a rough profile, and a gold earring. In San Francisco, the earring and the leather could mean literally anything — Hell's Angel; gay; leather fetishist; or I suppose even gay Hell's Angel leather fetishist. I wasn't in the mood to translate. I stared up at the reflection of the Christmas lights in the gold-veined mirror but I could still see him. He looked me over in a too-explicit way as he picked up his glass and brought it over to the bar. I straightened my back and projected mental images of third-degree black belts.

"Ms. Bogart?"

I gave Joe a filthy look when he delivered the gin and tonic, assuming he'd spilled the beans. He gave me a wide-eyed shrug, wiped a damp cloth across the bar, and leaned within earshot, pretending to read the *Sporting Green.*

Without any encouragement, the stranger went on: "My name is Bramwell Turlough." He slid onto the stool next to mine. Great. My new tenant. Director of the shelter. My personal Trojan horse.

I took a mouthful of my gin and tonic.

"How did you know who I was?"

"Someone told me tall, red hair, standoffish expression."

Score one for the guy in the black leather jacket. "How do you do, Mr. Turlough," I said primly. "I hope the studio is satisfactory."

"I haven't seen it yet," he said. "I flew in this morning from D.C. and went straight to the group home."

There was a long pause, which surprised me a little. My limited experience of social worker types is a never-ending stream of self-righteous, activist chatter. He drank his beer and I took another uncomfortable sip of my drink, feeling extremely standoffish.

The bar mirror reflected us both surrounded by the eerie glow of the Christmas lights. I looked tired, which I was. And I needed a haircut or something. He had a small scar over one eyebrow that looked like a built-in frown. He lifted his head suddenly and saw me checking him out. My reflection looked disconcerted. I've always been an easy blusher.

"We want to be a good neighbor, Ms. Bogart. How did the letter go over?"

"We didn't discuss it fully." No need to expose our skirmishes to a stranger.

"Maybe I could come to one of your

meetings to field questions. Not that there's anything you all can do; our first resident moved in this morning."

I turned to him. "I heard."

"And three more this afternoon with their kids. They're having fun helping to finish the painting —" He paused. "You heard about the accident?"

I nodded and somehow didn't say that I had seen Tim fall.

He shook his head. "At least the kids are having a blast. The women, not so much. One of them grabbed her ten-year-old and ran when her husband wanted to sell him for sex. Another is fresh out of a drug rehab program and wants to stay clean so her kids won't have to go back to selling drugs for their uncle. You can understand I don't much care if the people around here are uncomfortable." He drained his glass and signaled to Joe for another beer. I couldn't think of anything to say that wasn't inadequate.

"Thanks for renting me the apartment," he said, a little less forcefully.

"It's okay," I said. I could take credit for it, even if I had no idea at the time that's what I was doing. Besides, I'd told all my neighbors I was in favor of the group home; maybe they'd see my blunder as putting my money where my mouth was.

"Considering how your neighbors probably feel, it was a brave thing to do. Can I buy you a drink?" I shook my head. "By the way —" He reached into the pocket of his jeans, pulled out a wallet, and slid a ten-dollar bill toward Joe.

"Yes?"

"There's some boxes and furniture the property managers say belongs to people renting storage space. No one's paid anything for some time, and the stuff's in the way, so —"

"They've been told to get it out by Saturday."

"Okay. Thanks."

"There is one thing," I said, and he paused. "I don't know much about how to run a women's shelter, but aren't the locations usually secret?"

"It's more like a transitional group home, although we inevitably have women there who need a safe haven. The guy who rented us the building thought he was helping us by enlisting the locals on our side. You can see how well that idea worked out. First our cover's blown, then our painter falls out a window. What was the name of the captain of the *Titanic*?" He rubbed one hand over his jaw. "I guess I shouldn't make light of it.

I ought to get in touch with the painter's family. Do you know him?"

"He didn't have any family," I said. "I can ask everyone to keep the group home secret."

He shook his head once in a decided negative. "It never works. There's always someone who can't resist mentioning it at work or over dinner. We have a couple of weeks at most to find a more secure location for our most critical cases. Some of these women are in fear for their lives. They're all from other cities in California, but homicidal husbands can be very determined."

I felt myself go very still. It's odd how often things come up that remind me of that fact.

He looked a question at me, and when I didn't respond he finished the rest of his beer in one swallow. I was saved from further conversation by Nat's appearance. He was still on a high from the entertainment value of the association meeting.

"Figured I'd find you here," he said with a smile. He reached out a hand and untucked the hair from behind one of my ears and fluffed it up gently. "That's better. Have another to keep me company."

"I need one," I said truthfully, tucking the hair back behind my ear.

Turlough watched the byplay and I was about to introduce the two men when he said good night to me and left. Nat raised one eyebrow at me. "Good-lookin' guy," he remarked.

"You think so?"

"Mmm-hmmm."

"Short, don't you think?"

"Not especially, you giraffe. He's my height. Well-built," he added appreciatively. "The guy seemed interested. Hair's a real turn-on for straight men; would it kill you to let it loose? You know him?"

"Interested? No, he's my new tenant. I found out tonight he's the one putting together the group home or whatever it is in number twenty-three."

"Theo, no!" Nat hooted with laughter.

"All right for you," I said rudely. "But they're going to skin me. Ah, what am I worried about? By the time they finish with that property manager —"

When we left Coconut Harry's nearly an hour later I was the worse for three gin and tonics on an empty stomach. Determinedly not hearing the slight roaring in my head, I said good-bye to Nat and headed in the direction of Mr. Choy's grocery store on the corner. By this time it was nearly eleven. Mr. Choy was reading his newspaper with his glasses propped on his forehead.

"Ah? Good evening. Can I help you?" he said to me, the same as always.

"Milk-Bones," I said, already halfway there.

"Aisle three, next to baby formula," Mr. Choy said automatically, and returned to his paper. He announces the locations because nothing in the store makes any sense. He occasionally mentions his fortune-teller, and I think this fortune-teller is the marketing whiz who tells him to put tins of sardines and laundry detergent on the same shelf. His cash desk faces away from the door because the fortune-teller told him it was the most auspicious direction when he opened the store eighteen years ago. He sits on a stool surrounded by hanging displays of lightbulbs and huge tins of canned peaches. The rest of the canned fruit is next to the toilet paper and the Hamburger Helper. In among the baby formula, brass polish, and Pepto-Bismol he has Chinese patent medicines with dragons and peach blossoms on the packets. The patent medicines reminded me of Derek's mission to grow his hair. I went to the counter with my box of Milk-Bones. "Do you know much about traditional Chinese medicine, Mr. Choy?"

He put down his paper and reached for the cash register. "My late father used to deal in Chinese medicines from his pharmacy in Chinatown. Four employees. Very successful. I studied, but some things I didn't want to sell, so I go into Milk-Bone business instead," he said as he handed me my change.

"Sexual things?" I hazarded, otherwise at a loss to explain his embarrassment.

"Sometimes," he said, and wouldn't be pressed further, all of which heightened my interest in Chinese medicine.

I went home to take Lucy out for her bedtime walk in the garden. I wasn't sure why, but for the first time in a very long time, I was sorry to be going home alone.

CHAPTER EIGHT

The street was shiny with mist, the street-lights haloed. The foghorns on the bridge moaned softly and an occasional car swished past but otherwise everything was quiet. I shifted the box of dog biscuits under my arm and shivered a little inside my jacket as I automatically put a little more effort into my stride coming up the hill. The city is like a gigantic, undulating staircase, following the hills to the ocean in one direction and San Francisco Bay in the other. I sometimes wonder what it will be like to be old, pulling a wheeled shopping basket behind me up these slopes. By the time they're seventy, the old ladies around here must have legs like marathon runners.

I walked past the window of Aromas to my front door. I was careful, as always, to have the keys in my hand, to avoid making myself a dithering target for any would-be assassin who might be lurking in the shadows. The ex-policeman who ran my defensive violence class taught us things like that. Because of him, I was in the habit of gripping my keys with the points protruding through the fingers of my hand, like a set of brass knuckles. Even so, I wasn't sure I could work up the nerve to gouge out someone's eyes with my house keys. He also suggested we carry a three-inch length of galvanized pipe in our dominant hand to add some strength to our punches. I suppose I could wear body armor and a helmet, too, but you have to draw a line somewhere, even in a country where it's legal to carry loaded rifles into Walmart. I'd made peace with the keys but they were as far as I was willing to go along that road. I ran up the stairs calling to Lucy after locking and chaining the front door carefully behind me. Lucy jumped off the mattress (I heard her rotund little body hit the bedroom floor with a squishy thump) and swaggered down the hallway to greet me, yawning hugely. Having waited for me to scratch under her chin, she turned around and went back to bed.

I made myself a cup of tangerine spice tea and ate a chunk of cheese with some bread to help dilute the gin and listened to my jazz playlist as I leaned against my kitchen counter. The kitchen was nearly completed, but it was littered with open-topped cartons of dishes and kitchen tools, left over from when I'd emptied the old green-painted cabinets to replace them with the pale maple ones Nicole had chosen for me.

I folded a load of towels in the utility room and moved to a perch on a stepladder in the living room to drink my rapidly cooling tea. The flat, mostly empty and somehow starkly beautiful, seemed enormous. Accustomed to the tight quarters in the downstairs studio, I watched the watery shadows on my wall from the streetlight outside my window and felt as if Lucy were sleeping somewhere on the next block.

I exchanged contact lenses for a pair of glasses and whistled for Lucy and then, because she ignored me as she always does, I went to get her. She snarled at me automatically as I plucked her off the mattress. She was still grumbling as we headed down the back stairs. The wooden steps were bare and it was difficult to be quiet. Haruto and Bramwell Turlough would have to lump it, if they were home.

Stupidly, I left the utility room door open when I went down. I don't know why I always do that when I'm so careful about the front door. I think it's because the garden is so private and there's no other access to the building at the back. The buildings in Fabian Gardens are shoulder to shoulder from the street side, but they have outside staircases about halfway back to give us all a second way out, in case of a fire or other emergency (for which, read: "earthquake").

The back-door landings are nothing much, but big enough for a trash can and a few potted plants for those of us who are so inclined. I have some dispirited herbs, their leaves curling and protesting at the fog they're expected to deal with when they long for Mediterranean sunshine. The buildings have a variety of dressy facades at the front, but they're plain and flat-roofed, like shoe boxes, from the garden side. Because of the hill and the staircase effect, the buildings step down gradually so my back landing is level with next door's rooftop. If I wanted to, I could step past my pots of oregano and parsley onto my neighbors' flat gravel roof. In a sunnier climate, we'd use the roofs as sundecks; here we abandon them to the seagulls and an occasional laundry line.

Lucy and I spent ten minutes in the darkened garden; me hissing at her to hurry up and she, furtive and uncooperative, taking exactly the same amount of time as usual. I could hear occasional muffled noises. Sabina's grandfather, known as Professor D'Allessio, although he'd been retired for a decade or more, goes out after dark to crush snails and slugs. Around the time of the Open Garden, he redoubles his efforts and spends half the night out there, creeping up on unsuspecting gastropods. As if to confirm it, I heard the faint metallic ringing of his hoe.

If I'd been paying attention to what I was doing, maybe I wouldn't have been blind-sided by what happened next. But as I made my way back up three flights of wooden stairs, wondering if I should soundproof them with sisal matting or something, my mind was dealing with Nicole's promise to get her act together, and the new group home, and Bramwell Turlough, and, periph-erally, whether I thought him as good-looking as Nat did. I was carrying a little plastic bag containing the result of Lucy's expedition and remembering an argument I once had with a neighbor, who hates ani-mals and what he calls their "leavings," and trying to recall if it was the oregano or the parsley I'd poured a mug of water on the day before. Lucy's self-important little white bottom led me up the stairs in the pitch dark. I picked up the pot of oregano, at the same time pushing the door wide open. The unshaded bulb in the utility room ceiling flashed at me like the beam of a lighthouse.

An overweight man in a business suit was standing on my washing machine.

Every cell in my body lurched to a standstill. My eyeballs refused to recognize what I was apparently seeing; my synapses vaporized; my muscles locked. My heart stopped beating, and then started beating so fast somewhere up in my throat I thought my body would explode.

He was about fifty, with pitted skin the color of dust. His forehead was glistening with sweat and he was opening and closing his mouth like a sea anemone. Like me, he was paralyzed, wide-eyed and apparently frozen in place. He had a short red strap in his hand; it was ragged and torn at the ends. Tacky. Time suddenly wound down with an almost audible whine and I had time to think "tacky red strap" twice.

Everything about him stood out like neon. The navy blue suit. The pale blue handkerchief peeking coyly from his breast pocket. The shamrock lapel pin. The stylish inch of French cuff showing at the sleeve of his jacket. The malachite cuff link. I looked down at his feet for some reason. He had trampled and jumbled my pile of neatly folded towels. I felt a surge of panic, as if a towel trampler could be capable of anything. He took a step toward me and stumbled on another towel. I instinctively swept back my arm, flung the pot of oregano at him, and produced a loud, terrified scream that hurt my throat. The ex-policeman had told us to make as much noise as possible, so I kept screaming as I tripped in my panicked exit out the door, collided with the trash can, and fell crashing into the pots of herbs. I landed on my side, with half my body extended onto my neighbors' roof. Horribly, the image of the falling Tim Callahan blocked out lucid thought.

"For Christ's sake, shut up!" the man shouted. I heard him jump off the washing machine and stumble into the trash can. I shut up, but not voluntarily. The screaming turned of its own accord into hysterical hiccupping. I rolled over clumsily, preparing to sweep him off his feet with a scissor action of my legs. But he was down beside me on one knee, with a grimy mixture of potting soil and blood streaked down the side of his face. It didn't improve him. I groped for another pot to hit him with and came up with Lucy's plastic bag. Out of options, I froze in terror. The small part remaining of my rational mind told me that my last sight on earth might be the filthy face of my killer as he bent over me again to hurl me to my death. I would plunge through the air like Tim Callahan and land in the garden. Dead.

He lurched away from me into the wall and slid down into a squat, clutching his head. "Jesus! All right. Don't get up."

Of course I immediately sat up and then my muscles tightened into mean little knots. My field of vision narrowed and I could only see one thing at a time. First was the lapel pin. It was a green enamel shamrock. He waved the red strap aimlessly at me and I memorized how that looked. It was red nylon webbing. He jabbed it carelessly into his pocket as if he didn't know what to do with it and pulled it out again. If he had a gun in that pocket I was going to have to jump off the damn roof to avoid getting shot. Which was worse — bleeding to death from a bullet or being squashed by a head-first landing onto a garden bench three floors below?

Lucy snarled and made a lunge at his shoes, and he raised a threatening fist at her. I grabbed Lucy — her ego is the toughest part of her — and tried to contain her furious squirming little body in my arms.

"Where the hell did you come from?" the

man groaned, waving the strap again. Sweat was shining on his bald head like a layer of oil. His glance roamed vaguely past me and he mumbled: "The place is empty for months. Jesus. The luck of the Irish."

The flowerpot to the head must have dazed him; he was muttering to himself, not to me. His behavior so far was frightening, but unthreatening. Suppose he was a harmless nut, climbing on people's washing machines all over the city? Dealing with the public has given me unique life skills; a nut I can always handle. I opened my mouth to humor him, when he froze me rigid by reaching into his jacket pocket.

I thought: "Godammit, I can't jump off the roof," and frantically tried to remember some of the self-defense moves the ex-policeman had taught me. None of the examples we practiced began with the victim clutching a twelve-pound terrier in her arms, while the attacker squatted on the floor clutching his head. I heard a tiny grunt, and risked a quick look at his face. He was dabbing at the dirty mess oozing down his cheek with his immaculate, neatly folded handkerchief. He looked at the results and said, "Jesus," again. Then he heaved himself to his feet and stepped over me onto the roof next door.

He was several strides away when I blurted: "Wait, where are you going?" When he turned back with narrowed eyes I could have bitten off my tongue.

"Shut up, lady. Don't push it. Shut up!" His voice rose higher with every word until the last was a near squeak. Incredibly, he looked as if he might burst into tears any second. His jowls quivered.

It gave me another spark of courage: "Hey! Who the hell do you think you are? And what were you doing on my washing machine?" Dammit. I sounded unhinged, even to myself.

He made a ferociously crude gesture involving a clutched arm and a fist and trudged away across the roof. I watched him, openmouthed until good sense made a comeback. I grabbed Lucy even tighter in my arms, dived back inside my own back door, and slammed it shut behind us. If I'd had a drawbridge I would have pulled it up. Instead, in unconscious imitation of the man on the washing machine, I slid down inside the door, squatted on the floor, and shook.

CHAPTER NINE

My hand shook even more as I began to call 911. It shook so much I hesitated and then I snapped the phone off. I told myself nothing much had happened. And having cops in the house, with their thick-soled shoes and their creaking leather belts and buckles and their ton of attitude, was more than I could stomach. I waited for the trembles to pass and called Nat instead. Like the good friend he was, he heard me out in silence — I didn't give him much of a chance to talk — and then he said: "I'll be right over," in a muzzy, sleep-filled mumble. I heard something fall with a thump off his bedside table.

I felt consoled immediately. "It's okay. I just wanted to talk to you."

"Theo, I'm comin' over; I'll be there in ten minutes," he said more sharply.

While I was still pacing through the apartment trying to figure out what my burglar had been doing, Nat came up the back stairs three at a time and after asking me permission with his eyes, nearly crushed the breath out of me in a bear hug.

"Are you okay? What did the guy do?"

I had to mumble into his cashmere sweater. He felt warm and smelled of woodsmoke. "Nothing. He didn't do anything."

He loosened his hold a little. I was still going to have bruises on my arms. "Are you sure you're okay?" he said more gently.

I felt tears start into my eyes and it made my reply harsher than he deserved. "The stupid bastard dug around in my fireplace, trailed soot all over the house, climbed up on my washing machine, and scared the life out of me when I came upstairs," I said.

"Sounds like he's a coupla sandwiches short." He held me at arm's length and watched me carefully.

"That's what I thought. Just a crazy. Do you want coffee?" But I felt a wave of relief and anticlimax that was almost like a blow in the face and the kettle trembled against the kitchen faucet like castanets.

Nat took over the coffee making and all he said was: "This looks like the French almondine I gave you six months ago."

"You're the only one who drinks it."

"Hmmm. What did Lucy think?"

"She tried to eat him." I watched him grind the coffee and fuss with the press he'd bought me in a (futile) attempt to change my preference for tea. "Do you honestly think he was only a nut?" I asked him as the water boiled.

"What else?"

I swallowed hard and felt slightly sick. Aftershock, I thought, like the trembles that follow an earthquake. He walked with me into the utility room.

"I'll start the telephone tree tomorrow and post it on the Facebook page," he said thoughtfully. "Did you get dirt all over or was that him?"

"Me. I threw a flowerpot at him."

Nat's eyes lit up. "Good for you."

I bit my lip. "I guess everyone ought to be warned. Don't make too much of it though." He gave me an understanding grimace and I knew we were both thinking of the same thing. I was able to get away from a knife-wielding robber last year because Nat came into Aromas through the back door, heard my screams, and hit him in the back of the head with a gallon jug of shampoo. It dazed him, we made our escape, and the guy bolted.

Nat had rescued me. Nat who had somehow managed to do what needed to be done before he fainted at my feet seeing the small amount of blood on my arm. It was a debt he never mentioned, and one I'd never be able to repay.

Even though I was a newcomer to the neighborhood, thanks to Nat I had been embraced as one of their own and for days after I came home from the ER I didn't need to cook a meal or spend an evening without company. Very soon I'd felt suffocated and asked Nat to have everyone stand down. I couldn't face that again.

I pointed out the streaks of soot on the washing machine, and we followed the sooty trail backward through the kitchen and the dining room to the living room fireplace. There were handprints on a couple of the walls and footprints all over my refinished floors.

We got back to the kitchen and he poured out two coffees, opened then closed the refrigerator door, and rustled in one of my stylish kitchen cabinets.

"There's some artistic, irregular lumps of brown sugar in there somewhere," I said.

He heaved a mock sigh. "I bought that for you, too. I don't guess you have any half-and-half or hazelnut creamer?" I shrugged and he sighed. "No, of course not. What about the cops?"

I hesitated. "My grandmother used to say worse things happen in a war. Nothing much happened I guess. Now I'm more pissed than anything."

He touched my shoulder lightly. "No cops. Okay. Here's your borin' black coffee. Only you could drink tea for breakfast and coffee at midnight." He handed it to me and glanced around the kitchen. "You know, if you'd organize this kitchen . . . you've got a golden opportunity now everythin's new and bright. I'll even come over and do it for you. For example: always keep the dishes as close to the dishwasher as possible — makes emptyin' it so much easier. Look —" He took half my plates and dishes out of a cabinet as he talked and stacked them neatly into an empty cabinet over the dishwasher. He kept working, finishing by organizing my paltry, mismatched collection of pots and pans, his expression that of a craftsman forced to work with substandard equipment. "See? Much better. Although you should buy some Le Creuset — enamel on cast-iron, lasts forever. The forest green would look good in here. No, maybe the cobalt. We can decide later. In the meantime, I can't find the damn sugar."

"I think I ate it all. Nat, you don't have to

do this."

"Of course I do," he said more seriously, and draped his spare arm loosely around my shoulders. "What did he look like? Maybe we could have a drawing of him done and e-mail it 'round. If You See This Man Call The Cops," he said in obvious capital letters. "Was he young? White? Asian? Black? What was he wearin'?"

"He was fifty-ish. A white guy. Sort of fat and bald. In a suit and French cuffs for God's sake."

Nat snorted into his mug and managed to splash coffee onto his sweater.

"Shit!" he said, and dabbed at it frantically with a wet sponge. "Dammit, Theo, don't make me laugh. Look at me!"

I grunted in amusement; I couldn't help it. He looked up ruefully. "All right. I'm shallow. But it's cashmere! Besides, no one has burglars who look like insurance salesmen! What else do you remember?"

I hesitated. "There was something about his pronunciation. He said 'Jaysus,' as if he might be Irish. And he seemed mad — not crazy, but angry or upset."

"A hot-tempered Irishman. He should be easy to find," he said brightly.

I punched him lightly in the arm and he pretended it hurt him.

"What the hell could he have been doing? If he was after valuables, he came to the wrong place, the bastard," I said.

"You're beginnin' to sound more like yourself," Nat drawled.

I was beginning to feel more like myself, too. "Thanks to you," I said.

He shrugged it off and blotted his sweater again. "I forgot to tell you earlier, did you hear Sabina is havin' collagen injections to make her lips fuller?" he asked innocently.

It was my turn to choke on my coffee. "Who told you that?"

"No one has to tell me; I'm very intuitive," he said. "I'm thinkin' of giving her a nickname — um — Collie? That would remind her we shared a secret without tellin' everyone else."

"Collie!" I spluttered. "You can't!"

He snickered. "I met her comin' out of 450 Sutter the other day. That temple to the medical profession — full of fashionable quacks. I took her to the Redwood Room for a drink afterward — Perrier for two, twenty-one dollars, honey — and she confessed and swore me to secrecy." He twinkled at me.

"She'll kill you if she finds out you've told anyone."

"I haven't told 'anyone.' I've told you. Do

you seriously think she'll get violent? All that black leather —" He shivered happily. "No one tells me things they expect to keep quiet anyway. Ask Derek. Although he did make a point of askin' me again to keep quiet about the hair thing. He'll probably never share anythin' ever again. Besides, you know you love it; you need someone like me to keep you up-to-date on the important things." He yawned suddenly.

I was stricken. "You fainted this morning. I shouldn't have kept you out drinking, and then dragged you out of bed."

"The danger in being hemophobic — as opposed, always, to homophobic — is that people don't often arrange soft surfaces for me to keel over on; the kimonos were a nice touch." He yawned again and shook his head as if to clear it. "I'm going to be a wreck tomorrow. What time is it anyway?"

"It's past one. Go home, Nat. I'm okay. Truly." He ignored me and began to unpack another of my cabinets. I took some of the dishes and began piling them in the cabinet he indicated.

"Come on, Nat. Enough is enough. I'm fine."

Still with his back to me, he said in a completely different tone: "Can I ask you somethin'?"

"Anything."

"Do you think Nicole is having an affair with Derek?" His voice cracked and I looked at his back, horrified and disbelieving.

"What! No, I don't, Nat. Derek is head over heels for you."

He turned around. "They go way back to art school, and she was with Derek for the umpteenth time when I got home tonight and I lost it, Theo. I bitch-slapped her and threw her out of the flat. What the hell was I thinkin'?" He groaned and put his face in his hands. "Then Derek and I had this gigantic fight."

"What did Derek say?"

"He said I was out of my mind, that he loved me, then he put me to bed in the guest room with an ice pack and a sleepin' pill. In the guest room, Theo!"

"Honey, I saw him today when you passed out in the kimonos. Believe me, the man loves you. Was the guest room his idea?"

Nat looked a little shamefaced. "I told him I wanted to sleep there. But he could have talked me out of it! You don't think he and Nicole . . ."

"Definitely, definitely not," I said firmly. "Besides —"

Nat raised a hand. "I know what you're

going to say, but Derek is bi— he's told me about a couple of other women."

"Even so. Definitely, definitely not."

"Okay then. I guess I owe both of them an apology," he said gloomily. "That's goin' to go well." He ran fresh water onto the sponge and pulled the sweater away from his chest to look at it with dismay. "If I soak it in cold water, do you think it will keep the stain from settin'?"

I smiled. "I bet it will. Thanks for coming, Nat. There's nothing wrong with being a little in love with your best friend, is there?"

"Nope. I love you, too. And I must, because I'm going to sleep here and I'll have to share that damn mattress with you and Lucy."

"No. You're not staying."

"I am."

"No." I shook my head.

"I know that look. I'm not winnin' this one, am I?" He didn't sound happy, but the last thing I wanted was to make too much of a minor incident. Or to rely too much on anyone, even Nat.

He insisted on washing up the mugs, then going around with me to all the windows and doors, and checking the closets and the bathrooms, to make sure the flat was empty of uninvited visitors. He did it before I asked, without making me feel ridiculous for wanting him to do it. He gave me a kiss on the cheek and another hug before he reluctantly started to leave.

I said: "Seriously, Nat. There's no chance that Derek is cheating on you with *anyone*."

He nodded. "Yeah, okay. I trust your judgment, Theo. Thanks, sweetie."

Lucy and I went to bed, but between the coffee and the excitement, I didn't sleep much. I decided as dawn broke that the man on the washing machine had done me a favor. For the past year I'd wondered if I'd have the courage to put into practice what the ex-policeman had taught me. Now I knew and I'd won a small victory.

CHAPTER TEN

Nicole didn't come in to work the next morning and Davie showed up with a split lip and a black eye, courtesy of his father. As always, he begged me not to interfere.

"It doesn't hurt," he insisted as I clumsily bathed his mouth in warm water and peroxide and held a cold water compress gently on his eye. "He doesn't mean it."

Fury made my voice shake. "Davie, it isn't right."

"It's okay. It doesn't hurt. He needs me," he said anxiously. "Don't tell anyone, okay? He'll be pissed if CPS gets in his face again."

The first time Davie showed up with bruises, I flew at Mr. Rillera like a ballistic missile. It was like trying to reason with Jell-O. Hungover and remorseful, he sat with his head in his hands while my rage broke over him like a storm. When I gritted my teeth and called the police, they compared Mr. Rillera's 130 pounds against Davie's bulk and checked me off as an overprotective busybody. Child Protective Services did an investigation, but since Davie and his father both denied the abuse they did nothing.

Davie's mother opted out by hanging herself when Davie was six years old. A shelter like the one Turlough has opened might have saved the whole family.

I spent the time between customers fielding calls from friends who grilled me for more details than Nat had given them about my break-in, and who apparently wanted to be prepared in case the man on my washing machine broke into their places and started tap-dancing on their microwave ovens or something.

Sabina came in to pick up some body lotion and listened to my story without comment. Her hair was its usual tempestuous riot of red ringlets but her expression was sulky. Her black jeans were even tighter than usual, and I wondered how she breathed in them. I glanced furtively at her collagen-enhanced lips, but they looked the same to me.

"No work today?" I asked her as she wandered around the store running bubble bath beads through her fingers like gold pieces.

"I was offered an overnight to London. I turned it down. I thought of going to the health club for a workout."

"I could use a session in a nice hot whirlpool myself," I said, easing what felt like a permanent neck ache.

"Oh, I've given that up. Bad for the complexion," she said. Then she added more warmly: "It's been a while since we did anything together."

"Too long," I said, surprised that it was true.

"How about, oh, lunch or something? My schedule's pretty flexible. I'm thinking of selling the bike and going into some other line of work. I'm tired of racing around the city breathing in other people's exhaust and spending half my time on airplanes."

"How about brunch next Sunday? The shop is closed and . . . Sabina? Honey, what's wrong?" I added when she was silent.

She sniffed and said awkwardly: "Brunch on Sunday would be good. I'm nervous about your prowler, I guess. And Tim Callahan falling off the building. What's the third thing?"

"Third thing?"

"You know — bad luck comes in threes."

I didn't want to think about the possibilities, so I didn't reply. "Tell your grandparents about the prowler, okay?" I said instead.

"I've bought a beautiful new knife," she said abruptly. Sabina collected artisan-made knives. I found them disturbing, but I recognized that some were genuinely works of art. "I'll bring it to show you."

"I'll look forward to it," I lied.

I was putting her lotion, at her request, into a recycled paper bag when she said: "You know what, Theo?"

"What?"

"He sounds sort of familiar. The suit, and him being bald and everything, and looking like a bookkeeper or something."

"Insurance salesman, but you've got the idea," I said. "You think you've seen him before?"

"I caught a glimpse of some guy, you know? And I rolled over and went back to sleep because I thought I was dreaming. I mean it didn't make sense, right? A guy in a suit, with a gym bag —"

"A gym bag? What kind of a gym bag?"

"A kind of nylon barrel bag. Like you might carry workout clothes in. It was last month, remember when I was in bed with that bug? It was sort of early in the evening and I woke up and looked out the window and saw this guy walking around on the roof

131

a few houses down. I fell back asleep so I thought I was dreaming or feverish or something."

"A few houses down. Near my place?"

"It could have been," she said slowly.

"What color was the bag?"

"Red, I think. Or orange. Like I said, I didn't think much of it. Weird, huh?"

So weird, I didn't want to think about it much either. After she left, I made myself a cup of tea and sat at my desk in the office while Davie blundered about in the shop. My head was already aching, so it wasn't long before I was making a hash of the month's work schedule for the fifth time. Nicole's nonappearances of late have added to the complexity of the task; I have to pretend that she's coming in, while still having Haruto or Davie available in case she doesn't. I vigorously applied my shrinking eraser to the schedule yet again.

An overcast sky delivered on the promise it had been making all morning and rain began drumming on the window. Davie, complete with his black eye and split lip, a brand-new lightning bolt shaved into his short bristly hair, and an amethyst stud in his nose, pushed through the piles of boxes into our crack-in-the-wall office and stood in the doorway.

"What's up?" I said.

"Did that asshole hurt you?"

Damn. He looked more worried than a kid his age should have to be. I wish I'd explained things to him before all those telephone calls from my neighbors. "No, honey. He got into the flat when I wasn't there and he ran away when I got home. Don't worry."

His face cleared and he gave me a shy smile. He seems to feel I need protecting, which is one of life's little ironies. I tapped my papers into a neat pile. "I'm nearly finished," I lied. "Everything okay out front?"

"Can I help with the customers today?" He didn't ask very often, and I loved him for wanting to help somehow.

"Sure, if you'd like to," I said. He effortlessly picked up a forty-pound carton of soap dishes and carried it out to unpack.

I heard a customer come in and started to get up, but I heard Davie say: "May I help you?" in his politest voice, and I watched him through the two-way mirror. The customer's eyes flickered between Davie's lightning bolt — not to mention the split lip and black eye — and the lace and satin shower caps she was asking about. I went back to my scheduling, scowling at the

133

calendar of classes Davie had given me at the start of the semester so his time with us wouldn't conflict. I was glad he was with me. The man on the washing machine had given me the creeps and revitalized some long-buried anxieties. I penciled in Davie's name with a query mark for Monday morning, too.

I heard the spring bell on the front door and looked out in time to see the customer leaving with an Aromas bag tucked under her arm.

"Good for you, Davie," I said.

He was playing it cool, but he was delighted. "She bought three shower caps."

"Three! I'll have to put you on commission," I said. He grinned and went back to unpacking the soap dishes. Kidding aside, I was impressed. The shower caps cost nineteen dollars each.

After that successful sale, the rain came down even harder. Haruto was on the schedule that morning, but he telephoned at about ten-thirty to tell me he was having a crisis with a design for a bamboo fence and did I mind if he came in later, because business was bound to be slow there at the store, and the rain released his gamma rays (or endorphins or some damn thing), which helped him to think, and if he didn't get this fence designed his client was going to have cat fits. The storm had pulled in some giant waves at Ocean Beach, so I figured he was headed there with his surfboard. I didn't mind as it happened, apart from the shower caps, business was nonexistent, but I grumbled anyway.

I eventually gave up on the schedule. I put out a bucket of folding umbrellas I was trying to get rid of at a bargain price, then moved on to dusting shelves and re-arranging the displays of by-the-ounce potpourri. One of them is called Spring Rain, which was depressingly apt. Several dripping people came in during the morning and dawdled around hoping the rain would stop. Two of them bought umbrellas. At about twelve-thirty, I handed Davie two twenties and told him what to get me for lunch. "Get yourself something, too," I said as an afterthought. His shower caps sale deserved a little celebration.

"We gonna have lunch together?" he said eagerly. He usually headed out to the Mc-Donald's a few blocks away, in spite of my best efforts.

"Sure. Get whatever you'd like and we'll have lunch together." I didn't feel like eating alone anyway.

A short while later he lumbered in the

front door dripping wet, carefully shielding several Styrofoam containers inside his jacket. We sat in the office — me with an ear cocked for the spring bell, and one eye on the two-way mirror — and ate our quiche and drank our sodas, and listened to the rain. The quiche wasn't bad but the salad was slightly limp and the rain was flooding down the shop window. If it keeps up, I thought, I'll be able to count the day's profit on one hand. It was days like this that I missed my life as a freelance photographer. The light outside was interesting; passersby on the sidewalk, backlit by a ray of sunshine coming from somewhere, had turned into silhouettes and I felt the urge to pick up a camera again.

"You know what?" Davie said happily. "This is fun."

I opened my mouth to snort, and then looked at him. His eye was blooming into a deep pansy purple. He was perched on a carton of shampoo jugs like an enormous elf on an undersized mushroom, stabbing at his plate with his plastic fork, stuffing great green bouquets of salad into his mouth and chewing vigorously. Huge gulps of Coke followed each mouthful. I handed him my half-eaten quiche.

"Thanks," he said, and wolfed it down.

This was only a snack; he'd eat three more times before the day was over. Basically everything I paid him went straight into his stomach.

And if no one came into the store all day I wouldn't have to be diplomatic with shoplifters, or be stern with Jehovah's Witnesses, or apologize for running out of pink orchid soaps and having only blue orchid soaps left. For the first time since I'd come in that morning, I relaxed. I smiled at him. He was right. It was kind of fun.

"So what do you think about the man who broke into my apartment?" I asked him.

He swallowed his latest mouthful. He looked thoughtful and frowned. It made him look shifty, which is unfortunate because he's anything but.

"Maybe he was taking something into your apartment, not taking something out," he said, and he laughed at his own joke. Davie laughs like an asthmatic: "Heh, heh, heh, heh." He stuffed another forkful of salad into his mouth.

The first customer of the afternoon came in as the rain stopped. It must be a good omen, I decided as Davie trudged out to serve him.

He was wearing a yellow rain hat, which caught my eye in the two-way mirror and made me smile. He bought more than eighty dollars' worth of stuff, too. ". . . and two tins of Gibney talc number seven," I heard him say.

"Will there be anything else, sir?"

"No. How much?" He was gruff, but I was in a mood not to mind. Eighty-seven dollars and he could be as gruff as he liked. Davie was doing well. "Is Nicole here?" the customer said as he counted out the money.

"Nicole's not here today," Davie said.

Until then I hadn't looked at him closely, except for his dorky hat and his eyes when he first came in. I always look customers in the eye and taught Davie to do the same. It makes customers feel you're warm and sincere, but I do it because troublemakers give themselves away with their eyes. It's hard to explain, but now I can usually tell. I hadn't yet learned that skill when the guy tried to rob me last year.

But this fellow had calm, mud-colored eyes. I moved to the office doorway, ready to give Davie a well-deserved pat on the back, when my jaw dropped with an audible click as the customer left the store. He was taking off his rain hat and rolling it to put in his pocket. There was something about his back, and the way his bald head looked as he walked away from me. The last time

I'd seen this man he was stomping away from me across my neighbor's roof.

I started mouthing air like a landed fish, but he'd pulled open the door and left the store before I could say anything.

"Davie! That's the man on my washing machine — watch the store! Call the police! I'll be right back!" And I vaulted the counter and ran out. I heard something crash and break as the door slammed behind me, but I didn't care. I didn't even spare a thought to what I'd do if I caught up with him.

The sidewalk was still glossy from the morning's rain, but there were a few young mothers barging around with strollers, and office workers hugging go-cups of cappuccino from Helga's coffee shop. I looked both ways and caught a glimpse of him passing the hardware store at the corner. I could see his bald head and thick neck above his black raincoat like a new mushroom popping out of a plant pot.

But, now I had him, figuratively speaking, I didn't know what to do. Accost him? Follow him? Our local beat cop wasn't in sight. He was probably flirting with the girls at the flower shop.

So okay, I could follow him.

I felt glaringly conspicuous for the first fifty yards or so. I was wearing my shop apron — a fairly eye-popping turquoise — and pink ballet slippers. Not that anyone in the neighborhood gives odd outfits a second glance — or that by local standards the outfit was even all that odd. A guy with purple hair and thigh-high white boots passed me. He made up my mind. No one was going to notice me. I took the apron off, rolled it, and tucked it in the back waistband of my jeans.

I managed to keep at least one person between us and followed him, feeling exhilarated and faintly ridiculous at the same time. It reminded me of the days when I'd spent untold hours stalking reluctant celebrities to capture photographs of them and their newest inamorata. Apparently I'd been lying to Lichlyter; there was still something seductive about the thrill of the chase.

He didn't seem to be in a hurry. Every now and again I stopped to look in a shop window, and once, when he went into a bakery, I spent several minutes choosing an orange African daisy from a flower stall. He came out of the bakery carrying a grease-proof bag, and continued on in the same direction as before without looking my way.

After fifteen minutes we had passed the worst of the SRO hotels, with their front steps occupied by skinny boys in too-tight jeans and tank tops, and were coming up on another stretch of retail stores. There was more litter in the gutters here, and some of the windows had To Lease signs up. The man ahead of me was trucking steadily along, with his turquoise-and-white-striped Aromas bag swinging daintily from one hand and his bakery bag in the other. Then he stopped dead twenty yards ahead of me.

I did a quick ninety-degree spin next to a run-down Chinese herbal pharmacy, and stared intently through the window. Shops like it are all over the city, not just in Chinatown, in these enlightened days of holistic treatments and acupuncture cures for tennis elbow and childbirth pains. I'm always intrigued by the rows of unimaginable powders in jars and the chunks of unrecognizable and mysterious substances, and can't help being fascinated by a store where I recognize none of the merchandise. There was part of a thick horn or antler — or something that looked remarkably like one — standing on a shelf next to some glass jars of dried leaves. I buy artisan bread rather than commercial stuff because it tastes better, so I have no clear idea why mass-produced pharmaceuticals from mega-factories seemed more trustworthy than

141

whatever was being mixed up in front of my eyes.

I risked a glimpse at Mushroom Head. He was searching through his Aromas bag, as if for something in particular. I turned away, shielded my eyes with my hand, leaned against the herb store window, and looked further inside. A woman in a white pharmacist's jacket was standing behind the counter measuring a brownish-gray powder onto a scale. She already had a pile several inches high of different-colored ingredients, some looked like broken bark and leaves, and there were coarse crumbs of something that looked like chopped dried mushrooms. For all I knew, they were chopped mushrooms. The whole setup brought to mind Mr. Choy and Derek's hair tonics.

After I had been staring at her for half a minute, the woman in the shop began to look at me inquiringly and I realized I had to move on — or go in and buy a stomach powder or something — before she came out to ask what I wanted.

Mushroom Head disappeared into a doorway as I watched him from under my arm. I sidled up to the storefront he'd gone into and risked a quick look through the narrow Venetian blinds. It was an office of some kind, with a sagging sofa under the window and a waist-high fence a few feet inside like the kind in old-fashioned courtrooms. Six chest-high cubicles in two rows took up most of the space, and a small glass office at the back of the room took up the rest. There was a woman wearing a red sweater across her shoulders in the glass office. All but one of the cubicles was empty. My man was halfway down on the left, his back toward me, in the act of hanging his raincoat on a hanger and hooking it over the top of his cubicle wall. I pulled hastily back out of sight as he turned around and sat down. What was he doing? Somehow I'd never thought people like him — whatever that meant — had day jobs. Did he wander around the city all night like some sort of twisted supervillain and, come daylight, turn into a mild-mannered — well, a mild-mannered what?

It occurred to me to look up. The sign hanging out over the sidewalk above my head said:

Acme Tax.

The man on the washing machine was an accountant.

CHAPTER ELEVEN

I lingered on the sidewalk holding the daisy and positioned myself so I could see into his cubicle. Fortunately neither he nor the woman in the back office looked up. He was staring at a computer screen looking exactly the way I look when I'm fooling with the Aromas computer — bored. Every now and again he tapped his teeth with the end of the pencil he was using to tap on his keyboard. He had a muffin or something in a drawer and he was chewing lumps of it and compulsively gathering little piles of crumbs and pressing them together and sucking them off his fingers. I watched him in frustration. It felt anticlimactic to leave, but I couldn't think of anything else to do. I'd been known to shinny up drainpipes in my quest for the right photo, but I couldn't see that helping me much here.

I looked around for inspiration. There was a tiny shop across the road with brightly colored plastic merchandise spilling onto the sidewalk outside — cheap laundry baskets, dishpans and kiddie chairs, and toilet brushes standing upright in a plastic wastepaper basket shaped like a flower. Everything was sheltered under a clear tarpaulin puddled with raindrops. I gave Mushroom Head another quick glance and crossed the street to ask them — whatever I could think to ask them.

The place smelled strongly of plastic and was jammed with shelves almost to the ceiling.

The Asian woman behind the counter smiled and bowed as I crossed the threshold, and watched me carefully as I knocked over a pile of plastic sandals in little gold plastic mesh bags.

"Sorry," I muttered, and stooped to straighten them. I could have used a pair; my ballet slippers were soaked, scuffed, and sorry looking. My feet were freezing, too.

"Okay, okay! Can I help you?" She was slender and bright-eyed.

"Uh, not . . . I was wondering about the place across the street."

"Empty store? To lease?" she said.

"No. The tax place."

"Ah. They very good." She said something unintelligible, which I realized must be someone's name.

"Tell her we send."

I looked at the bilingual card she handed me. I was evidently in the Happy Day Company, Marilyn and George Goh, proprietors.

"I prefer to deal with a man. Is there a man there?" I offered my apologies to the potentially vengeful goddess of working women and held my breath as Marilyn — only the owner ever controlled the cash register in mom-and-pop stores like this one — paused to consider.

A faint shrug. "Mr. Obwiyen."

"Mister — ?"

"Obwiyen."

I thought rapidly, anxious not to offend. "O'Brien," I said firmly. She nodded. "Mr. Obwiyen. He okay." Again, the faintest of shrugs.

What had my burglar said? Something about the luck of the Irish? "Is Mr. O'Brien a short, bald gentleman?"

She nodded again. "No hair. But no short."

I judged her to top out at five feet, so it could still be my quarry. "Well, I'll look around if that's okay."

"Sure."

I walked up and down the tiny aisle, worries about my own abandoned business beginning to resurface, but still thinking about what the hell an accountant could possibly . . .

I watched Marilyn as I peered through the wavy lenses of a pair of neon green plastic sunglasses. She was pretending to straighten her counter display but one eye, at least, was following me. This was stupid; it was time I got back. I reluctantly considered calling the police. But without a report of the original incident, would they do anything? Besides, now that I'd seen him respectably at work, I was having my doubts.

I put the sunglasses down and started to leave, carefully skirting the pile of plastic sandals, when unbidden, a hasty, daring little plan sprang full-formed into my mind. I ran my fingers over a display of hair ornaments. O'Brien saw me once, for a couple of minutes in the dark, when his night vision was destroyed by the utility room lights and when I was wearing glasses instead of my contacts. I picked up a pair of the sandals. But I didn't have my wallet. I automatically patted the front of my jeans. The change from lunch and my daisy purchase was crumpled in my pocket. Well, I thought with a sort of inner shrug and an undeniable tremor, maybe the thrill of the hunt was more addictive than I knew.

I picked up some of Marilyn's ridiculous merchandise on my way back to the cash register, paid for it, and asked if I could use her restroom. She nodded toward the back of the store. It was typical of the minute spaces we spare from the selling floor — two folded strollers in plastic bubble wrap took up most of it, and a gargantuan plastic pack of toilet paper rolls took up the rest. Not that I felt superior. Most of my similar facility was crowded with folded cardboard cartons and Davie's bicycle.

I ruffled my hair and worried the bangs until they stuck out at odd angles, then pulled it back at one side and checked the effect in the mirror. The change from dignified shopkeeper to wild woman was a little surprising. I made a small grin at my reflection.

I gave the orange daisy to Marilyn and left the little store with a few cents in my pocket, and the memory of her gratified, if puzzled, expression.

Four pairs of eyes glanced up at me as I walked into AcmeTax, and a man with his back to me was pouring coffee into a Styrofoam cup. The office needed some TLC — there were faint patches on the beige walls where old posters or memos had been torn off leaving little scraps of paper and tape, and a few of the floor tiles were curling at the edges. Computer cables, attached to the floor with duct tape, snaked across the aisle between the two lines of desks. The place was murmuring with the sound of tapping keyboards and it looked — ordinary.

O'Brien's black raincoat, meticulously buttoned around a wooden hanger, still hung behind his desk. His dark gray suit looked freshly pressed. A peak of pale blue in his breast pocket looked spiffy with his navy blue tie, not to mention the freshly laundered pale blue shirt with charcoal and white stripes, complete with impeccable French cuffs. He was still intent on his computer screen, but every now and again he made a little rat-a-tat on his desk with the eraser end of his pencil.

"Bay I hep yew?" the receptionist said miserably. She had "Maryanne" embroidered on the collar of her blouse.

"I'd like to see Mr. O'Brien," I said.

Charlie O'Brien, alias Mushroom Head, aka The Man on the Washing Machine, looked up at the sound of his name, scuffed his files together in a pile as I approached, and half rose from his seat. He looked at me expectantly but, I was relieved to see, with no hint of recognition. I sat gingerly in the folding metal chair he waved me into and took a deep breath.

"I'm planning a small business and I need someone to help me with my books and taxes and so on. I happened to mention it to someone and he gave me your name." I licked my dry lips. I was more nervous than I expected. Suppose he recognized my voice?

Folding his pudgy hands together on the desktop he simply said in a completely even tone: "What kind of business are you in?" He was resting his sleeve in a small pile of crumbs.

"Uh . . . small baked goods. Cupcakes. Muffins. Things like that."

He grunted and reached into his desk drawer and pulled out a printed form of some sort.

I watched him closely. I'd never seen anyone who looked more like an accountant in my life. The lines in his face were different from the night before, slack, instead of anxious, and definitely unhostile. It made him look different. I experienced another tiny doubt. Maybe I was wrong about this. He picked a pencil from the pot in front of him and reached for a yellow legal pad. The pot was decorated with little shamrocks. And he was still wearing his shamrock lapel pin. And now I could see a bruise on his forehead where my pot of oregano had made landfall.

"And the address?"

"Excuse me? Oh. Before I go into that, I was wondering if you could give me a couple of references. Clients," I added when he looked at me blankly. "You know, people for whom you've worked."

He looked vaguely around the surface of his desk, as if a few of them were going to materialize next to the telephone. "Well, lemme see. Around here, d'you mean?"

I nodded. I'd been thinking about it. This guy had been skittering around on our roofs. And if Sabina's fever-induced memory was right, he'd been there more than once. Climbing up there from the street was impossible without a man lift or scaffolding; he must have been in one of the buildings backing into Fabian Gardens. So he had a client, or a friend or knew someone in the neighborhood, didn't he? I'd gotten that far when I realized I still didn't have a clear motive for what I was doing. If I didn't plan to tell the police I wasn't going to put anything I learned to any practical use. Still, he might not know it, but I'd paid him back for the fright he'd given me.

"Sure. Well —" He nibbled the end of his

pencil. "I'll write down a couple and . . . er . . . I guess you could ask them if our work is okay. Is that what you mean?"

"That'd be great," I said, and fiddled with my sunglasses.

What could he possibly have been doing in my nearly empty apartment? I was trying to look unconcerned and doing my best to read his file folder labels upside down, when I heard a vaguely familiar voice. I ducked my head and pretended to adjust my hair-comb. I could feel the nylon antennae quivering and the tiny pearls bobbing around.

"Thanks a lot, Maryanne," the voice said, and the owner of it — complete with rough profile, leather jacket, and gold earring — threw his Styrofoam cup into a wastepaper basket and started in my direction. I bent to adjust one of my new plastic sandals and he hesitated as he drew level with Charlie O'Brien's desk, but his stride picked up and he passed me. I heard him say something and the young receptionist giggled, the door closed, and I breathed easier. Not that I expected my new tenant to recognize me; we'd only met once and at that in the half dark of Coconut Harry's. Still, I was glad somehow he hadn't seen me in my fantastic plastic.

152

"I wouldn't get all hot and bothered, he's probably gay," someone said from the front of the office.

I almost opened my mouth to argue before I realized the remark wasn't aimed at me.

"He id nod!" Maryanne said indignantly.

I wouldn't bet on it either, I thought. I'd have to ask Nat what he thought. And then I wondered why I cared.

"Here's a list of some of my clients," Charlie O'Brien was saying. "I'm sure they'd give us a good reference."

He didn't actually look all that sure; he erased one of the names, blew the eraser crumbs all over me, and handed me the list. I stuffed it in my bag and stood up.

"Good to meet you, Ms. Er—"

"Holmes," I said. And barely stopped myself from groaning aloud.

"Good to meet you, Ms. Holmes. I hope you'll be in touch." He held out his hand for me to shake and I took it as briefly as I could. It was soft and warm. His small brown eyes looked smug and unsuspicious. I decided I had pushed everything as far as I could. There was no point in lingering.

And then the whole charade blew up in my face.

I got halfway across the aisle toward the

front door when I tripped over a computer cable. My sunglasses flew off in one direction and my haircomb in another, and both pieces of finery slithered along the floor out of reach. Maryanne picked up my haircomb.

While I was trying to grope for my sunglasses without showing my face, Charlie O'Brien took a few heavy steps in my direction.

"Hey, wait!" he said.

I pushed the glasses onto my face and turned back and he held out my plastic shopping bag — the one with my ballet slippers and Aromas apron in it.

"You forgot your bag," he said. He was frowning. I clutched it to me hastily.

"Thanks. Thanks very much. Talk to you soon."

"Here's your cobe," Maryanne said. "Are you okay?" She giggled.

I grabbed it and threw it in the bag.

"Thanks. Gotta go. Thanks, everybody," I babbled, and blundered through the door and onto the street.

Charlie O'Brien was still standing in the aisle. I saw his expression change as I ran past the window of AcmeTax.

He looked as if he'd been kicked in the stomach.

CHAPTER TWELVE

When I got back to Aromas, Haruto was alone in the store, sweeping something off the floor. Obviously his bamboo fence had gone well, or the surfing had been good, because he was humming to himself. He was wearing a green kimono jacket over his jeans and his ponytail was wrapped into a samurai knot with raffia. He looked up with a professionally bright smile as the doorbell jangled. His change of expression when he recognized me was comical.

"Let me know if — ? Theo?"

"It's okay, Haruto. What got broken?"

"The Waterford jar of lemon soaps is no more, a hundred and seventy-four bucks, retail."

"Damn."

"Davie said you flew out of here at a speed a notch below supersonic — I'm paraphrasing, but that's what he would have said if he'd thought of it. Said you knocked it over as you leaped over the counter like Wonder Woman." He grinned at me.

"Right, I remember now." I limped into the office and collapsed into my chair. My walk home from AcmeTax had been sobering. I'd done a reality check and drawn a couple of conclusions, none of them comforting. Charlie O'Brien was a nut. Maybe a dangerous nut. If he crawled around on rooftops regularly, maybe he was the one who shoved Tim Callahan to his death — if Tim was murdered, which Lichlyter had implied was all too likely. So Charlie O'Brien was a nut and a possible murderer. And if I'd judged his expression correctly, he'd recognized me. And he knew where to find me. I groaned and put my head in my hands. I felt sick from adrenaline rush and my head was thumping.

"Theo?" Haruto's soft inquiry from the doorway made me jump. His eyebrows almost disappeared into his hairline.

I tossed my pearl-and-antennae haircomb, the lipstick, and the sunglasses into the plastic bag and pulled out my apron. My ballet slippers were ruined, so I kept the beige plastic sandals on my feet. I threw the bag and its contents into the trash basket and stood up to wrap my apron around me. Haruto filled the electric kettle. Wisps of steam were drifting from the spout by the time I'd run a comb through my hair and returned it to its everyday smoothness.

"Tea?" he said blandly.

"Please."

I was staring into space when he put the mug of tea in front of me. I jumped again.

"Not the unflappable boss lady today," he said thoughtfully. "Let's see. You disappear and come home disguised as a mall moll. Davie departs the scene the instant I appear with a garbled excuse about a bald washing machine or a bold washing machine. Some kind of washing machine. A large cop appears and asks me what the trouble is. I stand in the middle of the store shrugging and he stomps off in disgust. And that adds up to what exactly?" He wrinkled his brow. "Darned if I know." He hesitated, as if waiting for me to explain.

I replayed a mental image of an enraged Charlie O'Brien throwing me off my own roof. It wasn't a reassuring image. "What do you mean?" I said faintly. "Isn't Davie here?"

"Nope. Gone with the wind."

"Where?"

"No idea. He ran out — near mowed me down on his way out."

The bell jangled out front. Haruto patted

my hand. "I'll get it," he said. "Drink your drink. Cool shoes," he added with another grin on his way out the door.

But it wasn't a customer; it was Davie. I heard Haruto's half-scolding, half-teasing tones. "Where have you been, little brother? Mama's back and she wants to know what you've been doing."

But Davie was uncharacteristically stubborn about saying where he'd been and started to get upset at Haruto's insistence. I decided I didn't care and told them to cut it out and keep quiet. While they served customers and kept my business afloat I shut myself in the office and sipped my tea and worried about Charlie O'Brien coming to — well, to do what? He knew where I lived. He knew where I worked. What was I going to do? I retrieved the list from my pocket and anxiously read through the references he'd given me. I didn't recognize any until I got to the end.

The last name and address was Aromas. Crap!

I snatched up the telephone as if jabbed by a cattle prod and called the police. I asked for Inspector Lichlyter, but she was "unavailable." The officer I spoke to was suspicious. There's no other word for it. If I knew this man, why didn't I report the incident last night? Since I had alerted him, he might have run away, he said, managing to suggest that I had been both negligent and meddlesome at the same time. I hung up the phone, damp with apprehension.

Charlie O'Brien had asked for Nicole by name. Maybe I should start there. But she didn't pick up when I called and when I stopped off at her apartment after closing that evening, she either wasn't there, or didn't answer her door. I called again later, but had to content myself with leaving a message. I got a little heated toward the end, snarling: "Call me, damn it!"

I felt as if my nerves and my emotions were being amplified through a vaguely malevolent magnifying glass. It felt like motion sickness. I wanted someone to talk to, but all I reached was a variety of "leave a message" messages. I paced up and down through my empty apartment, with an uneasy Lucy at my heels. Her little nails clicked on the bare wood floors, and every now and again she looked up at me anxiously.

As seven o'clock came and went, I heard the cicada-like chattering of the sprinklers, as Professor D'Allessio turned them on to make sure everything looked perfect for the next day's Open Garden. The sprays of water set the white Christmas lights ducking and bobbing in the trees. Silence fell an hour later as the sprinklers were turned off. I opened my bedroom window and the smell of moist earth rose up toward me. I saw the professor's shadow slip past a hydrangea, hoe at parade rest, at the ready for wayward snails.

In spite of my argument with Nicole about the gun-shaped soaps, I own a .32 caliber revolver. Chrome-plated and almost pretty, it was my grandfather's idea of an appropriate Christmas gift for me when he moved here last year. It had never been out of its little felt bag. He gave me a box of bullets for it, too. By eight-thirty I'd persuaded myself it would be a good idea to find it.

I dug it out of a carton in the bedroom closet and loaded it, reading from the instruction booklet and wishing I'd taken advantage of his other gift — a marksmanship course at his private club here in town. The club is a Beaux Arts mansion on Nob Hill with a no-women-members policy, which is galling. All the same, I wished I'd taken the course.

Once I got the thing loaded I sat with it gripped in both hands for half an hour, listening with every pore for Charlie O'Brien's step on the stairs or the sound of

160

breaking glass somewhere. I hated holding that gun, but the brass-knuckle keys weren't going to be adequate defense against anything.

When I heard a step on the back landing, my blood pressure nearly shot out through the top of my head. But whoever it was knocked lightly when they tried the door-knob and found the door locked.

"Who is it?" I said, clearing my throat and trying to sound threatening.

"Your door's locked!" Nat's indignation would have been funny another time.

I unlocked the door. Nat's lovely face was drawn and tired, with purple shadows under his eyes like bruises. And no wonder, I thought guiltily. He was up all night comforting hysterical friends. He saw the gun and his eyes widened.

"Hi, Theo. How stands the union?" he said cautiously.

I laid the gun carefully on top of a towel on my washing machine. "Am I glad to see you! Come in." I clutched him in a fierce hug.

There was a pause. "Are you okay?" he said, and added urgently: "Has anythin' else happened?"

"I saw the fellow who broke into my place last night."

"He broke in again? Holy —"

"No. No," I interrupted him. "I saw him. He came into the shop."

He looked aghast. "Did you have him arrested?"

"I tried, but the cops acted as if I was doing him an injustice. I guess if they get around to it sometime tomorrow . . ."

He rubbed his long, flexible fingers over his crinkly hair in a thoughtful gesture. "Is that why you're huddled in here? You're waitin' for him to come back?"

"Not too bright, I know."

"Typical anyway. Come spend the night with me and Derek."

He knew I'd refuse, but I appreciated the offer. "The hell with him; he's not frightening me out of here."

"Come on, Theo. No use toughin' this out alone." He looked definitely uneasy and for some reason the more alarmed he got, the more confident I began to feel.

"I'll be fine. I have Lucy, and I have my gun, which, granted, would be more useful if I knew how to use it. Anyway, Charlie O'Brien would be an idiot to come back. The cops will get him."

"I can teach you how to use the gun."

"You know how to shoot? Why didn't I know that?"

He snorted. "I'm from Texas. We shoot at each other to say good mornin'. I was given my first handgun for my twelfth birthday."

I gaped at him. "Your *first* —"

He looked mildly exasperated. "It never came up before. I knew you wouldn't be comfortable with it, English."

I rolled my eyes. "Are you and Derek going to the Open Garden?"

"You don't fool me with your changes of subject, girl," he said. Then he raised both hands in a gesture of mock surrender. "Derek's workin'. He's tryin' to get a commission finished. But I'll be there for a few minutes, to show I care." He did a slow double take. "Wait — who's Charlie O'Brien?"

"I thought this was Derek's evening for kendo. That's the burglar's name."

"Not this week. How did you find out his name?"

"It's a long story. Believe it or not, the guy's an accountant."

He came back into the kitchen from the guest bathroom, where he'd wandered to admire himself in the mirror. "What? I didn't hear you."

"Yes you did; you just couldn't believe it. He works at a place about twenty minutes' walk down the wrong side of Polk Street."

"How do you know all this?"

I told him the story of my lunchtime pursuit. When I'd finished, he was staring at me. "I'll be damned."

"I know — what's an accountant doing breaking into —"

"That isn't what I meant." He paused. "He recognized you?"

"I'm fairly sure he did."

"Okay, so the cops arrest him and that's it; he's done."

"My word against his?"

He looked meaningfully at the sooty streaks near the kitchen door that I hadn't had time to wipe away. "Fingerprints?"

"Fingerprints! Hell, I've got whole handprints and footprints, too," I said. "Nat, you're a genius."

He tried to look modest. "I know. That'll give the cops somethin' to work on. And I bet O'Brien remembers the fingerprints, too; he won't come back — he's probably in Tijuana by now." Except, I thought and didn't say, he went into work today as if it was a normal day and wasn't worried he'd left incriminating fingerprints everywhere.

"Anybody home?" Haruto called from the back door, which I'd left open of course, and I waved him inside. He looked sideways at the gun on the washing machine, but he

164

didn't say anything. "Thought I'd take a look at where this crazy guy broke in last night," he said. "You doing okay, Theo?"

"The gun's in case he comes back. But I think he's halfway to Mexico by now."

I hope.

"Wish I'd been home; I might have heard something."

"I appreciate the thought, but he wasn't violent; it was, well, weird."

We followed the trail of sooty smears through the kitchen and dining room into the living room.

"What did the cops say?"

"Oh, the usual thing," I lied. I heard someone else on my back stairs and went into the kitchen where I found Sabina, her red mane pulled back into a wild and glamorous knot.

She smiled at me but her face fell as we heard Nat giving Haruto a tour of the sooty trail and explaining my "burglar" all over again. "You have company."

"They came by to look at my burglar's sooty footprints. Would you like tea or coffee or something?"

She looked puzzled. "You've had a burglar?"

"I meant last night's prowler."

She still looked puzzled, and then her

brow cleared. "Oh, right."

"Still on for brunch next Sunday?"

"Brunch?" she said blankly. "Oh! I don't know. I'll let you know."

Right. I cast around for some other topic while she stood in silence and looked around the kitchen. "Er . . . how's Kurt?" I said finally.

"Damn Nicole anyway!" she burst out.

"Nicole?" I repeated stupidly.

"She's a —" Fortunately, words failed her.

"Nicole and, er, Kurt?"

"Not the way you're thinking, but I swear there's something. And he's being sort of a jerk about it. And of course Helga, who's like a kicked puppy every time she sets eyes on him, which he does absolutely nothing to discourage," she said irritably.

"I'm sorry," I said diffidently. I somehow felt responsible for the lousy behavior of my partner and my ex-lover. What the hell was wrong with me, anyway?

She looked around the kitchen and made a visible effort. "This turned out beautifully. You have a good eye for design."

"Thanks," I said awkwardly. It didn't seem the right time to praise Nicole's contributions. "You need some decent dishes though," she said, tipping her head to one side and looking at the contents of one of my open kitchen cabinets.

"What's wrong with my dishes? Nat's making me buy some French enamel pans —"

"Le Creuset? They're great."

"— does everyone know about these pans except me? And you know how he is, he's got more kitchen utensils than Emeril whatshisname and I have no sales resistance. He'll talk me into getting two of everything. Do you know he and Derek have a set of brochette skewers with little steel cows on the ends? I didn't even know what a brochette skewer was!"

Sabina's lip twitched. "Time you learned, chickie. You and I need a date to go to Macy's and see what we can get you in the way of dishes."

"Can they be white at least," I said in mock despair.

"Any color you like. We'll ask Nat to go with us."

"No, please, not that. He's already choosing the color of my pots and pans."

She laughed, which kicked Kurt out of the room. After heavy steps on the back stairs announced another arrival, Helga made her way through the utility room and brought Kurt right back in. Sabina scowled. Helga was wearing her pink Crocs and had added a matching neck scarf tied in a jaunty knot. She'd also exchanged her usual baggy cotton whites for a pair of snug white jeans and a long-sleeved white T-shirt. She made *zaftig* look good.

"I see you've already got more company than you can handle," Helga said with a snort. "I brought you some fruit tarts. I've been hearing about your prowler all day."

I smiled. That was Helga all over. She produced brownies or croissants whenever anyone had the slightest mishap. She wasn't socially adept and food seemed to be her way of expressing concern. She moved into the kitchen, grabbed a plate off a shelf, and shook the tarts onto it, then leaned back to place the baking tray on the washing machine. "Um —" she said as she caught sight of the gun.

Feeling like one of those performers down at Fisherman's Wharf who juggle live chain saws and bowling balls, I said: "Thanks, Helga. I'm fine. The gun is in case anyone else breaks in. Those tarts look great. Nice outfit, by the way. I was about to make some coffee," I lied. "Would you like some?"

I could hear Nat's high, clear voice telling Haruto a rambling and funny story in the living room. It was the one about Nicole's assault on the Adelphi Club with a busload of Birkenstock-wearing protestors and the subsequent relaxation of the color bar. Was there no escaping Nicole?

Helga blushed and glanced down at herself. "I won't stay," she said. Her eyes shifted toward Sabina and she made a faint grimace at me and wrinkled her nose. So I guessed she and Sabina wouldn't be starting a mutual admiration society anytime soon. Kurt didn't deserve all the fervor. "I'm up early to start the ovens. We can't all travel to Europe on someone else's dime," Helga added.

Sabina ignored her. She unzipped a couple of zippers and reached inside her jacket and pulled a frightening knife from a hand-tooled leather sheaf. "I brought the new knife to show you. I bought it down on Haight. What do you think?"

I took the knife gingerly from her hand. It was exquisite and looked lethal. The handle was inlaid with gold-flecked lapis. The blade was eight inches of gleaming steel with a malevolent-looking curve at the end. When I looked up, Helga had left, and I didn't blame her.

CHAPTER THIRTEEN

"Sabina okay?" Nat said when we were alone again.

"She and Kurt —"

"Kurt?" He looked startled. "I thought she was seein' that guy with the limo."

I shook my head. "Old news. Kurt's the man of the moment. Haven't you ever noticed the way he stares at her when she isn't looking? He's besotted. He just doesn't know it. Come on," I said. "I'll walk down with you. Lucy needs to go downstairs and I have to get out of here before anyone else shows up." I locked the back door emphatically. He eyed my spread-keys brass knuckles with respect and followed me down the back stairs. "Hard to believe that tomorrow's the Open Garden." I felt as if I'd lived a month's worth of emotion since the association meeting the night before.

"Great," he grunted. "You can have hoojigger O'Brien arrested in between Haruto's compost turnin' and the bonsai demo."

I started to chuckle, and then something in his tone of voice made me ask: "Are you and Derek okay again? You seem — I don't know — worried?"

"I do?" He squeezed my shoulder gently as we picked our way down the dark stairs. "Guess I'm tired. Can't imagine why, huh? You look as if you slept a full eight hours and breakfasted on dewdrops; I don't know how the hell you do it."

"Nothing else?"

"Derek and I had another argument, this time about nothin'. He's so pig-headed!" he added in frustration. "It sunk as low as do-you-think-cashmere-sweaters-grow-on-trees. I feel ridiculous tellin' him I'd sleep in the park as long as we were together."

"Where does he think the sweaters came from before you met him?" I said dryly. "You weren't exactly —"

"On Queer Street?"

I snickered appreciatively. "— sleeping in the park. You were selling high-ticket jewelry to the matrons at Neiman Marcus."

"Hush. He likes to be the provider. He wants — well," he gave me a crooked smile. "He wants everythin'. With a capital E. For both of us. The Jag is about to get a twin brother, so we can each drive the twelve blocks to work, I guess." He shook his head, but indulgently.

We were at the back door of the studio and after a second's hesitation I knocked. Turlough was putting on his leather jacket as he answered the door. Lucy, huddled in my arms, gave him a ritual growl.

"Hello, Ms. Bogart," he said with what looked like a genuine smile. It was a really nice smile. Nat nudged me. His eyes sparkled. He was vivacious. I sighed and began introductions.

"Bramwell Turlough —"

"Call me Ben," he said, and offered Nat his hand.

"Delighted, Ben," Nat said, and held on to his hand a little too long. "I'm Nat for a real good reason, too. Nathaniel. Aren't parents a kick?" Bramwell — Ben — gave a short laugh in apparent agreement.

Nat's enthusiasm was one of two things: either Ben was a fellow traveler and they were exchanging signals, or Nat was messing with the straight guy's head. Either way, I could have wrung his neck. This didn't seem the time to get his take on whether Turlough was gay or straight.

I remembered the "Ms. Bogart" almost too late. "Er . . . Mr. Turlough. I wanted to let you know we had a prowler last night.

Not dangerous, I don't think," I added. At least, not to anyone but me.

"Ben. Thanks for letting me know. Did you report it to the cops?"

"They said the usual kind of thing. He probably won't bother us again."

"Good." He looked about to say more, but caught Nat's eye and changed his mind.

Nat said ridiculously: "Enjoy yourselves, kids. Good night, Ben," and wandered into the garden and home. His departure seemed to leave us with nothing to say to each other. I put Lucy down and self-consciously told her not to go too far.

"Thanks again for telling me about the prowler. I'll keep it in mind," he said. "I'm heading back over to the group home." He closed the door behind him and we went out into the garden together. He said a gruff "Good night" and strode off across the garden. I watched him leave, still unsure whether I thought him attractive. He walked with a slight hitch in his stride, looking more like a longshoreman than a social worker. I damped down the flicker of mild interest, but it still smoldered. I felt as if I were reawakening after a long sleep.

I could hear the heavy bass of a rock record thumping out through a closed window somewhere behind me, and the hollow chinking noise of Professor D'Allessio's hoe. He was a college professor in Italy before he came here to teach twenty-five years ago. His English is still a little faulty but apparently in some circles he's famous for his books about an obscure Renaissance dramatist. Now he's single-mindedly devoted to the Gardens. His snail killing took two forms; sometimes he crushes them with his hoe and sometimes he plucks them by hand to grind them up as an ingredient in his snail repellent formula. I tried not to know the details, but he told anyone who would listen all about it. I pulled my sweater around me and made my way along the damp path to the bench we'd bought with money one of our members gave us. It had his wife's name on a little bronze plaque on the back.

Lucy rustled her way around her usual haunts. She usually works her way around me in ever-increasing circles, coming back to check that I'm still here at short intervals. The white lights were still twinkling in the trees. They gave the garden a fairyland-at-night atmosphere it only has in the summer. I thought of going over to Nicole's apartment to talk to her, but her apartment windows were dark. Then I thought of Charlie O'Brien, and hoped Nat was right about him being in Tijuana, although I'd have settled for the Hall of Justice downtown.

Professor D'Allessio came around the corner of a shrub, his hoe resting over his shoulder, his step buoyant. He stopped when he saw me. His shock of white hair gleamed in the moonlight, and his walnut skin looked black.

"It's you," he said.

"Good evening, Professor," I said, and because he lingered, added: "How's the garden?"

He jerked his head. "We need rain," he said. He always says that.

"Ah," I said, and looked around for Lucy.

"This soil, no good for growing," he said morosely.

Politely turning away, he spat. The city is built mostly on sand dunes. That, and the rotting remains of sunken ships. The first Spanish settlers thought San Francisco was uninhabitable due to the fog and blowing sands. Not exactly a gardener's paradise.

"I guess not. But you work wonders, Professor. It's a gift you have."

He looked sour, but he was pleased, the old fraud. He sat down heavily next to me on the bench and we sat in silence for a few minutes. "Well, I think I'd better be getting in," I said after another few minutes. "Have you seen Lucy?"

"Open Garden tomorrow," he said, as if I needed reminding. "People out here. At night even, interfering," he said darkly. "When we need them to work, where are they?"

"Ah," I nodded. I didn't have any idea what he was talking about, but it was probably the opening salvo in another feud. Last year half the gardeners were at daggers drawn over whether to plant radicchio or fingerling potatoes in the vegetable patch.

"I tell them, don't you worry," he said, "or maybe the young man is gonna tell them."

His number-one assistant, Haruto, was always only "the young man."

"He's no good, that one. He's gonna make trouble for us, fighting all the time." He was so adamant all of a sudden that his cheeks were quivering.

"Haruto?" I looked at him in surprise.

He waved an impatient hand at me. "Not him. Him. The other one. The earring one. He bring trouble."

I wasn't sure if this was criticism or not; Professor D'Allessio thrives on trouble. He enjoys infighting and he's Nat's only serious competition in the gossip stakes. He also refuses to call anyone by name so that we're all referred to by a series of more or less unflattering nicknames. I'd heard from others that I'm "the soap one." For some reason Helga is "the princess." Poor Nat is "the furry one." I'm uncertain about the professor's reasoning there. Nat professes to believe it's because his body hair is so silky; I think his trademark cashmere sweaters are a more likely reason. Several men around here wear earrings and studs in various places, not to mention the women, but I'd never heard about "the earring one" before, so I was betting on newcomer Ben Turlough. That Professor D'Allessio had taken a dislike to the man didn't surprise me — he hates newcomers and changes of any kind. I'd lived here for months before he deigned to nod to me in passing.

"Who does he fight with? What do you mean?" I said.

"Never mind who. Everyone, that's who. Yelling and shouting last night." He got up, muttering to himself.

"Wait, Professor. Who was yelling and — Professor, who was he fighting with? What do you mean?"

But the old man was shaking his head. He left me there staring after him into the darkness and hearing the swishing noise of his hoe swiping at random weeds as he made his way toward the other end of the garden and home.

"What do you mean? What fight?" But all I heard was a faint swish off in the distance. A rectangle of light appeared as he opened his back door, then the door slammed behind him.

Something in me snapped. "Silly old fool," I muttered.

"Mad about something?" a new voice said out of the gloom. Ben slumped down on the bench and inspected his outstretched legs.

"I thought you'd gone over to the shelter," I said, and wondered if I sounded as ungracious to him as I did to myself.

"That was nearly an hour ago. I'm back," he said mildly.

"It was?" No wonder I was cold.

"What were you and the old man arguing about?"

"We weren't arguing. He was telling me something and wandered off in the middle of it. God, old people can be crazy."

"Young people, too."

I looked at him sharply, but he looked noncommittal. "I guess," I said. "He said you'd been in a fight with someone."

"Oh? Maybe he means when some character leaped out of the bushes at me last night and started ranting and raving about raccoons and dogs."

"Probably Haruto," I said. "He gets pretty wound up before the Open Garden."

"Nice, peaceful place you all have here. I didn't see the old man though."

"He creeps around at night, hunting snails. He says they can hear him coming unless he's very quiet."

I heard someone else walking through the garden behind us, and a low growling sound that might have been Lucy arguing with a raccoon. We have a resident mother and kits who drive her nearly mad with frustration because they climb up onto the roof of our tiny toolshed where she can't get at them. They get in the trash cans at night, and drive the human beings mad, too — especially Haruto. We have a fine metal screen hiding under the surface of the koi pond to prevent them using it as a sushi bar. They're another bone of contention between the residents who hate them and those who feel they're a welcome touch of the natural world in the middle of the city. Like the coyote that showed up in Golden Gate Park recently. Everyone was sentimental about it until it ate a Pekingese, and then half the Richmond District was out for its blood.

"Lucy!" I hissed. "Leave them alone!" I was more afraid for her than for the raccoons, who have the strength and attitude of teenage boys and the emotional stability to match. She slinked over to me, still protesting and rumbling somewhere in her chest. She plunked herself down at my feet with ill grace.

"It's pleasant out here," Ben Turlough said. "Quiet."

I wasn't sure if that was sarcasm, or if he meant it. He didn't say anything more, but he didn't leave either. I tried to think of something neutral to talk about.

Nothing came to mind.

"Your name is Theophania, someone told me," he said suddenly. "Not Theo?"

"Theophania's a bit of a mouthful," I said awkwardly and wondered if I'd told him he didn't have to keep calling me Miss Bogart.

"Pretty, though," he said. "Unusual."

He sounded curious, which was vaguely alarming. I chose "Bogart" from the actor's role in an old noir film about San Francisco; I probably should have given up my first name, too. "So — er, how did you get to Ben from Bramwell?"

"It's a family name. When I was a kid, everyone called me Bram. Then in seventh grade everyone found out that Bram Stoker wrote Dracula. My life wasn't worth living."

The lights in the trees suddenly blinked out all over the garden, and the darkness became almost absolute. I could see the faint sheen of his eyes, a couple of feet from mine.

He cleared his throat. "I was in AcmeTax to see about having them do our books," he said finally.

"Ah, er, um," I said intelligently, and lapsed into an embarrassed silence. If he'd recognized me there, why didn't he say something at the time? And how did he find his way there? "Did — er, did someone recommend them?"

"Must have. Can't remember who," he said after a minute for thought.

Interesting. He sounded . . . evasive. I tried to think of a way to ask him why he wasn't more concerned about my "prowler." Isn't that exactly the kind of news the director of a women's shelter dreads? Before I'd thought of anything that didn't sound like an MI5 interrogation, he stood up.

"I hope you'll ask your residents and their kids to come to the Open Garden tomorrow," I said politely as we parted at the door to the studio.

"I didn't know they were invited."

"It's open to all Gardens residents and

there's no admission charge for them. The kids might meet some children their own ages."

"Thanks. I'll tell them." He smiled. It transformed his face and I found myself smiling back.

CHAPTER FOURTEEN

As I left my back door the next morning, the garden sloped gently up and away from me, looking like an illustration in a children's book. The rose beds tucking into the herb garden, the raised vegetable beds, and the lawn with its koi pond, all were divided and enclosed by the sinuous curves of the paths like the lead seams in a stained glass window. Five or six kids were already swarming over the jungle gym.

I took my donation — three dozen flower-shaped soaps — over to the sale table. It also held some straw sun visors from the hat shop; little glass vases from Donna Marie's Best Buds; and a selection of potted plants, courtesy of Professor D'Allessio's squad of garden helpers. Mrs. Jupp, who used to sell slicing and dicing machines at carnivals, was, as always, in charge of the sale table. The hardware store had donated a set of garden hand tools for the raffle and

I had given them one of our kimonos with a rose embroidered on the pocket. We were also selling cold sodas from Mr. Choy's store, and hot chocolate, cookies, and croissants from Helga's — all the usual suspects, in fact. This was only my second Open Garden, but from what I can tell it's the sameness of the event that draws people. Chaos and confusion may reign in the rest of the world, but here in the Gardens, they know what to expect.

The driveway gate is usually padlocked, but it was made welcoming with hanging baskets of blooms today. Sabina was sitting on a folding chair at the entrance, gathering five-dollar entry fees and crocheting something large and yellow in between arrivals. Watching her made me realize why knitting had made Dickens's Madame Defarge so sinister; there's something single-minded and inexorable about knitters and crocheters. Sabina looked up and waved with her hand tangled in yellow yarn. I waved back.

I walked around the toolshed into the vegetable garden and found Professor D'Allessio, hand shading his eyes, scrutinizing the garden. He was holding his hoe like a bishop's crosier, handle down, swan-neck blade level with his shoulders. With his silver hair and sun-weathered skin, he looked like an implacable Old Testament prophet. He rubbed a grimy hand through his hair as if to clean his fingers. "Where's the earring one?" he said abruptly.

"I haven't seen him yet," I said, and kept moving. Whatever his argument with Ben, they were on their own. "Maybe he's over at the shelter. He'll probably be out later."

The professor looked irritated and fell into step beside me. "The earring one," he said testily. "He no suppose to fool around in garden. I tell him. To hell with him. Earring or no earring."

"He said it wasn't him, professor. I asked him." Damn. Why can't I stay out of these things?

"Ah? The liar. I saw." The old man shook an admonishing finger at me.

"The garden looks great," I said hastily.

He expelled a breath and closed his mouth tight like a goldfish then inhaled deeply and looked around his domain. "Not bad. I gotta go," he said. "You tell that earring one —" He didn't finish whatever it was he intended to say. He growled and flapped a hand at me instead. I was dismissed.

A cluster of visitors milled around at the entrance to the garden, chatting and looking around brightly. I could tell the women were first-timers; they were wearing heels and hats, prepared for something like the Pacific Heights Decorator Showcase. Next year, they'd show up in sweats and sneakers, like everyone else. I was wearing my usual — jeans and a cotton T-shirt with a wool jacket I could discard if the day warmed up. The jacket was new. And then, because he was next in line, I watched with a sigh as my grandfather paid his entrance fee. He was wearing a fine tweed suit, Harrow School Old Boys tie, and highly polished brown lace-up oxfords. I gave him a cheerful wave and headed in his direction. He nodded at me and strode over to meet me halfway.

"Theophania," he said briskly, and bent slightly to allow me to kiss his cheek.

"Hello, Grandfather," I replied dutifully, schoolgirl manners coming to my rescue as usual. "You know you don't have to pay. You can be my guest."

"It's chilly today," he observed, following a pause in which my opening gambit was ignored. He looked around the garden like a grandee on vacation.

"Yes sir, it is," I agreed. We were in danger of sinking into complete silence after that sparkling exchange. "It's supposed to warm up later," I added.

"Ah-hum." He cleared his throat and gave

me a pitying look.

"Would you like some hot cocoa?" I said a little desperately.

"Thank you. I don't care for chocolate drinks." The rebuke was mild, but unmistakable. *Were* there any other chocolate drinks? He probably knew about some obscure concoction enjoyed by the Aztecs.

"I see you've brought your shooting stick," I said, as if I'd just noticed it. The old-fashioned perch-seat disguised as a walking cane had made its appearance at every open-air event for as long as I could remember. I gave myself a mental shake.

"No point in standing, when I can sit," he said austerely.

"No. I can see that," I said, and felt helpless. I'm not sure why he wanted to come. There must have been some attraction besides my unworthy self. I tried to imagine him having a guilty passion for one of my elderly neighbors and failed. As I struggled to think of something else to say, Mrs. Jupp over at the sale table caught my eye and waved me over.

I went over to find out what she wanted.

"The old gentleman" — she nodded at the table where the bonsai demonstration would take place — "says someone stole his favorite machete this week. He wanted us all to keep an eye out for it."

Since I couldn't imagine anyone waving a stolen machete around in broad daylight, I thought our chances of catching the culprit were probably slim. But I nodded anyway and stopped to say hi to Helga, who was putting out mugs for the hot chocolate. She was wearing her white jeans with a white sweater and a green camisole, which were both stretched to the limit. As she dipped to pick up a couple of mugs she provided an eye-popping display of what Nat would call boobage.

I hastily bent to help her empty the cardboard carton and arranged some of the mugs on the table. "Someone else would have done this for us today; you don't need to be out here with everything you've had on your mind," I said.

She bit her lip. "It helps to keep busy," she said, and her eyes filled with tears. She wiped them with her sleeve, half crying and half laughing. "I guess I was still Daddy's little girl. I always felt he stood between me and the world, you know?"

She looked lost, and she obviously wasn't sleeping if the dark shadows under her eyes were any clue. "I lost my dad, too," I said abruptly. "I know it's hard. But you're doing great."

"I don't know why people share things like that," she said, straightening the rows of mugs, not looking at me. "It doesn't help. You have friends; you have your grand-father; maybe other family, too. And that Ben guy is all over you. I don't have any of that. My father was all I had."

Ben wasn't all over me. And she didn't know about my family. And if she thought she didn't have friends, she wasn't looking closely enough. But it seemed kinder not to argue.

"I'll guarantee you, no one thought the compost turnings would be our most popu-lar event," Haruto said with a grin as I passed him on his way to the compost pile.

"What's the temperature up to?" I asked, because he was hoping I would and I didn't have the heart to disappoint him. The heat generated by the compost pile was a source of wonder during his demonstrations. Haruto was its custodian, but we all contrib-uted our vegetable scraps and the gardeners added their weeds and trimmings, so it was a communal effort and an impressive size.

He flushed with pleasure. "One hundred forty-two degrees. It's cooking." He hesi-tated, then added: "Those women from the shelter who came by this morning to help me have been great."

"What women?"

"Bella and AnaZee came out here at eight. Said they saw me working from the window and did I need any help. I put them to work finishing up dead-heading roses and raking the paths."

He nodded in the direction of two young women near the toolshed. One of them had a rake in her hand, and the other was returning a pair of garden shears to the toolshed. The taller woman had aged bronze skin and hair like a wedge of chocolate cake; her companion's skin was like uncooked pastry, with lank brown hair tied back in thin ribbon like a piece of string. I remembered Ben Turlough's brief histories of his residents and wondered, inevitably, which story went with which woman. Ben appeared beside them with two mugs of hot chocolate, which they took with shy smiles.

"Nice work, Haruto," I said. He threw me a wink and strode off in the direction of the compost pile, looking even more eager than usual to show off his pride and joy. I saw Davie over there, his black eye blooming. He gave me a big grin, which made me smile back. I turned as I heard a faint musical chime behind me.

"Cold?" Nat said. One of his pale blue cashmere-clad arms came gently up around my shoulders.

"Not now," I said cheerfully. "This reminds me of the fairy tale about belling the cat," I said, picking up the pendant and letting the tiny chimes run through my fingers.

"A fairy tale, huh?" He smiled down at me, his eyes sparkling with amusement.

"Where's Derek?" I said.

"Waitin' for me in the car. I only came by to say a quick hi. He wants to get over to the workshop and I get to watch adorin'ly."

"You love being needed," I said.

"True. I'd be pissed if he hadn't asked."

"You guys made up?"

He waggled his head from side to side. "I'd say we're mostly good. He's worried about gettin' this job finished for Professor D'Allessio."

"Oh?"

"It's a surprise," he whispered. "For Mrs. D for their fiftieth anniversary."

"It may be more of a surprise than he thinks; I think Ruth is hoping for an anniversary cruise."

He grinned and looked around brightly. "So what's the latest with Sabina and Kurt? I couldn't overhear a damn thing last night."

"Sabina seems to be having a hard time dealing with his exes." He gave me big eyes. "Not me, you idiot, mostly Nicole, who he's apparently cozy with, and Helga, who isn't an ex — is she?" He shook his head. "— but who has that thing for him. Look, have you seen Nicole? I haven't seen her for a couple of days and I think she's avoiding me."

His grip loosened as he looked in the direction of her apartment. "Not since I basically threw her out of the apartment the other night." He looked a little ashamed of himself, then he leaned down and sniffed ostentatiously. "Pretty perfume," he said after a few seconds.

"Thank you," I said, mistrusting his innocent tone.

"Makeup too?"

"A little blush."

"And mascara. And a teeny touch of eye shadow. Very tasteful."

I heard the women from the shelter laughing and then Ben left them and came in our direction across the garden. Added to the scar over his eyebrow, his earring made him look like an Elizabethan rogue.

"Everything looks beautiful out here," Ben said with that smile as he reached us. It made him look years younger. He wasn't coiled tight today; he seemed relaxed for the first time since we'd met.

"You're probably seeing it in daylight for

the first time," I said, and blushed. Damn!

"Advance plannin'," Nat said solemnly. "The gardeners give a little tweak here, a tweak there. Like makeup on a pretty woman. Gotta run." He blew me a kiss and darted off. Jackass.

My cheeks still felt warm in spite of the cold morning. Ben frowned around the garden, much as the professor had done earlier. Fortunately, the old man was nowhere in sight.

"It was good of you to let Bella and AnaZee lend a hand. They said everyone's been friendly," he said.

"That was Haruto's doing."

He raised a surprised eyebrow. "The same Haruto who leapt down my throat the other night?"

I made a gurgle of laughter. "He's a bit whimsical," I said.

"Bella and AnaZee are smitten. He must be schizophrenic."

We found them near the swings and he introduced us, by first names only. The women were guarded, with watchful eyes. Bella pointed out her daughter playing on the swings. The child had long blond hair and purple shadows under her eyes. I asked the women if they'd seen a machete while they were working around the garden, but they hadn't.

"This is a nice place for kids," AnaZee said, looking around at the enclosing buildings. "A safe place."

I heard what she meant; I know how necessary it is for a terrified woman to feel safe.

"Come and show me around, Theo," Ben said next to me, and we left the two women to whatever comfort the garden gave them.

"Tell me about the fuzzy, snaky-looking red plant over there," he pointed. "Don't think I've ever seen it before."

He was making conversation. Nice. "It's an amaranth, which sounds sort of boring, but it's got a great common name."

He smiled at me. "What is it?"

"Love-lies-bleeding." I walked blindly into one of the rosemary topiaries. I needed to stop looking at his face and pay attention to where I was walking.

He took cigarettes from his jacket pocket, and offered me the pack. I shook my head. He lit one for himself, inhaling the smoke as if he'd been waiting a week. "Trying to quit," he said.

"How's that going?"

He chuckled. "Not great. I notice Californians don't smoke much."

"It's pretty unusual. Once you've been

here a while the universal condemnation will get to you."

"I doubt it," he said, and I thought he was probably right.

I walked him through the main areas of the garden, most of the time watching his face more than where I was going. Lesson not learned apparently. He took my arm a few minutes later to prevent me from walking through a rosebush. As we finished our circular tour I pointed out the compost pile and its custodian. Haruto was checking his thermometer again.

"That's Haruto?" Ben said. "It was dark the other night but I could have sworn the guy I saw out here was bigger. I don't remember the ponytail, either."

"When Haruto's defending his compost pile, he's nine feet tall," I assured him.

Ben hesitated.

"Why?" I asked. "Do you see anyone else it could be? Almost everyone is here."

"No." He thanked me for the tour and left me to talk to another one of his residents who had come down to join in the festivities. By now there were about forty people in the garden, several of them taking tours led by Gardens residents and others waiting expectantly near the compost pile for Haruto's demonstration. I sipped a hot chocolate, all plans to leave forgotten because Ben was still there. It had been a while since I took pleasure in simply watching a man move.

At exactly ten twenty-five, Grandfather planted his Swaine Adeney shooting stick firmly in the ground a few feet in front of the compost pile and sat on its leather seat. The rest of the audience used him as their polestar and gathered around him. Every now and again he waved an imperious hand at anyone arrogant enough to get in his line of sight and they respectfully fell back. We'd have the same performance at the bonsai demonstration if he was up to his usual form. I tried not to watch.

Ben walked over to join the audience and I hovered on the outskirts on a slight rise of ground that gave me a good view of Ben in the compost audience and of Helga serving hot chocolate and Mrs. Jupp enjoying herself at the sale table. Two young men walked away wearing sun visors; one of them was carrying a bud vase.

Haruto began the show; he was in his element, giving his little speech about aerating the compost to jog all the little microorganisms into doing their duty. He showed them the thermometer, the kind that looks like a metal lollypop, stuck into one side of the pile, neatly shaped like a square, a good five feet on each side, and over four feet tall. I heard his voice, fading in and out with each turn of his head.

". . . up to . . . and sixty degrees . . . steams on a cold day."

There were murmurs from the crowd and Haruto looked gratified. He indicated his watering can (a Haws, naturally) with which he sprinkled the compost after he lifted it, forkful by forkful, and replaced it in neat layers, like a cake. He uses a hose normally, but the watering can looks better for the demonstration.

". . . careful not to . . . too wet. Like a squeezed-out sponge is . . ."

Haruto loves it when he gets questions from the audience so I knew he'd be delighted with the opener from a young guy with his arm around a girl: "Can you put dog and cat poo in it?"

Grandfather says Americans are euphemistically inclined.

". . . glad you asked . . . the answer . . . no . . . harbor bacteria . . . don't want to hear about . . ." The crowd laughed.

Everyone watched intently as Haruto's face grew a few degrees pinker with each heavy forkful. A few people, I knew from experience, would be startled by the smell. Grandfather, accustomed to the perfume of the stable yard, wouldn't flinch.

Then three things happened more or less simultaneously. Haruto flung aside a particularly large forkful of compost, Grandfather did flinch, and someone produced a high, thin scream. A man with a mug of hot chocolate stood between me and whatever was happening. His cup slowly tipped and the cocoa dribbled unnoticed onto his trousers. Next to him a woman in gray and black sweats relaxed her grip on the string of a yellow helium balloon. It floated lazily away above her head.

What the hell was happening? Was Haruto injured? I stood on my toes to see over the crowd, but Grandfather was sitting rigidly on his shooting stick, blocking my view. And then he stood up abruptly and I could see all too clearly.

A woman's body lay partially exposed in the crumbly brown compost. Her throat was cut through to the spine, her head bent backward so that the wound was an enormous gaping smile above her abbreviated neck. Haruto's grip on the pitchfork wavered and he collapsed in a graceless faint.

The dead woman's hair was plastered with blood to her bare shoulders, so at first I thought she was naked. But then I saw that the rivulets of burgundy-brown stain only partially covered the glimmer of sequins. Blue and gold sequins. My stomach heaved and the ground felt watery beneath my feet. Someone gripped my arm to keep me from falling.

In awful slow motion, Nicole's bloody head flopped forward and a tiny avalanche of half-rotted vegetables fell out of her mouth.

CHAPTER FIFTEEN

The garden stopped looking like a children's book and started to look like a painting by Hieronymus Bosch. Oddly mismatched groups stared blank-eyed at the tableau around the compost pile. A teenager with a blond Mohawk solemnly handed his can of Coke to an elderly woman who sat on one of the children's swings, her face sagging with shock.

"Oh, God, the children!" I said, suddenly defrosting and looking wildly around.

"They're fine," Ben said, and touched my arm as if he thought I planned to take flight. He pointed at Sabina, holding a toddler in her arms, leading a cluster of young children farther down the garden, away from the horror. She was being trailed by an assortment of distraught parents like the tail on a comet.

The murmuring people closest to the compost pile were prevented from approaching it by my grandfather. He stood at parade rest with his back to her. No one, his uncompromising expression said, should even *want* to see her.

And then everyone, including Grandfather, was shooed away by uniformed police officers who materialized out of nowhere. An enormous, lurching fire engine crept slowly through the narrow entrance into the garden. With its red lights flashing and Klaxon blaring, it drove ponderously through the rose garden, crushing the bushes. Petals scattered, and the canes broke and splintered and lay slowly down under the wheels.

A sob caught in my throat.

"Theo?" Ben said.

I cleared my throat and wiped tears off my cheek with the flat of my hand. "The roses," I whispered. "Nicole loved them."

He frowned. "Wait here," he said, and left. He came back with a mug of hot chocolate and wrapped one of my hands around the mug. When the warmth reached my fingers I inspected the chocolate in the mug carefully, but didn't drink it until he raised it to my lips. I couldn't taste it.

God, Nicole!

I looked vaguely at the people nearest the compost pile. Helga was resting against Mrs. Jupp's shoulder, staring unblinkingly at the compost pile. Haruto had come out of his faint in the care of a paramedic and was sitting on the ground holding a hand over his eyes. They were all going to need therapy. A woman in a familiar red jacket was speaking to the man in the cocoa-stained pants. He looked pale and shaken. He'd dropped the cup at his feet and he had his glasses in his hands. He was wiping them meaninglessly, over and over, on the tail of his shirt. Inspector Lichlyter came across the garden to where I was standing.

"Miss Bogart." The depressed lines at the corners of her mouth were deeper than ever. She consulted the notebook in her hand. She was brusque with barely contained anger. I didn't get it and couldn't force my brain to work; why was she mad?

"The deceased was your business partner?" She didn't look up from her notebook.

"I think — I'm pretty sure — I mean I know it is because — Nicole."

"Does she have family?"

I tried to get my brain to focus. "No. Yes. An uncle, but I don't know his name. She only has — had a married sister in Wisconsin, or Minnesota I think."

She wrote that down in the notebook. "How are you doing? I have some more questions —"

"Right now she's going to sit down," Ben said, and he was right; I needed to sit down before I fell down. I couldn't remember the last time I took a breath and inhaled audibly. He took off his leather jacket and laid it over my shoulders without saying anything. It felt heavy. The satin lining was warm. I pressed it against me and absorbed the warmth. I hadn't realized I was so cold.

The inspector looked up from her note-taking and inspected him. "Try one of those benches," she said. "We won't be needing you for a few minutes yet," she added to me.

"I'll wait," I said vaguely, not very curious about why she might need me.

Her glance shifted beyond my left shoulder and I became aware of Grandfather standing composedly by my side. He took hold of my elbow in a courtly gesture and we walked slowly away. I looked back over my shoulder. A uniformed police officer was videotaping the scene immediately around the compost pile while another was taking photos. Haruto's pitchfork lay across Nicole's partly excavated body like a fallen spear and Grandfather's shooting stick was still planted firmly in the ground next to her.

Ben and Grandfather sat on either side of

me on a bench facing away from the compost pile. I hunched inside Ben's jacket and
thought of absolutely nothing. It felt as if
my mind had simply shut down. I didn't
think with any clarity about Nicole, or our
friendship, or the terrible sight I had just
seen. I didn't think about it, but I saw it as
if through a telephoto lens. Every tiny detail
was present in front of my eyes, even when
I closed them. Shock and sorrow were war-
ring with revulsion and seemed to be cancel-
ing each other out.

After clearing his throat a couple of times
and evidently thinking better of it and laps-
ing into silence, Grandfather said finally:
"The police will want to know when you
last saw your partner alive."

"On Friday," I said. It helped to have
something to concentrate on. "She came
into the shop to borrow some money. She
needed to pay her rent. I wish I hadn't . . ."

"Hadn't what?" he said sharply when I
didn't go on.

"I gave her fifty dollars and a ton of
righteous disapproval."

Nearby, a knot of uniformed officers were
talking in voices quiet enough to make
individual words indistinct. For a few
seconds, I tried to make sense of the murmurs, but the sounds remained confusing. I

looked aimlessly back at my grandfather. His dark gray hair, impeccable as always, was slicked back with military precision by fifty strokes daily from a pair of oval, silver-backed brushes. A disobedient tuft of hair peeked coyly out over the top of his ear. His earlobes were very long. In early photographs of him, his earlobes were smaller. Age, I thought, makes strange changes.

His long face grew even more disapproving than usual as I stared at him. "Theophania, pay attention," he said. "Your partner was stealing from you?"

"For about two months," I said. "I told her it had to stop, or . . ."

"Or what?" He aimed a worried look at Ben. The two men had unexpectedly developed a rapport that required no speech.

I felt confined by their book-end presence and excluded from some exclusively male understanding. I considered standing up to make some sort of point and decided I felt too tired.

"I don't know. I hadn't figured out what to do. We had another fight. Oh, hell." I leaned forward onto my knees. Gradually becoming aware of a certain quality in the silence, I looked up. Ben was staring over my head to the compost pile; Grandfather was chewing the inside of one cheek and frowning ferociously.

"I think I will telephone Adolphus," he said finally. "My solicitor," he added to Ben.

"I'm an attorney," Ben said, with no relevance that I could see. Grandfather grunted.

They didn't talk anymore after that. Ben continued to stare over my head, and Grandfather chewed his cheek meditatively. I don't think he would have kept doing it if he'd been aware of it.

After what felt like hours, I watched our visitors slowly file out of the garden past Sabina's table, where two uniformed police officers sat, talking to each person. They inspected credit cards or driver's licenses and wrote down the answers to a series of questions before anyone was allowed to leave.

"Names, addresses, and telephone numbers," Ben said. "Routine."

He got up and stuffed his hands in the pockets of his jeans, watching the scene behind my back with undiminished attention.

I heard crunching steps on the bark chips of the path and Sabina appeared and knelt down beside me.

"This is so awful. Poor Nicole!" Her voice cracked a little. "Are you okay, Theo?" she whispered.

"Not too bad," I lied. "How about you?"

She grimaced. "Not great. Kurt threw up."

Kurt did? I would have thought a doctor would be immunized against most horrors.

Grandfather cleared his throat and she looked at him in confusion and then at Ben. "Mr. Pryce-Fitton, I didn't see you. And, er —"

"Ben Turlough," he said economically.

"Oh, right," she said vaguely. "I guess I'll be getting back to the kids and Kurt if you're okay, Theo. Are they finished with you? Are you going up to the apartment?"

"The police," I croaked. I cleared my throat and began again. "They want me to stay and talk to them when they get finished. They asked me if Nicole had any family, but I couldn't tell them much except for her sister."

Sabina's brow crinkled. "She was married twice, but I don't know anything about her exes. There was a cousin or something," she said.

"An uncle, I thought."

She nodded. "Right. An uncle. Had a weird name. A nickname? It reminded me of horses."

"G.G.?" my grandfather said unexpectedly.

Sabina looked at him doubtfully. No point in explaining to Grandfather that Americans don't understand arcane English patois. But Sabina's face cleared. "Oh, right. No, it wasn't that. A kind of horse, maybe? She only mentioned it once and that was years ago."

"I didn't know you knew her that long," I said.

Her color was suddenly brilliant. "Not as long as some people," she said, and made a peal of penetrating laughter that rang like a bell in the silent garden. Heads turned in our direction. The laugh had obviously surprised Sabina, too. Her eyes went wide and she covered her mouth with her hand.

"Is Haruto okay?" I asked, anxious to get off the subject of horses and inappropriate laughter in case Grandfather hadn't run out of suggestions. The guessing game was too frivolous for the occasion; a nickname wasn't going to tell us much anyway and the police would find what they needed from Nicole's phone contacts.

Concern for Haruto reclaimed Sabina's earlier manner.

"Ruth D'Allessio has him wrapped in a blanket somewhere." She sounded approving. "I'd better get back to Kurt. The police have told us we can leave. I'm going to cook for him to take our minds off things — I'll make plenty and bring some up later, okay?"

"Sure. Thanks," I said, and tried not to observe that Nicole's death was already bringing Kurt and Sabina together. She gave me another hug and left.

"Nice young woman," Grandfather said with more approbation than I'd heard in his voice in years. He obviously didn't recognize her as the leather and motorcycle-helmeted object of his disapproval a few days before. He was probably blinded by her knowledge of horses. When I was three years old, he had held me up on his beloved and enormous hunter, and I'd screamed in terror. Later attempts had the same result. Because he gave me no choice, I eventually learned to ride competently, but I never learned to love horses as he did and, I'm convinced, they learned to despise me.

"They've put a screen around Nicole's body," Ben said some time later. All I'd been aware of in the meantime was the silence all around; even the birds had stopped singing, frightened away by the fire engine's raucous arrival. The only thing unchanged was the sweet smell of the hundreds of flowers in bloom all over the Gardens.

"Ms. Bogart?" Inspector Lichlyter had approached quietly. "I wonder if you'd make a formal identification?"

"Isn't that usually done with photographs?" Grandfather said with a frown.

Lichlyter gave him a considering look. "Not always," she said. "We've moved her so she looks less distressing," she added unexpectedly to me.

"Distressing" wasn't the word I would have used, but I appreciated the sentiment and clung to it as we rounded the screen shielding Nicole's body. She was lying in a long, black plastic bag, with an opening that went only as far as her chin. Supported from behind by some fortuitous bump in the terrain, her head still looked attached. She was puffy, soft and swollen and unnaturally pale, especially her lips, which were almost gray. My treacherous memory presented me with a reminder of Haruto's pride in the temperature of his compost pile.

I felt the swimming-ground motion I'd felt when she first fell forward out of the compost and my stomach pitched in the same way. This time the grip on my arm was the steely fingers of Inspector Lichlyter.

"Okay?" she said briskly.

"Yes. It's Nicole," I whispered. "Nicole Bartholomew," I added more formally. "She used her maiden name. Is that all you need

210

me to say?"

I felt unable to move. She turned me away from Nicole the way my nanny used to when I was defiant as a child, by grasping my hand and walking around me so that I was forced to follow her lead.

"She didn't have any identification on her. We need her address," she said when we'd traveled a few yards.

"Eleven-A Fabian Gardens. Over there." I pointed at the ground-floor apartment.

"Right. I know that was tough. You did fine." It sounded like ritual reassurance. "What's your full name and address?"

I looked at her without answering and at the young officer with the video camera who was now filming me. I turned away slightly but he followed my movement so that he stayed directly in front of me.

"For the record," she explained.

"Theophania Bogart. Thirty-two Fabian Gardens. On the opposite side of the garden." My stomach rolled again, a little more emphatically. "Is that all you need?"

She frowned. "For now," she said, and underlined something savagely in her notebook. "You can go, but I want to talk to you again."

"I'll be at home."

When I did throw up, I managed to be

alone behind a large acanthus. Someone handed me a handkerchief and I automatically wiped my mouth, hating the bitter taste and the loss of control.

When I looked up Ben was politely staring at the fire engine.

CHAPTER SIXTEEN

By unspoken consent Ben, Grandfather, and I went up to my flat together by the back steps. Lucy came to the door to greet us, but for the first time since she'd known me, I ignored her. Ben stroked her head and she followed him into the kitchen, looking up at him and rubbing her head against his leg at every opportunity.

The flat welcomed me as if I had lived there for years instead of days. I took off Ben's jacket, and folded it on the kitchen counter, and wished I had a few chairs for people to sit in. If interior designers are right about a person's living space revealing state of mind, my mind was currently full of sharp corners and hard surfaces. Ben perched on the end of the kitchen counter, but Grandfather was clearly nonplussed. He leaned his shooting stick against the dishwasher and folded his arms.

"Does anyone want some tea or coffee?

Or there's a bottle of wine in the fridge," I said. I felt at some obscure advantage on my home court, even if I didn't have any furniture.

"Sure, I'd like some coffee," Ben said easily. He'd become less watchful in the last few minutes, like a doctor whose patient has come out of a fever. I wondered what that meant exactly; I've known people who are only interested in wounded birds, not strong, healthy, able-to-fly birds. I hunched my shoulders self-consciously, as if testing my flight feathers. They felt strong again.

"The coffee press is over there. There's some coffee in the cabinet. You'll have to drink it black; mugs are behind you. Help yourselves and I'll be right back."

Sounding a lot more in control than I felt, I left them to it.

I went into the bathroom, where my white towels were like slabs of snow and somehow comforting. I rinsed my mouth, washed my hands and face, and ran a comb through my hair. I stared at my reflection. It was like looking at a stranger. My eyes looked huge and dark in my pale face. The high neck of my black T-shirt gave my head an uncanny resemblance to Nicole lying in the body bag. I leaned on the bathroom counter and gripped it until the queasiness passed. I splashed some more cold water on my face and dried it with a towel, but it still felt clammy.

When I returned to the kitchen, there was a fresh pot of coffee brewing but Ben had left. Maybe there were some broken wings somewhere to be fixed.

"I have some Earl Grey tea, or Darjeeling if you'd like some," I said to Grandfather. "But no teacups, only the pottery mugs," I went on, unable to stop myself. "I bought them at a street fair from the woman who made them." His teacups were early nineteenth-century Crown Derby. A set of twelve and their matching saucers without a single nick or chip.

"Nothing, thank you," he said distantly. The expression in his eyes sharpened. "I — er, hand-thrown pottery can be very appealing."

"I'm sorry there's nowhere to sit," I said impulsively.

He waved my regret aside. "No need for a lot of chairs you don't use."

"No," I said, not sure I liked his easy assumption that I never had guests who would want to sit down.

"The renovation —" I started to say.

"Yes, of course," he said a little impatiently. "I'm going downstairs to see —

when you can expect that inspector person," he said. Perilously close to admitting to an unseemly curiosity, he was pink cheeked and vigorous; stimulated by recent events rather than crushed.

I hid my understanding by pouring a mug of coffee for myself. I looked up, expecting him to offer his cheek for a kiss and leave without further ado. Instead, he hesitated. It was like seeing a Grenadier Guard out of step with his regiment.

"Are you feeling better?" he asked a little tentatively, but as if he wanted to know.

"Yes, I am," I choked.

He held out his arms stiffly and after a brief hesitation I stepped into them. He closed one around me and pressed my head gently to his shoulder. I couldn't stop the tears from coming and felt comforted when he rubbed his hand up and down my back.

I heard a minor commotion on the back stairs, wiped the tears and blew my nose on a neat handkerchief Grandfather handed me, and went to the door to see what was happening. Davie and Ben were struggling with a folding card table.

"Hi," Davie said cheerfully, apparently unaffected by the events of the morning. "Ben said you wanted a table and chairs so the lady cop could sit down."

I opened my mouth and then shut it again. He was right. I couldn't let her conduct the interview while we lounged on the bed like Roman courtesans or sat cross-legged on the floor by the fireplace. Unreasonably, Ben's tact was beginning to annoy me.

"Fine," I said. "Thank you," I added to Ben.

"You're welcome," he said, dry as the Sahara.

They set the table up in the dining room, and went back downstairs to collect four folding chairs.

"Someone gave us these for the game room at the group home," Ben explained as he unfolded the last of the chairs. "We can do without them for a few days."

"I won't need them that long," I said. Nicole had been planning something sleek and modern for my empty dining room. I hoped the wobbly card table wasn't some sort of portent. It looked full of ominous significance.

Inspector Lichlyter appeared in the back door. "Is it possible for our conversation to be private?" she said without preamble. As before, the order was masked by the polite question. Unisex police academy courtesy, or the usual woman's diffidence about giving orders? I looked at her determined expression and decided it had nothing to do with diffidence. I heard heavier footsteps on the stairs and a man's head rose behind her back like a slow sunrise.

"Sergeant Mackintosh will make a record of our conversation if you have no objection," she said, starting to dig around in her shoulder bag.

"I'd like to stay," Ben said suddenly, "to represent Ms. Bogart." I hadn't expected that. He and Grandfather exchanged a look, a mere seconds' glance, and Grandfather prepared to leave.

"You're her attorney?" the inspector asked.

Ben nodded. I opened and shut my mouth without saying anything when I caught my grandfather's eye. As clearly as if he'd spoken I heard: "Only fools, Theophania, don't accept help when it's offered." I didn't say, of course, that I thought his new chum might have his own reasons for wanting to hear what I had to say to the inspector. Maybe now wasn't the time, but we'd been together in the garden and it still bothered me that he hadn't asked anything about my "prowler."

"I have no objections, Mr. Turlough," she

said. "But Mr. Pryce-Fitton and Mr. Rillera —"

At first I didn't realize who she was talking about, but Grandfather said his good-byes with uncharacteristic meekness and Davie sidled up to me to whisper: "Don't worry, Theo. It'll all be okay. I found that guy."

"What guy — ?" He shuffled outside and he was stomping down the stairs before I could gather my wits. I clamped my lips shut. I could only think of one guy he might mean. Charlie O'Brien.

"Wait!" I said hastily. "Er — Grandfather." He paused in the act of picking up his shooting stick from where he'd leaned it against the dishwasher. Feeling ridiculously like a child imparting a secret, I muttered hastily in his ear as he bent courteously toward me: "Ask Davie about the guy he found." I kissed his cheek.

"I'm sure you have nothing to worry about, my dear," he said distinctly. And then he closed one eye in a grave wink and he left.

I took Inspector Lichlyter into the dining room and we all sat around Ben's card table like an ill-assorted bridge foursome. Inspector Lichlyter took out her battered notebook and pressed it open on the table. It still bulged with extra papers and reused enve-lopes covered with penciled notes. She didn't write in it much however, merely referred to it occasionally. Sergeant Mackin-tosh had an iPad. His fingers tapped stolidly throughout the interview and I never heard the sound of his voice.

Inspector Lichlyter didn't ask questions, she imperceptibly encouraged me to talk. And whether from relief or the aftereffects of shock, talk I did. An hour later, I felt I had exposed every conceivable detail about Nicole's personal life, our friendship, and our professional dealings.

I mentioned the missing machete and all she said was: "We found it underneath the metal screen in the fish pond."

"Is that how she was killed?"

She flipped back through a couple of pages in her tattered notebook. "People are usually killed by someone close to them," she said conversationally. "A husband. Lover. Business partner." She paused. "It makes our job easy quite often."

"It can't always be like that," I said anx-iously.

"Ms. Bogart, do you know what a tontine is?" She didn't seem to expect a reply so I kept silent and tried not to fidget while she wrote something fairly lengthy in her notebook in faint, hard pencil. She looked up. "What sort of a partnership agreement did you have with the deceased?"

I looked at the top of Sergeant Mackintosh's head as he bent over his iPad; his hair was thinning. I kept my voice level. "A fairly standard one. I had capitalized opening the store, so officially I was to be paid back out of the profits, but we didn't make much in our first year and this year, in practice it was usually fifty-fifty."

"Losses as well as profits?"

"Of course."

"And in the event of one of your deaths?"

"The survivor . . ." I hesitated.

"Takes all?" Inspector Lichlyter sounded mildly inquiring.

"It's a standard provision. Nothing unusual, and hardly a tontine," I said. I could feel perspiration gathering on my upper lip. "My death would have benefited Nicole slightly, since she wouldn't have to pay me back," I said earnestly. "But her death leaves me pretty much where I was before."

"But of course it did rid you of an awkward partnership with a partner who could have run up some significant debt, which you would have had to pay."

There was no denying it. I wondered what else she knew.

She flipped several pages of her notebook and studied one of the pages. "You argued, I believe, the last time you and the deceased met?"

"We had a slight disagreement," I admitted, "it wasn't important." Then I remembered the telephone message I had left on Nicole's phone, rehashing the conflict. I had been furious by the end of the message — and sounded it.

"About money?" she said, as if I hadn't spoken.

"It was nothing new. It had been going on for —"

"Ms. Bogart has been more than cooperative," Ben said suddenly. "She's had a serious shock and needs to rest." He looked sleepy, even bored, but the inspector folded her untidy notes into her notebook, thanked me, and prepared to leave.

"Before you go — this is going to sound melodramatic," I said uncomfortably. I glanced at Ben and he still looked bored. But I had seen lawyers look bored before — it was the deceptive calm of a lazily swimming shark. I liked him better when I thought he was a social worker.

She said thoughtfully: "You think the death of Mr. Callahan and the death of your partner are connected."

"Don't you?" I said in surprise. She made a slight moue with her lips.

"There's something else," I said. She waited. "Can you tell yet when Nicole was killed?"

She looked at me without answering. "Why?"

"I was thinking that if it was two nights ago, I had a — a sort of prowler here that night. Yesterday he came into the shop and asked for Nicole by name. I followed him and —"

"You did what?"

"I followed him. His name is Charlie O'Brien and he works for a tax service called AcmeTax."

Ben stood up suddenly, then rubbed his fingers into his temple as if he was massaging away a migraine. "Doesn't mean they're connected," he said. "You need to stop talking now."

"No, I know, I thought . . . he was here, and . . ."

Lichlyter took off her glasses and gave me an unsettling, lopsided stare with her blue and brown eyes. "We'll check into this, Ms. Bogart. And now I'm going to ask you something that will sound as if it comes out of left field, and I'd appreciate it if you'd keep it to yourselves." She waited for nods

223

of agreement from me and from Ben. "Do you know anything about rhinoceros horn?" she said.

For a long moment, I thought I'd misheard her. She might as well have asked the question in Urdu.

"Er," I said intelligently. "Do you mean — what do you mean?" Where else had I heard mention of rhinoceros . . . rhino. Her notebook. It said "rhino" in the notebook she left at Aromas.

"Anything that comes to mind." Her tone was casual, but she was watching me intently.

"Um — let's see. It's made of some sort of compressed hair material or keratin, not horn or ivory; some rhinos have one horn and some have two; I know there are different kinds of rhinos, white and black and some other kind from somewhere besides Africa. Sumatra? No, that's something else. One kind has a pointed lip; the other kind has a sort of square mouth. Um — I know some rhinoceros are endangered and near extinction and poachers shoot them for their horns. But — oh, I know, Arabs use the horns as dagger handles or something. Is that right?"

"And that's everything you know?"

"Isn't it enough?" I said, a little wildly.

"Mr. Turlough?"

"That about covers what I know, too." He was looking a lot less bored.

She gave him a speculative look. "It's a part of the Chinese pharmacopoeia. An expensive part," she said. She looked expectantly at me, but I was still bewildered. She shut her notebook and rose. "Okay then. No one knows anything. We'll have a word with Mr. O'Brien." She gathered up the silent Sergeant Mackintosh and left.

"Rhinoceros horn?" I said incredulously to Ben. I wasn't sure what to do next. I felt oddly exposed in my foundling chair. Ben seemed uncertain, too. He ran a hand through his hair and I watched it fall back against his skull in undisciplined waves. He had blunt, powerful fingers. The occasional gray hair in the black curls made him seem vulnerable and I felt a tug of physical attraction. He began to say something when a noise from outside interrupted him. I was relieved. He was making me more and more uneasy. I couldn't decide whether his involvement was social worker routine or specific to me. Impossible to ask. Impossible not to want to know.

Grandfather came back with Davie and I gave everyone coffee. They sat on cardboard boxes and ate rice cakes and honey. It

225

seemed like a time for sugar and they were the only sweet thing I had in the glamorous kitchen cabinets. Even Grandfather had one, perched on a cardboard box like a fantastical tweed insect, balancing a plate on his knee and appearing — astoundingly — to enjoy himself.

"Mr. Rillera tells me that he's found this fellow; the one you — er — followed the other day," Grandfather announced.

"How did you find him?" I asked Davie, who beamed when Grandfather called him Mr. Rillera. He was thoroughly at ease and relishing being center stage.

He wiped his mouth with his hand and swallowed. "I followed you when you left the store," he announced, and faltered at my astonished expression.

"But, why?"

"I was worried the asshole might hurt you, like before," he said anxiously.

I swallowed nervously. Ben frowned. "He hurt you?"

"He means something else," I said hurriedly. I concentrated on reassuring Davie. "It's okay. It's nothing like that. So what happened next?"

He went on more confidently: "You went back to the store, and so did I, but later I went back to where he worked and followed him home." I stared at him blankly. He swallowed a rice cake more or less whole, scattering crumbs all over himself, flicking them off unconcernedly and licking the honey off his fingers. "He lives around the corner from that place where he works. And you know what? I've seen him someplace around here." He looked at me triumphantly.

"Here in the Gardens?"

"Yup. Working on a computer. Through a window." He couldn't complain that he wasn't holding his audience's attention. We were all riveted. But that brought him to the end of his information. He helped himself to another rice cake and dribbled honey on it with a soup spoon.

"What window? Can you remember?" I said hopefully.

He frowned in concentration and shook his head. "Nope, but I'll think about it." He smiled radiantly. "Did I do okay?"

"Davie, you did wonderful!" I said. Grandfather winced slightly, but I didn't care.

I telephoned Lichlyter's office and left her Charlie O'Brien's home address. Learning something more about him made me feel as if I had regained a little dominion over my life. A very little, all things considered, but it cheered me enormously.

CHAPTER SEVENTEEN

After the coffee party Davie, Ben, and
Grandfather all left together when I insisted
that I was fine, that I wanted to get some
rest, that nothing was going to happen to
me, that I would call one or all of them if I
needed anything. It took some persuading,
but I finally got them to leave. It was late
afternoon and I barely resisted the tempta-
tion to get into bed and go to sleep.

I talked to Haruto, who was still shaken
but not inclined to talk much. I asked him
if he wanted company, but he said he was
spending the afternoon with a friend. Sabina
brought up a plate of hot food, but I didn't
ask her to stay and she soon left. I couldn't
face the thought of food, especially something that looked like lamb and raisin
couscous. I gave it to Lucy. We went downstairs briefly for her outing. Parts of the
garden were cordoned off. The compost
pile, the toolshed, the koi pond. The com-

post pile was still the center of some official-looking activity, but the rest of the garden was deserted. I looked over to Nicole's empty apartment. I couldn't make my brain believe I would never see her again — she had been a large part of my life here, and a mostly positive part of it. Her intense, enthusiastic friendship had given me Aromas; a connection to the art world I'd once loved; a relationship with a shady chemist — and a barely habitable apartment. I missed her already.

I spent the afternoon calling Nicole's friends; it was early evening when Nat arrived by way of my back door.

"Hey, English," he said breezily. "Coffee on? Derek's still workin' and doesn't want me hangin' around anymore so —"

He so clearly hadn't heard the news that I blurted it out. "Nicole's dead," I said baldly.

He smiled. "What now?"

"No, Nat. She's dead. Killed."

"Killed?" He was watching me warily. "Like a traffic accident?"

"No. Killed. Murdered."

"Oh dear Lord on a crutch. When? How?"

"Don't know. We found her this morning. She —" I gave him a sketch of the morning. He went grayish when I described how she'd been found, but I was too involved in the telling to spare him the details.

His reaction when I came to a halt was unexpected. "Trust Nicole to die so it causes the most possible trouble."

"You don't mean that." I gave him a glass of Chablis and he took a gulp, looking a little shamefaced. "Can you think of a reason for anyone to kill her? Or both Tim Callahan and Nicole, if the two deaths are connected?"

He grimaced. "Two violent deaths in less than a week? They have to be connected."

We talked about Nicole for another hour and then Nat yawned an enormous yawn and detoured into a non sequitur: "If you wanted to know something about Chinese medicine, who would you ask?"

"What?"

He gave me an apologetic look. "Sorry. My head feels like a cat pissed on my brain. But who?"

"Mr. Choy on the corner. His father used to keep a Chinese herbal place. I bet he could tell you what you want to know. Whatever that is," I added nervously. Why couldn't I get away from this Chinese medicine business? Only the promise made to Lichlyter kept me silent about the rhinoceros horn.

"I should have thought of Mr. Choy," he

said slowly, and faded into silence.

"What do you want to know about it?"

I thought nothing would make me smile on that ghastly day, but Nat managed it, deliberately or not.

"It sounds trivial next to Nicole, but it's those damn herbal concoctions Derek is taking all the time!" he burst out. "I keep telling him to get a real medical prescription if he's so damn worried about his hair — there must be something besides Rogaine — but he's takin' things I've never heard of and I'm afraid he's poisonin' himself! You can laugh," he added, when I could no longer keep myself from chuckling, "but some of them turn his pee purple."

I hugged him. "Get home to your man. And stop worrying. He's no fool; most of those herbal remedies are made of mushrooms and squid, like chow mein. Call me tomorrow, okay?"

Minutes after he left, Inspector Lichlyter telephoned and asked if I would accompany her to Nicole's apartment the following morning. They had determined, she said formally, that Nicole had not been killed there; they'd appreciate some input on whether anything was out of place in the apartment.

"Right," I said. "Of course. Ten o'clock?

See you then."

When I'd hung up, I almost fell asleep with the receiver in my hand, and jerked awake, wanting desperately to crawl into bed. I decided to take a hot bath before calling Nicole's sister in Wisconsin. I took my time, washing my hair and wrapping it in a huge towel so that I looked like a cross between a snowman and a Bedouin in my white terry bathrobe.

I couldn't remember the married sister's name, but I thought Nicole might have put her address in the Aromas laptop. I went down the back way in my bathrobe and slippers. The garden was completely quiet, although it wasn't all that late. The police had strung plastic tape around the diminished compost pile and I heard it rustling.

I turned on a couple of small table lights as I made my way to the office. At night, the flowery ceiling is mysterious instead of fresh and outdoorsy; the shop intimate and den-like. The front window was lustrous, shutting out the street. It gave me a vivid picture of myself as I stood in the center of the shop. I inhaled deeply. Nicole's death had somehow lifted a huge weight from my shoulders and I was having trouble feeling terrible about it. No, I realized in some alarm, I was having trouble not feeling euphoric. I caught my breath on a jubilant high, before my mood plummeted downward and I broke into racking sobs. I buried my face in my hands and wept. Tears ran over my hands and down my arms and dried. The storm spent itself and still I stood unmoving.

I eventually went weakly into the tiny bathroom. A glimpse of my red face and puffy eyes was all I needed to remind me that I'm not an attractive crier. I soaked some paper towels in cold water and held them over my eyes as I sat at my desk.

Footsteps outside hesitated and Ben stuck his head around the back door.

"I saw the light," he said. He was breathing hard, as if he'd been running.

"Looking for a telephone number," I said awkwardly, keeping my face averted by carrying the laptop over to the counter. Ben came into the shop and looked around.

"Are you okay?"

I didn't answer and he looked at me carefully.

"It's enigmatic in here. Suits you," he said.

"It's not so enigmatic in daylight," I said.

He reached out his hand so casually that I quite naturally gave him mine. He kissed my palm lightly. It was an intimate, unexpected thing to do and it left me breathless.

He raised an eyebrow at me and gave me that smile, then left without another word.

The shop was alive and beautiful in the lamplight. Like a bower.

I remembered why I was there and found the number. I hesitated outside the door to Ben's studio, but it was quiet within and I didn't quite have the nerve to knock. What if he asked what I wanted? Yet I felt in the mood for a shared gesture. On an impulse, I went back into the shop and filled a muslin bag with herbs — mostly rosemary, lavender, and chamomile — and left it dangling from the studio door.

I had been dreading the call to Nicole's sister, but I needn't have worried. Even though I soft-pedaled the details, she was only superficially interested. She and Nicole hadn't met for more than fifteen years, she said in her flat, Midwestern voice. She asked me to take care of what she insisted on referring to as "the arrangements."

"Should I let her uncle know? Doesn't he live out here?"

There was a brief pause. "You're right. He's a half brother to Nicole's father — we were only stepsisters, you know. Now what was his name?"

The pause grew so long that I said: "If you think of it, perhaps you'll call me —"

"There are a few pieces that belonged to our mother. If I text photos, will you have them shipped to me? I'll reimburse you of course."

I swallowed. "What about her other things?"

"You can have anything you feel is worth keeping, or I'm sure the Salvation Army could use it."

"There's a new women's shelter around the corner. How about that?" I said.

She gushed at me a little. So grateful, she said.

I asked about Nicole's collages and paintings, but I could have been speaking Martian.

"Her what?" Her tone was completely uninterested. I heard a young voice yelling in the background. The lady muffled the receiver and shouted back and then apologized. "You know teenagers," she said comfortably.

"Her paintings. Her artwork."

"Well," she said doubtfully, "are they any good?"

Her attitude was inexplicably heartless. Nicole's work was better than good. She was maturing as an artist, and her recent work was especially compelling. I agreed to send her sister some photos so she could make her own determination, and all I could think was: I'd want someone, anyone, to care more than that if I was murdered.

CHAPTER EIGHTEEN

Unreasonably, I slept like a log. Lucy and I were still asleep when Lichlyter arrived at 9:55 the next morning. She was wearing the red jacket and had two men in tow.

"While you and I are in Ms. Bartholomew's apartment, I'd like your permission for these two officers to search your flat here."

"Seriously? Why?" I was tucking my shirt into my jeans and felt less than ready to face the world.

"A matter of elimination mostly," she said blandly. "I could get a warrant, but I thought I'd ask first."

"But what are you looking for?" God, I needed a cup of tea and a bagel or something.

She screwed up her face a little. "There may be some small thing."

"But Nicole hasn't been here. I only moved back in myself a few days ago. It's been a construction site forever."

She didn't say anything.

I shrugged uneasily. "Fine. Why not? Be careful of Lucy, that's the dog," I explained to the two men. "She's little; but she's fierce. Don't upset her, okay?" They nodded without speaking. I couldn't imagine it would take them more than five minutes to hunt through the entire flat.

I tried prospecting for a glimmer of humanity in the inspector. "Can we walk past the coffee shop? I need help waking up."

"I haven't been to sleep yet," she said neutrally. "The first thirty-six hours in a homicide investigation are usually nonstop."

There was a sign on the door of Aromas reading Closed Due to Illness. A knot of people with too much time on their hands stood gazing from across the street, from which I deduced that the neighborhood bloggers and Facebook posters were in full cry.

She wouldn't let me buy her a cup of coffee and punctiliously paid for her own. Helga gave me my usual mug and asked the inspector if she'd prefer a return-deposit ceramic mug or a disposable cup. She took the paper cup, which raised my hopes a little. Maybe she didn't expect to be around long enough to need a mug of her own.

"How are you doing?" I asked Helga as she handed over our drinks. "You were pretty close to things at the sale table yesterday."

She shook her head. "Why bury her there? Why do that?" She sounded genuinely puzzled and I understood how she felt. It was disrespectful, making the murder even worse somehow. "Here," she said, "have a doughnut. On the house," she added awkwardly. "Fresh this morning." No wonder she looked shattered; after the emotional day yesterday I'd barely been able to drag myself out of bed at ten o'clock. She offered Lichlyter a doughnut, too, but the inspector refused, so I breakfasted alone as we left through the back door of the coffee shop and walked across the garden.

After a quick glance I avoided looking at the compost pile. Most of it had disappeared and when I mentioned this, Lichlyter said: "Evidence," as if that explained it. And perhaps it did.

"We didn't find any drugs in her apartment," she said suddenly. "It was one of the first things we looked for."

"Why?"

"Modern times," she said tiredly. She rubbed her eyes.

"She didn't keep it there," I said, acting

on a decision I didn't know I'd made. "Cocaine," I added baldly.

"There was none on her body, either."

"She carried it in a heart-shaped locket."

She pulled her notebook out of her shoulder bag with her free hand. "Can you describe it?"

"I can draw it for you." She handed me her pencil and I sat on a bench, balancing the notebook on my knee. "It was chased and engraved silver, quite large, with a clasp at the side. The engraving was of a cupid wreathed in roses; it appealed to her sense of humor," I said as I sketched. "She usually wore it on a black silk cord." I finished the drawing and handed her the notebook.

"Did she always wear it?"

"Nearly always. She wasn't wearing it on Friday. She wasn't really an addict," I added, feeling an obscure need to defend her. "It was fairly new."

She looked at my drawing. "We didn't find a locket in her things. How long have you known?"

"About the cocaine? For a couple of months, give or take." I wondered for the first time where Nicole's cocaine had come from. I had always connected it somehow with her art school contacts, but I had never asked. Now it occurred to me that her dealer might be more local than that. Didn't drug dealers make examples of deadbeats to frighten their other customers? I started to mention the theory, but we arrived at Nicole's apartment and I suddenly had other things to think about.

The apartment had a musty smell, even though the police must have spent hours there the day before. I asked Lichlyter for permission and when she nodded, I threw open a couple of windows before opening the door to the studio.

Most of her rooms relied on light wells for illumination, being on the ground floor and sandwiched between the buildings on either side, but the studio jutted out at the back. It had skylights and windows on three sides overlooking the garden. Nicole once told me those windows were her reason for taking the apartment.

I had been at her apartment for pizza and wine two weeks before, but I hadn't been in the studio. The portable paint box she used to take with her on excursions into the Marin Headlands lay open and crusty with dried paint. Her big wooden easel leaned against one wall. A jumble of baskets on a central worktable spilled over with foreign-language newspapers, colored rags, chunks of driftwood, small pieces of machined metal, even strips of animal fur. Several of her newest collages stood propped with their faces to the wall. I tipped a couple back to look at them. She had told me a few months back that she had begun a series called Extinctions. There were three of them here: huge animal-like shapes, elephants perhaps, splattered with bloodred paint and shreds of hide and lettering that didn't spell anything but that looked vaguely malevolent. As I stood them back against the wall I abruptly made a connection to the strange conversation about rhino horn.

Odd coincidence.

Fine arts magazines were piled on an armchair. I leafed through one and found the small review of her work I'd been looking for. Praise from a distinguished critic. We had both been so sure it would mean the launching of her career. I showed it to Inspector Lichlyter.

"I sat in that chair and watched her work the day the article came out," I said. I could almost see her at her easel — her canvas work apron and her hands daubed with paint, her curly hair escaping its confining ribbon. She'd been excited, busy, and fulfilled, looking forward to the recognition she was sure was coming. Except it hadn't, quite. A year after the review her art was still an avocation, not a career.

I dropped the magazine back on the chair and left the studio, followed by the silent inspector. Everything was exactly as it had always been in the rest of the apartment. She had three of my photographs in frames in the hallway, famous faces in candid close-up. The computer she'd used for Aromas' books was swathed in plastic covers in the small room next to the studio. I looked out the window at the garden and felt my eyes prickle with tears.

"I'll need to get at the computer fairly soon," I said. "It has Aromas' books and records on it. She always said we should keep them separate from the shop in case anything happened and we needed to reconstruct everything after an earthquake or a robbery or something."

"I'll let you know when," she said briefly. "We removed the hard drive yesterday and gave it to our forensic computer guys."

The bathroom was neat on the surface. Nicole used our hypoallergenic line of soaps and cosmetics and she had them all jumbled into the drawers. Lichlyter said, picking up a bottle of hand lotion: "She seems to have more than the usual quantity of things like this."

I looked again, sorting through all of the

drawers carefully, but it was the same as always. "She was always trying out new lines and had a lot of stuff around."

There were a few serious-looking books I hadn't seen before on finance and investing, which I mentioned to Lichlyter; small heaps of magazines and catalogs, but little clutter in the rest of the flat. A pile of unopened bills from credit card companies told its own tale.

She had a few pieces of good furniture, more inexpensive fill-ins from Ikea, most of them improved in some way with more skill than money. She'd gold-leafed and lacquered the coffee table. I'd always liked its ditzy grandeur and she'd promised to do one like it for my renovated apartment. The secondhand sofa was covered in airbrushed canvas. A couple of wood and canvas director's chairs at a Formica table in the kitchen served her for a dining room. I used to think her surroundings were simply a reflection of her taste. I realized for the first time that the cocaine must have been costing a good deal of money.

"Is there anything about the apartment that seems different or out of place?" Lichlyter spoke formally. "Anything that should be here that isn't, or vice versa?"

I hesitated, took a last look around, and

shook my head, filled with useless regret for a wasted life, for a friend in need. "Everything else seems about right." Which was ridiculous; there was nothing right about it. "Did you know she was once married to Tim Callahan?"

"We knew that. How long have you known?"

"Since a couple of days after he died."

"Do you know about any other relationships she might have had with the people here? We're trying to build a picture of her life, not only here and now but in the past."

"She and Derek Linton and Tim Callahan were at art school together," I said. "Professor D'Allessio was one of her professors at Berkeley. She used to say San Francisco is like a small town in some ways." I hesitated. "She was close to Derek and to Dr. Kurt Talbot."

"She and Dr. Talbot were lovers at one time, I understand."

I was genuinely startled. "Who told you that?" Lichlyter pursed her lips and didn't say anything. "She never mentioned it," I said. Not even when Kurt and I *were* lovers.

That felt weird.

When we got back to my flat she went into an immediate huddle with her two minions.

One of the men handed her a clear plastic bag and she held it up for my inspection.

"Do you recognize this, Ms. Bogart?" she said.

A heartbeat of incredulity was followed by a leaden and, to me, audible thump as my heart fell into my shoes. My drawing had been accurate; the silver cupid in its wreath of roses winked at me from its plastic shroud in her hand.

"It's Nicole's locket, the one I was telling you about." And then, because I had to know: "Where did you find it?"

One of the men consulted Lichlyter with his eyes and she nodded.

"In the laundry room," he said.

"But Nicole hasn't been in the flat for weeks," I said distinctly. I felt my face redden. Even I felt as if I was lying; I'm sure it looked that way.

Lichlyter folded the plastic evidence bag into her pocket. "Yes, I remember you saying that. Any idea how it might have gotten there?"

"None! I've no idea at all. The last time I saw her she wasn't even wearing it. It's impossible!"

"So it would seem," she said aridly. "Thank you for your help. I'll be asking you to come downtown to make an official statement later today or tomorrow."

As they left down the back stairs — and I was closing the door emphatically behind them — the front doorbell rang.

Inexplicably, a rolled-up carpet was propped against the wall outside. A man with a clipboard ran up the steps.

"Delivery for Bogart? Sign here, please." He proffered the clipboard.

"Bogart's my name, but I wasn't expecting anything. I think this is a mistake," I said. How had that locket found its way into my utility room? Someone must have dropped it there. But who? Nearly all my friends had been in and out of the apartment for the past few days. Dear God, was Nicole murdered by someone close to me?

He checked the clipboard. "Nope. Right address. Deliver to T. Bogart. Sign here, please."

"But I'm sure you've got the wrong person," I said in exasperation.

"Lady, I don't have time for this. Look. Delivery to T. Bogart. That's you, right?"

I nodded. "Yes, but —"

"Thirty-two Fabian Gardens. That's here, right?"

"Yes, but —"

"Sign here, please."

His smugness was infuriating. "Who sent

the damn carpet?" I snarled.

He sighed and flipped over a couple of pages. "Pryce-Fitton."

Grandfather?

The man officiously held out his clipboard. "Will you sign here?"

I signed.

"Jack!" he bellowed over his shoulder. Another man dogtrotted up the stairs and between them they bullied and cajoled the carpet into my living room. They cut the strings and unrolled a soft, glowing, and majestic Persian rug that covered almost the entire floor in deep reds, blues, and golds.

"Nice, huh?" the first man said as if he were responsible for the gift.

"Yes. Beautiful," I said blankly.

CHAPTER NINETEEN

Because I couldn't think of what else to do after they left and Grandfather's housekeeper said he was out when I called, after giving the carpet a last incredulous look I went down to Aromas. Davie was sitting on the front step spinning the wheel on his bicycle as it lay on the sidewalk. The yellow rose was dropping petals on his massive shoulders. He leaped to his feet when he saw me.

"Hi, Theo," he said cheerfully.

"Hi yourself. I'm keeping the shop closed for another couple of days."

He shuffled his feet and looked shifty. "I know. Can I come in and feed the butterflies?"

He keeps a small butterfly habitat in the shop and feeds them sugar nectar by unrolling their tongues carefully with a pin, the way a botanist at the Academy of Sciences showed him. He's starting to recognize what kind of butterflies he'll get from where he finds the eggs. I helped him to write a letter about it a few weeks ago. The botanist sent him some pamphlets and invited him for a tour, which thrilled Davie to the core.

While he fed them, I mechanically dusted shelves and rearranged merchandise. All I could think of was that damn locket. I was positive — as positive as I could be, anyway — that Nicole hadn't been in the flat for at least a month and I'd noticed her wearing it after that; so how had the wretched thing arrived in my utility room? Had Lucy found it in the garden? And if so, when? I wished a thousand times that I'd never mentioned it. Or drawn the damn thing.

Eventually I settled in the office staring mindlessly out into the shop and beyond to the yellow roses nodding over the front window.

"I've finished," Davie said from the office doorway.

"Okay then," I said, and got up to let him out.

"I could stay if you need me."

"Not really," I said thoughtlessly. His face fell and I had a sudden inspiration. "Why don't you see if Ben could use some help over at the group home?"

He chewed his thumbnail. "Will you ask?"

"Uh, okay." I listened to the phone ringing, rehearsing what I'd say when they put me through, but he flummoxed me by picking up himself.

"This is Theo Bogart," I said.

"I found your gift on my door."

I'd forgotten about the bag of herbs. "Good will from the local chamber of commerce," I said casually, hating myself for needing the pretense.

"Thanks anyway," he said.

"Davie wondered if you needed any help over there. We'll be closed here for a couple of days and he's at a bit of a loose end."

"He couldn't ask me himself?"

"He's shy, that's all."

"Sure, I could use some help." He paused. "How are you doing?"

"I spent the morning with Lichlyter."

"Next time call me; I'll come with you," he said gruffly, and went on in a different tone: "I wouldn't normally bother you about this, but —"

"What's wrong?"

"Nothing. Everything's fine. Except I promised the kids yesterday they could play in the attic here; I want to keep them away from outside, so I wondered if I could bring this stuff of yours over to get it out of here."

My head felt packed with rags. "What

stuff are you talking about?"

"The wooden crates marked with the name of your store. Everything else is gone; people came by on Saturday to get the things they had stored here."

"Wooden crates?"

"Right. Crates. Made of wood," he said slowly, as if to a deranged person. "You know — wooden crates."

"Of course I know what wooden crates are, but — forget it. If they belong to the store, I'll come and get them."

"They're too heavy to carry over. I'll bring them over in the van. Send Davie; he can help me load them."

They came with AnaZee, and the four of us unloaded the crates into the garage. Ben handled the crates with strong, practiced movements as if he was accustomed to physical work. He filled out his jeans nicely, too, which I may have noticed before. Clearly he worked out. It was difficult for me to imagine him in a law office.

Davie dusted off his hands. "I'm going to inventory the housekeeping supplies over at the shelter," he said proudly as he left.

I looked over at Ben as Davie left and said, "Thank you." He made a sketch of a bow. He was wearing a small gold ring in his ear, like a pirate. I admired the fit of his jeans again as he gave one of the crates a shove with his foot.

I gave myself a mental shake and thanked AnaZee for her help. The tall black woman with the chocolate-cake hair said quietly: "You're welcome. I'm sorry about your friend; it's real terrible."

And I had allowed myself to forget for a few minutes. She said she was about to begin her shift at the ecological center on the street level of the shelter.

She took a deep breath and glanced at Ben, who gave her an encouraging nod. "We thought of asking your association if they'd pay for, you know — sponsor — some new trash receptacles for outside the stores. We thought of a three-part container for glass, aluminum cans, and paper . . ." She trailed off a little uncertainly.

"You'll have a natural ally in one of our members, Tasmyn Choy," I smiled. "Shall I have Tasmyn call you over at the shelter? You can work up a presentation for our meeting next month." Maybe the project would forestall the usual argument over what to do with the proceeds from the Open Garden.

"I'd like that." She nodded shyly and left.

Ben stayed, adjusting the position of the crates along the wall. Much of the wall space was already filled with neat stacks of cartons and rows of plastic gallon jugs. The three wooden crates were nearly five feet long and eighteen inches deep. They were discolored — as if they'd traveled a long distance. Indecipherable printing appeared on them at random. The fluorescent lights overhead flickered. I half expected the crates to disappear.

"I think there's been some sort of mistake," I said.

"There's the name of the store along the side in black marker," Ben said, brushing his hands on the seat of his jeans.

"Mmm. I see it. That looks like Nicole's writing. But no one ships our sort of merchandise in wooden crates — too expensive. They weigh more than the contents."

Nicole had jealously overseen the inventory, and I had seen no reason to interfere. I'd no idea why these crates were in the attic at number twenty-three. She did occasionally store stuff elsewhere when the garage was full for some reason, but there was plenty of space at the moment.

Ben cleared his throat. "About last night."

I realized I had been silent for some minutes, perplexed by the enigma of the crates.

"Don't apologize," I said awkwardly, when

I realized he was referring to the kiss he had dropped on my hand.

He scowled. "I wasn't going to. I wanted to tell you — that I'd like to do something I might have to apologize for."

"Oh!" He had my full attention again. We exchanged wary glances, like foxes standing on our hind legs and sniffing the air for spoor.

He gave one of the crates a needless extra push and looked at me sideways. "I've been married, but not for several years." I tried to hear it as casual conversation, but I felt the warmth of awareness in my face. He touched my shoulder. A tremor went through me, followed by a tingling sense of profound surprise. Cautious by habit, I found I couldn't speak.

He withdrew his hand and flexed it, then frowned at it as if it annoyed him. "Do you want to look inside one of these crates?"

"What?" I felt dazed.

"If you've got a crowbar or something . . ." He bent down to inspect the fasteners holding the crate together, apparently fascinated by the problem of how to break it open. I collected my wits and found a claw hammer, which he used with unnecessary violence to pry the crate open, sending splinters flying all over the garage. Together we pulled the wooden lid apart, but all I could see inside was about an acre of wood shavings. I started to root around and dug out a tube nine or ten inches in diameter and over three feet long. It was very heavy. It had end caps with leather thongs wrapped around both ends and a single thong along the length of it, like a carrying strap. I shook it gently and it made a soft, slurry sound as whatever was inside fell through the tube.

"It's some sort of rattle," I said, and handed it to Ben. I was more puzzled than ever.

"I've seen them in Africa," he said unexpectedly.

"Africa?"

"Two years. Peace Corps," he said briefly. I waited for him to go on, but he didn't.

"It must be something Nicole was planning to add to the store." But even as I said it, I knew it didn't make sense.

Ben was making dull little *thwocks* on the tube with a tapping finger, then he tugged at one end of the rattle and it popped open. A shower of rice fell around our feet. He peered inside the tube and looked up at me with a startled expression. "Not unless you were planning to feature rhino horn," he said.

"What!"

He tipped the rattle and something — looking undeniably like a hacked-off rhinoceros horn — fell into his hand. He put the tube on the floor and hefted the curved horn thoughtfully in both hands before handing it to me.

I stared at it incredulously. "Lichlyter asked — but isn't this illegal? Isn't there some sort of international agreement?"

"The CITES treaty," he said absently. He broke open another crate and found another two rattles nestled side by side. I helped him lift them out of the crate and he pried off the end caps and looked inside.

"More of the same," he said.

Oh, Nicole.

With one crate left to open we had a row of four amputated horns. Four animals had died in agony somewhere in Africa for these things to be lying on my garage floor in San Francisco. It was repulsive. From Ben's expression, he was also finding the experience less than wholesome.

"These aren't yours," he said finally as we stood in what I assumed to be an atmosphere of identical disgust. I was glad he hadn't made it a question. He sounded furious. I shook my head. He made a neat pyramid of the rattles and the torn-off end caps. The rice and wood shavings would need to be swept into a pile. A breeze under the garage door was blowing tufts of it around already. It reminded me of something. I made a small choking noise. Ben turned around. "What's wrong?"

"The painter, Tim Callahan. There were wood shavings in his hand. These crates were in the attic room he fell from; he must have been looking in one of these when . . ."

"When the owner interrupted him?" There was something odd in his inflection.

"Nicole? She wasn't a violent person." Besides, I knew Nicole couldn't possibly have thrown Tim Callahan from that attic window. It took a man — or a woman — of considerably more strength than she possessed. Although, as I remembered Lichlyter's demonstration with the broom, maybe it hadn't taken much strength to knock him off balance. And he wouldn't have been on his guard with someone he knew. I looked around at the strange place my garage had become and at the crate remaining to be opened. I moved toward it, claw hammer in hand. I shoved it away from the wall to make the opening easier. The top was badly gouged.

"Someone's opened this one," I said. "There are big splinters missing from the side." I easily slid the top planks sideways.

This crate contained a bonus. In addition to two more rhino horns, we found a paint-brush, stiff and crusted with yellow paint.

Chapter Twenty

"I suppose I'd better call Lichlyter," I said grimly.

"You don't sound too happy."

"Oh? I'm overjoyed about implicating my dead partner in a — a rhinoceros horn smuggling gang. I can't believe this. It's ridiculous." I slammed the back door of the garage.

"You don't have to tell her about the rhino horn," he said abruptly as we made our way up the back stairs. "Possession isn't illegal; only importing it is. Once the stuff is here, there's nothing anyone can do. It has to be stopped at customs."

"What kind of a protective treaty is that?"

"Over a hundred countries signed the CITES treaty. It's hard to get that many countries to agree on anything. The idea was to arrest the guys shipping it out of Africa and into Japan and Vietnam and wherever, to stop the trade at its source."

"But what's it for?" I wailed. "Is there a hot market in San Francisco for Arab knife handles or something?"

"Like Lichlyter said, the horn is ground into powder and used in some Asian medicines. It's supposed to be good for fevers and arthritis and it's a heart tonic. The Vietnamese think it's a cancer cure."

I unlocked the back door to my flat. "Why ship it whole? Wouldn't it be easier to ship as a powder and pretend it's spices or something?"

"Quacks have tried to pass off counterfeit powdered horn; people insist on seeing the horn so they know it's authentic."

"You know a hell of a lot about this stuff," I said sourly.

"I'm putting together a library for the ecological center; you wouldn't believe the things I know!" He sobered. "I know one more thing. At today's prices, those horns are worth about two hundred thousand dollars each."

I thought of that row of dismal dead things, looking like detritus from a theatrical property department, and did some quick arithmetic. "That makes the entire haul worth more than a million dollars?"

Ben nodded, looking uncomfortable.

"Wow. Worth a phone call, anyway," I said.

"And she asked us about rhino horn! How did she know? And how in hell does this fit in with anything?"

But Inspector Lichlyter was out of the office. I asked if she could be reached, but the voice on the other end of the telephone wasn't encouraging. In the end, I left my name and number and a message and asked her to call. "Tell her I've found some rhino horns and a paintbrush," I said. Then I had to do some fast talking to convince the cop that I wasn't a prankster.

"A few hours isn't going to make much difference," I told Ben as I hung up.

"I hope you're right." He looked uneasy.

"I'll grant you things are getting weird, fast."

He took my hand in his and stroked the tips of my fingers thoughtfully. My stomach curled. God, this was getting complicated. I pulled my hand away with an effort.

"And maybe dangerous," he agreed, as if nothing had happened. As if I hadn't stopped breathing. He looked unaffected, which was galling. "I wish I didn't have to be away tonight."

I thought of saying that having him downstairs in the studio wasn't all that helpful anyway, or that I was accustomed to taking care of myself, but all I said was: "Away?

Where are you going?"

"I'm flying to Los Angeles in" — he checked his wristwatch — "ninety-seven minutes. I have a morning meeting. I'll be back around lunchtime tomorrow." He hesitated. "I wouldn't go, but —"

"Of course you have to go," I said, and tried not to sound wistful.

"Isn't there someone you could stay with?" he said in sudden frustration. "Do you have to be here alone?"

"Being alone isn't what worries me," I said.

But he refused to smile. "For God's sake, be careful," he said. And then he was gone. I couldn't be used to having him around so I told myself I didn't feel abandoned, even though I did, a little.

I took Lucy down into the garden for her evening outing, carefully locking the back door behind me. The light was failing and the garden was deserted. The fire engine's heavy tire tracks still defaced the rose garden. I expected the professor and his helpers to be cleaning up. Maybe the police had told them not to. Preventing them would practically take a court order.

I heard Nat before I saw him; he was toying with the pendant around his neck and I followed its faint, clear chiming around a shrub to find him sitting moodily on a bench with his long, elegant legs stretched out in front of him. He was holding the pendant and swinging it in front of his eyes like a hypnotist.

"Hey, Nat."

He brightened. "Hey, English."

"You'll put yourself in a trance."

He dropped the pendant and it nestled into the pale pink cashmere on his chest. "And do embarrassin' things, like eat dirt or cluck like a chicken?"

"That's the idea — all inhibitions released."

"How about releasin' your inhibitions with a drink at Chez Nat and Derek?"

I grimaced and shook my head. "I'm going back upstairs in a few minutes, lock all the doors, bar the windows, load my little gun and stick it under my pillow, and sleep for a week."

Nat stirred restlessly. I gave him an inquiring look, but he only shrugged. I watched Lucy rustling in the flower bed. "Come back with me," he coaxed. "Everyone and his brother is up in our flat. Derek is tellin' us all about Nicole's heroism as an activist fifteen years ago; Sabina and Helga are taking the position that activism does more harm than good, so Derek and Sabina aren't speakin'. Haruto is suckin' all the air out of the flat praisin' the virtues of Asian versus Western medicine. You'd expect Kurt to be pissed off about that, but he's just drinkin' Scotch as if he's crawled on his hands and knees out of Death Valley. I had to get out for some fresh air."

"What does Haruto know about Asian medicine?" I said blankly.

"Turns out he's turned himself into an expert herbalist by takin' courses all over town and he and Derek are chewing the fat — if herbalists chew the fat; maybe they chew ginkgo leaves instead — like a couple of old cronies. Derek is ready to invest in anythin' to make his hair grow back."

"Invest?"

"Emotionally speakin'."

"Is that the only reason you wanted to talk to someone about Chinese medicine?" I felt relieved of a nagging little worry.

"I wanted to make sure he wasn't poisonin' himself. Mr. Choy told me the things he's takin' are okay. They contain plenty of *shou wu*. Or maybe they don't contain any *shou wu*. I'm unclear on the details. Whatever. He said they might even do some good. He also told me about ginkgo leaves– you cook 'em up with a bunch of other disgustin' stuff to improve your memory. He implied mine could use improvin'."

I shook my head and smiled.

"Come on," he said. "Bring Lucy. It's a kind of impromptu wake."

"I'm not in the mood, especially if everyone's being crabby."

"Come with me, or I go up to your place with you and Derek tracks me down and everyone follows him and ends up in your kitchen."

I sighed. "Who's there again?"

"Everyone! Haruto of course — practically weepin' because he's lost all his precious compost. Sabina, too — she's taking Nicole's death hard for some reason and it's comin' out in bitchiness. She's almost invisible under that yellow thing she's crochetin'." He gave a delicate mock shudder.

"What is it, anyway?"

"Illinois, I think. Helga suggested it was sorta shapeless and Sabina went for her throat. Let's see, anyone else?"

"It's already way too many people for me."

"Prefer the company of one, eh?"

"Who are you talking about?" I said repressively.

"You know damn well. The handsome one with the earring. Where is he, by the way? I could invite him over."

"He's in L.A."

His face fell comically. "For good?"

"Overnight. Do you honestly think he's handsome?"

"Let's say I wouldn't throw him out of —"

"Jesus, Nat. Give it a rest."

He gave me a surprised look from underneath his eyelashes, raised an eyebrow, and said thoughtfully: "Well, well, well. Today's paper said the icebergs are breakin' up. Spring is a dangerous time of year in the North Atlantic."

I concentrated on looking noncommittal. With Nat in this mood anything I said was going to get me into trouble.

He looked disappointed. "Not playin' today, hmmm? At least you're over Dr. Kurt."

"I've been over him for a long time." And as I said it, I realized it was true. My heart hadn't been broken but my anger had been hard and real and hot. Not feeling it in the background was a relief of sorts.

"Come on over. I think we're all huddlin' together pretendin' not to care that some madman —" He abruptly shut up. "Sorry," he muttered. "My springs are loose today."

"Anyone else?" I said.

"There's no room for anyone else," he moaned. "Professor D'Allessio called —"

"That's it — I'm not coming!"

"— but he only wanted to talk to Derek about the big secret anniversary gift, so you're safe."

"Why wasn't I invited earlier?" I said vaguely. Why did I have the feeling that I was being stupid about something? Something about Nicole and the professor? Or did mention of him remind me of something else?

"No one was invited; they just all arrived! I was goin' to call you when it looked like you were the only person who wasn't goin' to show, but if you ask me we're all ashamed because none of us had been exactly gettin' along with Nicole lately."

"I didn't know," I said unhappily.

"No one wanted to upset you. Besides, if anyone had said anythin' you'd have frozen them out. You're very loyal. Upright, honest, and true," he added with a grin.

"Nice way to put it, but what you're saying is that everyone was too polite to point out the obvious to the village idiot," I said with a sigh.

CHAPTER TWENTY-ONE

He called out as we walked through the French doors into their two-story living room. "Look who I found!"

A chorus of welcoming cries greeted my arrival. Everyone was already pretty well oiled, judging by the general hilarity. Derek seemed relatively sober; at least he had co-ordination enough to apply a tiny screw-driver to a pair of glasses from his perch on the arm of the couch. He looked up to blow me a kiss. He looked more like the frog foot-man than ever.

Sabina was sitting slightly apart from everyone else, crocheting busily. Her afghan, or whatever it was, flowed over her lap and onto the floor in great yellow waves.

Haruto was arguing with Kurt about — saints preserve us — the compost taken by the police.

"You wouldn't use it on the garden any-way, after —" Kurt was saying with a distinct slur in his voice. I wasn't so sure.

"Another Coke, Sabina?" Nat said.

"Sure. Thanks," she drawled.

"Nothing stronger?"

She shook her head.

He picked up some paper cocktail napkins and a couple of empty glasses and took them out to the kitchen. He was compulsively tidying up as usual. Sabina leaned over and turned on the MP3 player. Someone sang "What Becomes of the Brokenhearted." Haruto and Kurt wrangled about whether it was the Four Tops or the Temptations. Neither of them bothered to get up and look. I knew it was Jimmy Ruffin, who was related to one of the Temptations, but I didn't say anything.

"What shall we do about the D'Allessios' anniversary party?" Haruto said to the room at large as a pause in the chatter was in danger of letting thoughts about Nicole and her killer creep into the room.

Sabina turned to me with a smile. "Theo's here, maybe she can tell us the right thing to do."

"What?" I took a grateful swallow of the gin and tonic Nat handed me.

"The fiftieth anniversary party," Haruto said. "Do we go ahead as planned next week or should we postpone? Ruth D'Allessio didn't like Nicole — sorry, Theo — but she thought it might be more appropriate to postpone it, for at least a couple of weeks."

"I guess it doesn't make much difference," I said with a flash of temper. "No one seems to be mourning her anyway." My sore conscience made me angry; I couldn't be said to be mourning her myself.

"At least we're not hypocritical," Sabina said with surprising venom. But she wasn't looking at me, she was watching Kurt.

"I liked her," Derek said, breaking the spell but with his eyes still on Sabina. "She'd still be coming round except —"

"Go ahead, blame me!" Nat said, surprisingly not making a joke of it. "Because I thought your little friend was a bitch —" His voice wavered. He took out a handkerchief and turned it into a campy gesture, and everyone laughed, if a little uneasily.

I started to get up to follow Nat out to the kitchen, but he threw me a wink over his shoulder and, not entirely reassured, I sank back into my seat. Derek finished his eyeglass repair and gave them to Haruto with a hand that shook a little. He and Nicole were friends and he was prevented from mourning her by Nat's jealousy. And Sabina's eyes were red. And Kurt was drinking in a way I'd never seen before. And

271

Nat's nerves were jumpy. And Helga was wearing a thousand-yard stare. No one looked particularly festive. I guess we were all mourning her in our own fashion.

"Sorry, everyone," I said contritely. "The last few days have been . . ."

"Yeah. They sure as hell have," Haruto said, and everyone looked relieved.

"We could all use some chamomile tea to soothe our nerves," Derek said, obviously trying to lighten the mood. "Remember that time Nicole made some and we decided to make rum coolers out of it? Yuk!"

We all laughed. "I remember when she was a firebrand, not a staid businesswoman with a sideline as an artist," Derek said fondly. "We even got arrested together in art school — man, she could get a crowd revved up quicker than anyone I ever saw! Believe me, at the end of one of her demonstrations, we all needed more than chamomile tea!"

"I'd rather have a Valium. All this herbal hocus-pocus — medical science has come a ways since ground-up lizards," Kurt said piously.

"No one gets addicted to lizards," Derek said, looking hurt.

"Besides, medicine and surgery can't cure everything," Sabina purred. She laughed and one or two of us joined in a little nervously. Kurt, the surgeon, didn't laugh.

I hastily brought the conversation back to Nicole. If this was a wake, dammit, she should stay in center stage. "What were her big issues when she was a student?" I asked Derek.

"She wanted to make a difference. She was ready to take on anyone over anything! The color bar at the Adelphi Club, rebuilding the Embarcadero, green spaces on the Presidio, getting toilets placed in the parks for the homeless — man, she was relentless." He shook his head with a smile.

Helga snatched up another beer; she lifted it to the room in a little salute before drinking it more or less in one gulp. "I've got to get back to my ovens," she said. I put a hand on her arm as she passed me. "Stay a little longer," I said.

She looked down at me blankly. "The croissants won't bake themselves."

"C'mon. Another half hour. What made you open a bakery, anyway? You work half the night."

"True," she sighed. "I was born a princess and, alas, an evil queen stole my fortune. Luckily I'm a natural night owl," she said. "Okay, half an hour." She picked up another beer, which she dispatched with equal efficiency. As far as I could tell they were having no effect.

"I'm sorry, honey; I know this isn't a great time for you," I said, but it was the wrong thing to say.

Her face darkened and she sniffed, rubbing the back of her hand against her nose in an effort to stop a tear escaping. It didn't work and she looked away from me over to Kurt, who was staring at the top of Sabina's head as she concentrated on her crochet hook. Crap.

Besides the obvious there was something wrong here that had nothing to do with Nicole's murder. The undercurrents — what a poet friend once called the ocean under the sea — were dragging me in directions I didn't want to go.

Nat came back with a bottle of Scotch in one hand and gin in the other. "Forget the herbal elixirs," he said cheerfully. "Let's all have another drink."

So I did. And another. And a couple more. The effects of alcohol, I've been told, are exaggerated by emotional stress. I was feeling seriously stressed. I'd been asked not to mention rhino horn to anyone — even before I found it; my suspicions about Tim Callahan's death being murder were presumably *infra dig* too; I was sorrier than I

274

could admit about Nicole, more frightened than I could admit about the idea of a killer on the loose; angrier and more worried than I could admit about Lichlyter not being on hand when I needed her. I forgot that I hadn't eaten for the best part of two days. And every time I picked up my glass it was full.

"This is a great idea," I said at about midnight. "That damn inspector has me tied up in knots." There was a chorus of "Me, toos" from everyone. "She's all over us like a blanket for days and when I have something to tell her, she's nowhere around."

"What are you going to tell her? Have you thought of something?" Kurt's cheeks were bright. He waved his half-empty glass for punctuation. I got a grip on my loose tongue and shook my head casually.

Haruto, whose ponytail was shaken loose around his face so that he looked more dis-sipated than usual, said: "The professor was trying to tell her something this morning, but you know how he is, he gets more and more Italian and hard to understand and he blames whoever he's talking to and —" Several people laughed. "— anyway, he decided she was an idiot and refused to talk to her. He called her 'the knows one.' "

"Nose? What about her nose?" Kurt said, looking puzzled. "I didn't notice anything about —"

"No, 'the knows one,' because she thinks she knows it all." Haruto shook his head fondly.

Speaking for all of us, Derek said: "What was he trying to tell her?"

"Yeah. What could he know?" Kurt asked a bit belligerently.

But Haruto either didn't know or wasn't saying.

I got up to go to the bathroom and on my way back down the hall I zigzagged drunkenly into the wall and stood there for a couple of moments trying to steady myself. I could hear fragments of an argument coming from somewhere; two voices so low and angry they sounded like cats hissing. I peered around the doorway into the kitchen, but the lights were off — no one there. Must be in one of the bedrooms, I thought, sluggishly, listening hard.

I crept quietly toward the back of the flat, feeling my way along the wall. I heard a burst of laughter from the living room.

"No! You're not getting it!" a woman's voice hissed somewhere close by. "Kurt's a bastard."

"You will, or I'll —"

"Or you'll what? Kill me?" A hysterical laugh accompanied a fumbling noise, followed by a small thump. Then Nat's voice: "Leave it!"

The bedroom door immediately in front of me burst open and Sabina marched past me, rigid with fury. I flattened myself against the wall but I don't think she even saw me. Nat came out into the hall almost immediately. He put an index finger to his lips.

"Everything okay?" I said.

"Couldn't be better," he said cheerfully. He offered his arm theatrically and we waltzed back down the hallway.

"Is anyone else thinking Tim falling had anything to do with Nicole being killed?" Sabina was saying as we got back into the brightly lit living room. "Otherwise it's all too weird."

Helga, who had decided to stay, slammed another beer. Those croissants tomorrow were going to be one hell of an odd shape.

I was trying to get back to my seat without falling over and succeeding only marginally, so I wasn't paying attention to what I was saying: "You want weird? What about those crates of — stuff — in my garage." I slid gracelessly to a stop. I didn't exactly cover my mouth with my hand, but damn near.

"Crates?" Kurt said, looking puzzled. "You mean like trunks or something?" He came over with the gin bottle.

"Sort of," I said casually, falling back into my chair and trying to concentrate on the lemon peel in my glass. Kurt topped it up with more gin and I smiled at him mistily. I had more attention than I wanted, even if everyone's mind was nearly addled from Nat's liberal hand with a bottle, and I tried to think of something innocuous to say that didn't involve wooden packing crates and rhinoceros horn. Derek's face floated in front of me. He was shaking his head. Fine. He never drinks so he could afford to look superior.

"I'm hungry," I announced.

"I think you're drunk," Nat said, plopping an ice cube into my glass. Why had he and Sabina been arguing in the bedroom? I tried to focus on his face. It looked the same as ever. No. He looked relieved about something.

"We're all drunk," I announced, with a swing of my arm that nearly decapitated a table lamp.

"When did you last eat?" he said.

"I told you I was hungry," I said wisely. "I don't remember. Breakfast. Doughnut." I waved at Helga, who looked vaguely disgusted.

Nat snorted. "Five gins on an empty stomach. Come on. Let's get you home."

Derek caught me as I lurched to my feet and nearly fell over the coffee table. Lucy growled from underneath it. "Maybe you should spend the night in our spare room," Derek said with a grin as he swung me over his shoulder. I thought fondly that friends who stay sober and can still be amused by drunks are true friends. Everyone laughed a little too loudly. Derek carried me down the hallway. Someone took off my shoes and I put my head on the pillow with a snort. This was a good idea. I nodded to myself and wished I hadn't. The dresser — complete with some of Nat's simpering Royal Doulton figurines — floated up to me and do-si-do'd back against the wall. I stared at the ceiling and concentrated very hard on making the light fixture stay in one place. I grabbed hold of Lucy as if she were a life buoy. Nat opened a drawer on the bedside table and I felt him slip something small into the pocket of my jeans.

"Whassat?"

"I told you — in case those icebergs keep breakin' up. Protection in fluorescent orange." I thrashed around trying to reach into my pocket to throw the small packets at him, but got tangled up in the comforter and gave up.

"Sleep tight; don't let the bedbugs bite," Nat's voice said affectionately from the doorway. The light went out.

"Hey!" I said. "It's dark!"

The moon came out from behind a cloud. I could see the pale outlines of furniture. "How's that?" Nat's voice said.

"S'very good. G'night. Smart-ass."

I heard him chuckling to himself as he went back down the hall. When I concentrated fiercely, the ceiling light fixture stayed still, and without noticing it, I drifted off to sleep.

I dreamed of machetes and koi ponds, of muttering voices and a glass breaking; of big silver lockets and a woman's voice, shrill and weeping. And a quieter argument between two men. The Brokenhearted.

My eyes popped open and I knew that the worst was about to happen. If I didn't get to a bathroom in the next fifteen seconds, Nat would never forgive me. Badly disoriented and still very drunk, I stumbled into a closet before tottering down the hallway to the main bathroom.

I threw up for the second time in twenty-four hours, and waited to see if a repeat performance would present itself. When it didn't, I felt a little better. I sat on the side of the whirlpool tub with my head in my hands and tried not to groan. I looked in the medicine cabinet for Alka-Seltzer and found dozens of paper packets with hand-written labels, some in English, some in Chinese, and some with only numbers. I had no idea what to take, or if one of them would grow hair on my tongue.

The bathroom was, like the rest of the house, immaculate and beautiful. The twin vanity mirrors had curved metal frames set with panels of luminescent agate. Derek's work. Various silver-topped bottles were in height-graduated ranks with pale powders, crystals, and lotions inside. Pastel green towels were folded on glass and agate shelves. I looked at my reflection. I was the untidiest feature of the room. I borrowed a comb and tried to return some semblance of order to the shattered wreck in the mirror. I had to open a new bar of soap to wash my face — Nat always keeps a silver bowl full of Aromas soaps. What the hell. I ripped open the wrapper and tossed it in the wastepaper basket in what I hoped was a sufficiently artistic position. Then, because it seemed important the way things do when you're drunk, I rearranged it. I washed my face and hands and patted them dry on one of the fluffy green towels without unfolding it.

The house was quiet and so far I hadn't disturbed anyone; I wanted to keep it that way. I crept like a thief back to the guest bedroom, and fumbled with my phone until it told me it was 2:15. I picked up Lucy, still sleeping soundly, and carried her down the hallway with exaggerated care so as not to wake Nat and Derek. I couldn't find my shoes and decided to leave without them. I wanted to get home. My heart failed me, however, at the thought of crossing the garden in the dark. I left through the front door — carefully closing it silently behind me — walked up the hill along the silent street and entered my flat from the front. I fell gratefully into my own bed and was asleep in seconds.

CHAPTER TWENTY-TWO

I woke suddenly on an intake of breath with a hammering heart, not knowing why I felt frightened and feeling the muzzy aftermath of alcohol and a nightmare. My bedroom was dark. I could see the outline of Lucy's head and pricked-forward ears against the window, where clouds diffused the moonlight into a soft-focus halo for her. I took a couple of deep breaths and stretched uncomfortably in my clothes; considered getting undressed; reflected that whatever the nightmare was it must have been a doozy to wake Lucy, too; punched my pillow back into shape and prepared to roll over.

Lucy gave a hesitant little yip and cocked her head at me.

"What is it?" I fondled her ear gently and listened carefully, but heard nothing. I checked the time. It was three o'clock. "It's okay, nothing there," I said soothingly, but stopped suddenly to listen again. There it was. A thud. It was coming not from inside the apartment but from outside somewhere. Lucy growled deep in her throat.

Thinking of Nicole, and the macabre burial ceremony that must have taken place in the garden only a couple of nights ago, I peered out of the window. All was quiet and apparently normal. The clouds parted. Hard, bright moonlight illuminated the inky garden for a few seconds before the clouds closed over the moon like a curtain. In those brief seconds I had seen the garden as if floodlit, and nothing was moving. I was halfway back to bed when I heard it again — a little louder this time and more easily located. I pulled on a pair of shoes.

The noise was coming from my garage.

Feeling melodramatic, I tried to remember where I'd put the little gun. Where the hell was it? I stood, irresolute, and heard another noise from downstairs.

I was still drunk enough to feel that what I did next was a good idea. I grabbed the brass-handled walking stick I keep by the bed and made my way stealthily down the back stairs. When I got to the bottom, I heard a pastiche of faint, muffled noises and whispers and as I hesitated, the world fell on me.

■ ■ ■ ■

A sharp clink of metal on metal was the first sound I heard when I woke up. Its tinny chink reverberated like a kettledrum in my brain. It swooped and roared like a furious eagle, coming to rest finally at the back of my neck where it lay throbbing and pulsating and flapping its wings. I passed out again gratefully.

By the time I was conscious for the second time, everything had resolved into an excruciating headache. I was lying awkwardly on my stomach. My eyes were screwed shut, which was hurting my eyebrows, so I opened my eyes. Nothing changed. It was as black outside my head as inside. I blinked slowly a few times. It hurt like hell even to move my eyelids, but things stayed soot black. The renewed clinking noise distracted me for a few seconds by causing tears of pain to start into my eyes and roll down my cheeks, but I still couldn't see. Had I gone blind? It didn't feel like it. Why couldn't I see?

I rolled over onto my back. I'd been lying facedown on something cold and rough. My mouth must have been open; there was grit on my tongue. Ugh. I tried to wipe my mouth, which is when I discovered something new. My hand was immobile. I tugged it uselessly and the chinking exploded into a virtuoso performance. Gritting my teeth, I used my free hand to grope along the length of my arm and came to — a metal ring? A bracelet? The feeling of unreality expanded. There was a short loose chain — a handcuff? My fingers continued to probe delicately and found the second half. I was handcuffed to a metal pole.

For a second, the relief was tremendous. I don't know why but it felt great to know something, even something that should have been alarming. The euphoria lasted long enough for me to pull myself into a half slouch against the pole. But the metallic chinking quickened. *Chink. Chink. Chink. Rat-a-tat. Rat-a-tat.* My hand was shaking and then my entire body was trembling. It went on for too long; nausea rose to the back of my throat. Why couldn't I see? Why was I handcuffed in the dark?

"Think!" I shouted aloud, and that helped a little.

That's what was needed here. Bring a little intelligence to bear on the problem. I started with the pole, which, literally and figuratively, was the only thing I could get a grip on. I clasped my hands around it. It was three, maybe four inches thick. But how tall? What if it only reached above my head and I didn't bother to check? I ignored the thumping in my head as best I could, pulled myself up, and dragged the handcuff up the pole as far as it would go. The stretch pulled air into my lungs; I expelled it in a tiny cough. But the pole went up higher than I could reach and the stab of pain caused by the effort nearly made me faint again.

After a few minutes' rest I leaned out as far as I could, straining against the handcuff until it pulled at my flesh, and the fine bones in the back of my hand felt about to snap. I circled the pole twice to be sure and waved my free arm around in all directions. Nothing. Nothing but cold air.

I slumped down again onto the floor and scrunched up my knees to rest my head on. None of this made sense. The last thing I remembered — what was the last thing I remembered? I'd been outside the door of the garage. Was I in my garage? I thought hard. I couldn't see, but I could use my other senses; what could I figure out about my prison? I could hear a faint humming noise that might have been a piece of distant machinery; an occasional chink from my handcuff as I shifted; my own breathing, quieter now. And something else. Every hair on my body rippled as I identified the other sound.

Someone was breathing near me in the dark.

Before I could catch another breath, a thick moan came from somewhere behind me.

"Hah? What — uh — can't move — what — ?" A furious thrashing noise followed. "Shit!"

"Haruto! Haruto, is that you?" My voice was sharp with fright.

"Hah? Theo?" His voice was thick and muzzy. "Tied up. Hands behind my back." He grunted.

The thrashing noise came again. "Why can't you — wait, are you tied up, too?"

"Handcuffed."

"What the hell's going on?"

"Do you remember anything?" We were talking in hoarse, macabre whispers, which did nothing for my composure, but it seemed wise, all the same.

"I was asleep. I heard a noise. Thought it was the raccoons in the trash, came outside — uh, maybe someone hit me. God my head hurts." He made a few more grunting noises. Having been through the process myself a few minutes earlier I could sympathize with the disorienting waves of clarity and fog. "How long you been awake? Where are we?" His tone was getting sharper.

"Not long. Not sure. Can you move?"

Some rustling noises, then: "Uh — tied to — uh, pipe maybe? With plastic padding."

"Can you reach anything?"

Shuffling, followed by a dull thump. "There's something — cardboard box, uh" — more thumps, smaller this time — "Bottles. Plastic bottles."

Relief flooded me. In unison, we said: "The garage!"

"It's not long 'til daylight. Someone will hear us then if we yell."

"Unless whoever put us here comes back first." He sounded dispirited. "Good thing this isn't creepy or anything. Do you think — well, that whoever killed Nicole . . ."

"Great, Haruto. Thanks a lot. What? You think he's gone home to find a machete?" I'd meant to be sarcastic, but I sounded frightened, even to myself.

"Maybe the guy on your washing machine killed Nicole and came back to get us, too."

"It's been so eventful around here lately I'd almost forgotten about him. It's funny."

"What's funny? Doesn't seem so goddam funny to me."

"No, I meant Charlie O'Brien, the man on the washing machine. I don't see him as a man of action. If I'd tried to grab him, I swear he'd have slipped through my fingers, he was sweating so much."

Haruto asked me something else, but I didn't hear properly. I'd given myself an idea. I interrupted whatever he was saying. "Haruto — can you reach those bottles?"

There was a short, offended silence, followed by a sandpapery sound as he shifted along the floor. "Yeah. What good are they?"

"Can you roll one over?" A slithering noise was followed by a faint bump against my hip and the familiar feel of a plastic gallon jug in my free hand. "Some of these body lotions and shampoos might be enough lubricant to get me loose."

"I'll be damned." He sounded surprised. "Nat always says you're smarter than you look."

"He means it as a joke."

"You're a genius. I always knew it. Is that one any good?" He grunted. "I think I can reach another one with my feet."

I unscrewed the cap and sniffed gingerly. "Perfect. Hair conditioner. High oil content."

It took too long, and I left several layers of skin behind, but my well-conditioned and tormented hand finally slid out of the handcuff and I was free.

I staggered over to the wall and felt for the light switch and the stuttering fluorescent light gave me a strobe-effect picture of Haruto leaning against the hot water heater intake pipe. He smiled at me a bit uncertainly and I grinned back. The grin faded as I looked around the garage. The neat stacks of cartons and Aromas merchandise were still there, but everything else — the wooden crates, the wood shavings, the rhinoceros horn — was gone. The thieves had even swept up the spilled rice.

I found a box cutter and cut Haruto loose. He rubbed his wrists where the rope had made rough blue indentations in the flesh. Those gouges must have hurt like a bitch but he hadn't complained. He walked around slapping his thighs to restore the circulation.

I looked over at the metal pole jack my architect's crew had installed to hold up the building. The handcuffs were puddled at the base.

Neat to the last, I recapped the half-empty bottle of hair conditioner and returned it to its place. Something glinted on the floor and I bent over to pick it up.

"What's that?" Haruto said curiously as I poked it with my index finger in the palm of my hand. "Looks like a four-leaf clover."

I was beyond surprise. "It's a shamrock lapel pin," I said.

CHAPTER TWENTY-THREE

I needed to pee. I found the brass-handled cane on the floor in the garage and used it to hobble upstairs to call the police. Haruto left me outside his apartment because he wanted to take a hot shower to warm up.

"Lock your door," I said.

"You, too. See you in a few."

I lay on my mattress, bruised and stiff, with my head pounding like a drum, listening to the soft city nighttime noises. My cell phone was dead. Hell. I needed to get up and tell Haruto to dial 911. In a minute. I blinked as sudden bright moonlight sent an ice pick through my brain and fell asleep before my eyes closed.

Something woke me with a start and I wondered how I could possibly have drifted off to sleep. I wondered sleepily what had woken me. It was still pitch dark, and Lucy abruptly sat up in the other side of the bed with her ears pricked and a low grumbling noise coming from somewhere deep in her chest. My heart beat a little faster, even as I told myself that it couldn't be — couldn't possibly be — another break-in. I reached for Lucy and hugged her and whispered softly. "Hushhhh, it's okay."

And then I heard an out-of-place noise so quiet and yet somehow so close, that I shot out of bed in one unthinking motion. I threw the covers over the pillows, snatched Lucy under one arm, and in two strides was across the room, behind the door, with my brass-handled walking stick raised over my head.

The on-again, off-again moon had completely disappeared behind the clouds, and the room was so dark I couldn't even see Lucy. I stood behind the door almost without breathing. I'd got to "one thousand and nineteen," and was beginning to feel foolish as my heart rate returned to normal, when I heard a quiet footfall in the hallway beside me. On the other side of the door I could hear him — or her — breathing.

Inches from my eyes, a gloved hand and the barrel of a gun peeked coyly at the edge of the door, pointed at the bed.

The gun made two deafening lightning cracks and something on the bed exploded with a repulsive thud. The gun barrel drooped slightly, appearing almost alive in its apparent indecision.

Fury made me reckless. A second's thought would have made me hesitate, but in less time than it takes to tell I thrust my leg at the door, kicked it with all the strength I could muster, and jammed the hand with the gun in the door. I flailed at it with the cane. The gunman screamed and dropped the gun. Staggering footsteps, no longer bothering to keep quiet, stumbled along the hallway and through the kitchen and crashed out through the utility room door.

I followed, but not quickly enough. My head hurt. I heard Haruto's door open and I made my way shakily down the stairs.

"Did you see him?" I grabbed his arm and he steadied me.

"See who? Christ, have they come back?" He looked down the stairs and then at me.

"Come up with me. Bring your phone."

The police dispatcher kept the line open until Haruto told me to open my front door; the officers had arrived, he said. In fact, there were five of them, loaded for bear, pounding up my front steps.

Half an hour later, it felt as if the entire San Francisco police force, the SAS, and the Israeli Secret Service were all crawling around on the rooftops with Uzis.

I was sitting on my front steps, wearing a raincoat over my shoulders and gripping my cane with Lucy on my knees when Lichlyter showed up.

"Ms. Bogart, you have an incident-filled life," she said.

"Bitch!" I said, and bent my head and sobbed into Lucy's fur.

"Yes," she agreed unexpectedly. "It's the lack of sleep."

She had someone make a pot of coffee and Haruto and I drank some. So did half the Delta Force who arrived about then. She made a quick movement with her head and suddenly we were alone. She tugged gingerly at my sleeve, exposing the torn skin and welts. My hand looked as if I'd been chewed by a moray eel.

"You said someone shot at you," she said.

"There was a sort of prelude." I told her about my adventures, starting with the drinking party and ending with the gunman in my bedroom.

"You called us after you escaped from the garage?"

"I came up here and fell asleep." I got up and plugged my phone into its charger. "My phone was dead."

"I see. Let's take a look at this garage of

yours," she said. Suspicion was sticking out all over her like brass doorknobs. I took her downstairs to show her the garage. The handcuffs were still where Haruto and I had left them.

"There's a lot of stuff still here. What was taken?"

"About a million dollars' worth of rhinoceros horn," I said, enjoying my triumph over "the knows one," even though it could only mean more complications. "I telephoned to tell you I'd found it, but you weren't in the office."

"I was given a message that you called. A paintbrush was mentioned," she said faintly.

"I also found this." I handed her the lapel pin. "I saw one like it on Charlie O'Brien. I told you he works at a bookkeeping service called AcmeTax; I told you where he lives."

"We haven't been able to find him," she said.

We went back upstairs and I told her about the horn cache and the rest of my evening while my flat was being swarmed over by more police than I'd ever seen — and I'd seen a lot.

"Let's sit," she said, and led the way into the dining room, where Ben's card table and chairs still looked like orphans.

She chewed her bottom lip meditatively.

"Is there anyone you'd like me to call?"

"Where's Haruto?"

"Mr. Miazaki is giving his statement. Is there anyone else?"

"I'm fine." I got up and found a bottle of dusty aspirin in the kitchen. I chewed several and swallowed them with a mouthful of coffee. I rubbed the palms of my hands on my jeans.

She looked around the shadowy room and through the archway to the living room windows, where dawn was beginning to glow faintly. "Okay then. We have the particulars of the rhinoceros shipment. It's possible that it was intended for a Chinatown distributor. We'll look into Ms. Bartholomew's possible connections with . . . with anything that seems likely to lead to contraband." She looked frustrated. I didn't blame her.

"Mr. Turlough was with you when you discovered the horn. I'll speak to him. He and Mr. Haruto Miazaki both live in this building, don't they? Mr. Miazaki is in the flat under you and Mr. Turlough is in the studio behind the garage, is that right?" She somehow managed to make that sound sinister. "He didn't hear any of this while it was happening?"

"Ben Turlough's not here. He's in Los

Angeles," I said. "He took a flight yesterday evening and said he'd be back this afternoon."

And I wish to God he was here, I thought. And then I had to stop worrying about Ben and Haruto and tell her I'd probably been shot with my own gun. "It looks like mine, and I couldn't find it earlier."

"Did you report it missing?"

"I didn't know it *was* missing."

"Will we find any fingerprints on it besides your own?"

I sighed. "Probably. The gunman was wearing a glove, but just about everyone handled the gun recently." I stopped. Suspicion was hardening again on her face like ice on a Vermont skating pond. I had a sudden mental image of her bringing my birthday presents to the state penitentiary.

"Tell me about the paintbrush," she said abruptly. "The message you left said something about a paintbrush."

I'd almost forgotten. "It was in one of the crates. The metal collar was bent — I think it had been used to pry open the crate originally. It had dried yellow paint on it."

"And of course it disappeared along with the crates from your garage." She sighed.

"Why do I get the feeling this isn't a surprise?" I said slowly.

She chewed her lip again. "We knew about the paintbrush in the crate," she said finally. "We knew about the rhinoceros horn, too. We've been working with Fish and Wildlife out of Burlingame hoping the owners — you and Nicole — would take it out of the attic and we could trace your customers and the customs officials involved in the illegal importation. I left my notebook in your store hoping it would shake you loose. We've been following the rhino horn. We saw Mr. Turlough, Mr. David Rillera, and Mrs. AnaZee Williams moving the crates from the attic to your garage. It looked like a bold move at the time, but I guess it belongs to someone else" — she looked at me sharply — "unless you shot your own pillow. Still," she leaned forward and passed a not-too-gentle hand over the back of my head where a lump was swelling nicely, "I guess you didn't hit yourself over the head."

She glanced at her battered notebook. "And from what you say, anyone at the party this evening could have put two and two together, realized that the horn had been discovered, and decided to steal it back. Maybe they decided you knew too much — or suspected you were on the verge of discovering his or her identity."

My head throbbed. "You've known this all

along and you suspected — me?"

"It didn't help that you're living here under an assumed name," she said sharply.

I rubbed my aching forehead anxiously. I suppose I'd known they would find out, but I hated the exposure. "I only wanted to keep my past quiet," I said.

"That's the usual reason," she said dryly. She raised a tired hand when I began to explain. "I know who you are now, but it wasted time in the beginning."

I gulped. I couldn't help it.

"And of course there's the crates of rhinoceros horn that Fish and Wildlife have had under observation since Nicole Bartholomew — not some random person, but your partner — picked them up at customs in Oakland."

"I see what you mean," I said, shaken by the weight of the chain of suspicion. Then: "Wait! If you've had the place watched, you must have seen who stole it from my garage!"

She bit off her reply through clenched teeth. "Where do you think those handcuffs came from? The officer we had on watch is in the ER."

CHAPTER TWENTY-FOUR

Minestrone was my mother's Saturday standby in the winters of my childhood when we'd spend a month in Switzerland. She'd make it on Friday night, leave it simmering all day Saturday, and we all helped ourselves whenever we felt like it. We had a fairly Bohemian style of living for that precious month each year. I've found the technique so practical that I still use it; I make large quantities of simple dishes, and reheat single portions until it's all gone. Since I only cook what I enjoy eating, I don't care if I eat the same thing for several days running. In the summer, I make a basil and tomato pasta salad or cold soups. I eat apples to make up the dearth of vegetables in my diet and somehow stay on my feet.

My mother found the minestrone recipe in a magazine. It earned so many hosannas from me and my father that she and our succession of cooks and housekeepers kept making it even back at our home in Belgravia, although it never tasted quite as good as the version we ate from mismatched bowls on the side of a Swiss mountain. It's probably not authentic minestrone, but it starts with a ham hock stock, skimmed and kept in the freezer. I toss in a mixed handful or so of lentils and various dried beans; some herbs — heavy on the oregano — a half cabbage, chopped; a couple of cans of Italian tomatoes; and as much sliced pepperoni as I feel like adding. This is heated until the beans and lentils more or less dissolve, and it's ready. I began to cook it when the last of the police officers left at around eight that morning. "Don't forget to lock your door," he said, looking at the splintered doorjamb where my gunman had forced his way into the flat.

Very funny.

I took Lucy down into the garden, and used some picture wire and nails to jury-rig a back door fastener, promising myself to have a dead bolt installed as soon as the hardware store opened. I left the soup to simmer on the stove while I took a shower, swept up about two acres of feathers in the bedroom, put the phone on vibrate, and fell into bed. I didn't wake up again until late in the afternoon.

Antonio Carlos Jobim was a genius. Almost anything can be improved by listening to his recordings. "The Girl from Ipanema" was insinuating itself around the flat when I took a bowl of the minestrone to the empty fireplace and sat on the floor, tearing chunks off a French loaf for dipping. Lucy sat next to me gnawing a rawhide chew. As I was about to take my first taste, I heard a knock at the back door.

I untangled my makeshift wire lock and found Ben leaning against the wall outside. Like everyone I knew lately, he looked tired. His eyes were shadowed with exhaustion. It was remarkably good to see him.

"Quaint of you to knock," I said.

Lucy was squirming and wriggling with joy and he leaned down to scratch her. He inspected the picture-wire lock carefully. "May I come in? Hello, Lucy."

"Do you want some soup?" I said impulsively.

"If it's no trouble," he said. "I haven't eaten since yesterday."

"Bowls in the cabinet over the sink. Spoons in the drawer to the right of the dishwasher. You'll have to share my bread and sit on the floor."

"That's starting to sound attractive," he said, almost to himself.

I reattached the wire after he was inside. When he joined me in the living room, holding his bowl and spoon, he sat down on the floor on the other side of the fireplace.

I missed the first tremblings of the house.

Ben didn't though. "What's that?" he said, and put the bowl on the floor. Out-of-staters are always more sensitive. We live with the earthquakes and it starts to feel like no big deal when the house shakes a little.

"Earthquake," I said. The tremor rattled the windows and shook the floor and we sat in that half-cautious, half-expectant way that people have in an earthquake waiting for it to stop, except that it didn't. It matured in intensity until every beam and nail and window frame protested like live things at the stresses tearing them loose from their accustomed places. I snatched up Lucy and scrambled for the archway to the dining room, trying not to hear the snapping and cracking and the terrifying low rumbling noise.

"Come on," I shouted at him over the din. "You're safer away from the fireplace!" I went back to grab his arm and pulled him over with me, and we stood in the archway with our backs to the walls on either side. With no fanfare, everything stopped shaking and the noise quieted and died. The house swayed languorously for a few more seconds, as if reluctant to give up the novelty. And then everything was impossibly, unreasonably mute.

"Jesus." Ben's face looked strained.

"I've felt worse," I said, but I was rattled, too.

"I haven't."

"It was probably less than a 6.0 and not on the San Andreas."

He looked at me with respect and I was reminded how arcane the commonplace can seem to an outsider. "You can tell all that?"

"More or less." I smiled faintly. "You seem like a guy who prefers data to poetry. I don't usually spout factoids."

He looked around the room as if to check on the devastation that such arrogant force had wrought, but I had no knickknacks to break and nothing on the walls, so everything looked the same.

"Is it safe to stay inside?"

"For now. Sometimes the aftershocks are worse than the original quake. They can go on for weeks. Months. This was probably related to that small one we had a few days ago."

"Good factoids," he said.

I kept trying to reassure him, remembering my response to my first earthquake.

"I've had shear walls put in and the place is bolted onto the foundation. All the modern conveniences."

He was staring at me, his expression unreadable. He touched my cheek with his open hand. It felt cool and hard. I closed my eyes in a gesture that was partly relief and partly surrender, and covered his hand with my own.

"I heard about last night. I was afraid I'd left it too late." He frowned at my hand, at the torn skin, and drew it toward his mouth.

I felt short of breath. "Left what too late?" I said.

For an answer, he kissed my wrist. It stung where the handcuff had scraped the skin and I started to draw away. He pulled me toward him slowly. I moved the last few inches under my own power and my mouth was hard on his before I could talk myself out of it.

After a long moment, I shucked his jacket from his shoulders and felt his tongue on the tender skin of my neck.

Nat's fluorescent orange condoms from the evening before caused a raised eyebrow and an accepting grin. We made love on the Oriental carpet in front of the fireplace, eagerly, as if we'd both waited a long time. And again, more slowly. Every second was sweeter than the last. And then we were quiet, draped around each other like eels, lying on a patchwork of underwear and sweaters and his leather jacket, watching dislodged soot drift onto the hearth like black snow.

I ran questing fingers along a scar that traveled down his back and disappeared underneath his arm. He rolled over lazily and answered the question I hadn't asked. "A friend of mine got into an argument with a drunk and a broken beer bottle. I tried to help him out."

"That was brave — and you were lucky."

He smiled. As always, it made him look ten years younger. "Not so brave; you'll notice he got me in the back. I learned a bunch of things though."

"Like what?"

"That the exercise gurus are right — running can save your life."

I gurgled with laughter. "What else?"

He was suddenly serious. "Faced with a friend in need, I forget everything I've learned." He stared thoughtfully at the soot dislodged by the earthquake, still drifting into the hearth from the chimney. He placed the flat of his hand gently against the scar on my arm. His eyes asked me the question.

"I'll tell you sometime," I said uncomfortably.

"Now's good. I'm not doing anything much. At least not for fifteen minutes or so."

But I couldn't bring myself to share the joke or answer the smile in his voice. "Do you want some hot soup?" I said, and wriggled into my jeans.

He watched me for a few seconds. He reached out and took my hand, not preventing me from leaving, but inviting me to stay. "We don't need to talk," he said gently.

The lack of pressure loosened my tongue.

"I was robbed not long after I moved here." I glanced at him quickly; his eyes were dark and unreadable. I felt a wave of something — encouragement? empathy? — coming from him and I went on more calmly:

"He came into Aromas early one morning when I was alone and forced me into the office at knifepoint. I didn't know what he planned to do, but —" Despite the effort it was costing me, my voice shook. "I was able to get away from him because someone came into the store and hit him in the back of the head with a gallon jug of shampoo." I chuckled without humor. "When he was half dazed, we were able to get away, and by the time the police arrived, he'd escaped."

Ben waited, still without speaking. I thought he might be regretting his curiosity about the scar, although I didn't blame him. It caught the eye.

"So this week was even harder on you than it seemed. Nothing like getting a reminder of how vulnerable we are."

My head was splitting and I felt as if I'd run a marathon. I tried to get my voice and breathing back to normal. "Thanks for being here when Lichlyter talked to me — when was that? It feels like weeks."

He responded to the change of subject and the change in my mood. "All part of the service — no pun intended."

He surprised me into a laugh. This was what I had missed; I was responding like a thirsty plant to some of the best parts of physical love — the relaxation of tension, the joy, and the first delicate tendrils of trust. I felt something in me relax, like a tendon held taut for too long, aching without being noticed.

Lucy, disturbed by the laughter, took it into her head to walk through the hearth; she left tiny sooty smudges on the pale floor as she wandered around the living room.

I stirred in his arms after a long time and pulled my sweater over my shoulders. He was partly dressed, like me, and I'd been lying against his naked chest. He was in good shape, with powerful shoulders and a taut, muscled stomach — I made a small involuntary noise. He looked down at me. "Are you cold? Shall we build a fire?" he said lazily, and kissed me.

I gathered my wits. "No, best not. After a quake the chimney ought to be checked for cracks, so that it doesn't —" I sat up suddenly.

"Doesn't what?" he said.

"The chimney!"

"What about it?"

"Charlie O'Brien left sooty smudges all over the apartment when he broke in here. Why did he do that? He couldn't unless he'd been . . ." As I talked, I crawled to the fireplace and peered up the flue, seeing nothing for my trouble. I reached up the chimney as far as I could. I waggled my fingers around and they caught on something. I tugged. When whatever it was remained stubbornly jammed in the flue, I tugged harder.

A choking puff of soot fell down into the hearth, followed by a soft-bodied, red nylon gym bag.

CHAPTER TWENTY-FIVE

The bag was smeared with velvety black streaks and the greenish zipper had a couple of broken teeth at one end. I picked it up gingerly by its only handle. The opposite side only had two torn patches where a handle had once been. I was willing to bet that the red strap I'd seen in Charlie O'Brien's hand would fit exactly.

"Aren't you going to open it?" Ben said impatiently as I continued to stare at it. "You're looking at the thing as if it was full of vipers."

The bag was limp and looked empty. No vipers. I dragged it onto the hearth, opened the zipper. I felt around inside and pulled out a cardboard envelope several inches square.

I offered it to Ben to look over. He flipped it over and handed it back. "Maybe it's a tarantula," I said.

"Too flat."

"A killer bee?"

"It's not buzzing."

"A letter bomb? Charlie O'Brien had an Irish accent."

He hesitated. "It could be, but my guess is something much more mundane."

"What?"

"Size and weight's about right for a CD or DVD. Or it could be a tarantula."

"You said it was too flat."

"A crushed tarantula. For God's sake, Theo, open the damn thing." I opened the flap warily and pulled out a plain and unremarkable CD with no labels or identifying marks.

"I was hoping for an emerald necklace," I said.

"Have you checked the heating ducts lately?" With a quick glance at my undoubtedly pale face, he added briskly: "I'm getting cold. How about some soup?"

"Let's think about it tomorrow, you mean?"

"Not tomorrow, Scarlett, how about in half an hour?"

He was right. The doughnut I'd eaten for breakfast yesterday wasn't making it as a foundation for rational thought. I was still hungry and some food might help me to think.

While he reheated our untouched soup, I washed the soot off my arms, turned up the thermostat, and found him a bathrobe in case he wanted a shower — a masculine quilted number in dark green. I thought of telling him I'd bought it on Haight Street for last year's Halloween costume party and decided not to; he could believe what he wanted.

He examined the disk. "No way to tell if this is music or data. We've got a computer set up at the shelter. Do you want me to have a look and see what's on it?"

"The laptop downstairs will work."

I put the disk into its envelope and stuffed it back into the gym bag. Then I put the bag in the copper tub of firewood next to the fireplace and arranged a couple of logs on top of it. Ben raised an eyebrow, but I said: "People have been marching in and out of here pretty much at will."

Ben took a spoonful of his minestrone and made an appreciative noise. "Ever hear the old army joke about an officer giving the command to fire at will?"

I shook my head, smiling.

"One of the recruits drops his rifle and runs for the hills. The officer says 'Who was that man?' And another recruit says: 'That was Will.' "

I snorted into my soup. "That may be the worst joke I've ever heard."

"I know a lot of worse ones. Did you hear the one about the golfer —"

"No, please. Not in my weakened condition. I need food." We applied ourselves in companionable silence. "I was hungry," I said unnecessarily as I put my bowl down a few short minutes later.

"Feeling better?"

I nodded.

"Good. You seem to be in the middle of this whole story. Why don't you try running through it for those of us," he nodded at Lucy, "who don't know what the hell is going on."

I took a minute or two to collect my scattered thoughts and began: "Charlie O'Brien had the bag's other handle, which connects him to the CD. For some reason he was afraid someone would find it or steal it, so he hid it in my chimney while the apartment was being renovated and basically empty for all those weeks and I was living in the studio downstairs. Maybe the workmen let him in for some reason; I don't think the lock was tampered with."

Ben gestured agreeably. "Go on," he said.

"Whatever's on it, it must be important. He came to retrieve it and it was just bad luck he chose the night after I moved back in. The bag was hung up on the damper so he couldn't get it out of the chimney. He heard Lucy and me coming up the stairs, panicked, and got as far as the utility room, which is where I found him. So far so good?"

"Hmmm. But where does it get us?"

"It ties together in the end, I think." I chewed my lip thoughtfully. "Is it too much of a stretch to think Nicole was killed because of that rhino horn?"

He corrugated his forehead and said: "I'll grant you that for now."

"We know Nicole was connected to the crates because her handwriting was on them. I found his lapel pin in the garage, so Charlie O'Brien is involved in the rhino horn smuggling with Nicole. And," I added with a sudden inspiration, "since there's a connection between them, he could have had Nicole's locket for some reason, which is why the police found it in my utility room."

Ben looked puzzled. "What locket?"

But I was unstoppable. "All of which means he could have been Nicole's cocaine connection, or at least fairly close to her, otherwise why would she give him her locket, and if he didn't kill Nicole, he probably knows who did because he and Nicole and their partners were all in the smuggling game together. And since he was involved with Nicole in the smuggling, maybe Tim Callahan found out so he killed him, too. That's a bit tangled," I apologized, "but I think it hangs together."

"What locket?"

I explained about the cocaine locket. Ben's face darkened. "The idiot!" He sounded unexpectedly savage. He visibly got a grip on himself and shook his head. "Why do you think he and Nicole had partners?"

"Charlie couldn't have moved those crates alone last night, no matter how much time he had. There had to be at least one other person." As I realized what I was saying, I fell silent. Who among my friends and neighbors did I nominate?

Ben looked dissatisfied. "It's a long stretch from a lapel pin to involvement in a murder. Those shamrock pins are cheap; anyone could buy one."

"Wait! Charlie O'Brien," I said in wonder.

"What about him?"

"Charlie O'Brien!" I said excitedly. "The initials! C.O.B."

Ben looked mystified. "C.O.B. what?"

"My grandfather used to breed Hunters

and Welsh cobs. A cob is a kind of small horse," I said exultantly.

"A small —"

"Remember? Sabina said —"

"My God. She said Nicole's uncle's nickname reminded her of horses." He looked at me grimly. "The man on the washing machine is Nicole's uncle?"

"Has to be!"

"And he killed her?"

"I guess that doesn't sound right," I said more uncertainly. "Except maybe they went into the smuggling together and had some sort of a falling-out. It's possible, isn't it?"

"Do you think he's the one who shot at you?"

"Who else do we have?"

"But why?" He looked dissatisfied again. "You said he didn't hurt you when you found him in here; he doesn't sound violent."

"Maybe he didn't know where Nicole had hidden the rhino horn, but somehow figured out I'd found it and wanted to make sure I was silenced?" It didn't sound all that unreasonable, and Ben made a face in which I read reluctant agreement.

"And I had those crates while all this was happening, or at least they were in the group home." He sounded mildly disgusted.

"What about his partners? And what does that CD have to do with anything?"

"I'll know when I've taken a look at it, or Lichlyter has. Maybe I should be looking for someone around here with connections to Africa for the rhino smuggling. Or maybe it's simpler than that — maybe I should find out if anyone around here knows Charlie O'Brien. It needs a direct connection —" My phone buzzed like an angry hornet out in the kitchen. "— Blast! I'd better pick up in case it's Grandfather. I should have called him after the earthquake."

Ben followed me out to the kitchen carrying the soup bowls and kissed the back of my neck lightly as I picked up my phone. I almost forgot what I was doing.

He put the soup bowls in the sink and went back to the living room. I could hear him getting dressed. While someone in my ear told me to hold, I spent a few pleasant moments imagining the getting-dressed process and rinsing out the bowls. My heart sank a little when I realized who the call was from. "I'm sorry, Inspector, I didn't hear you; would you repeat that?"

"Mr. D'Allessio has been attacked. He's in intensive care at St. Francis Hospital."

I felt the blood run out of my face. Ben landed another gentle kiss on my neck, whispered, "See you later," and left through the back door before I could call him back or gather my wits.

"How did it happen?"

"His wife found him in the garden an hour ago. He was stabbed with a fine-pointed weapon of some kind. It barely missed his heart," she said precisely.

I felt as if I couldn't stand for another second and slid down to sit on the floor.

"Oh my god," I whispered. "They're about to celebrate their fiftieth wedding anniversary."

"I'm glad to find you at home. Can you tell me where you have been today?"

My stomach knotted. I tried to remember that she didn't suspect me, that she had confided in me. "I slept until about two hours ago; since then I've been — Mr. Turlough has been here."

Her voice sharpened. "Is he there with you now?"

"No, he just left. And I — I've found something else."

"Oh?" Her voice was a masterpiece of reservations.

"I found a gym bag with a CD inside. There's a handle missing. A red webbing handle. Remember?" I said anxiously as she remained silent. "I told you that Charlie

O'Brien —"

"Was holding a red strap of some kind. Yes."

"He has an Irish accent. And I found that shamrock lapel pin."

"In your garage. Yes, I remember that, too," she said. "I'm returning now to Fabian Gardens — half my life is spent in that damn place." I heard her take a deep breath. "I'll come by and pick up this CD. Perhaps that will help." She sounded doubtful.

I made a stupefied attempt to prevent her from hanging up before I'd told her every-thing. "I think he may be Nicole's uncle," I blurted.

"Why do you think that?"

"Sabina said Nicole's uncle's nickname reminded her of horses. Charlie O'Brien's initials —"

"Ah. Cob. Yes, I see."

Her composure was infuriating. "If you're so damn smart, why haven't you questioned him? He probably killed Tim Callahan and Nicole; maybe he stabbed Professor D'Allessio, too, and took that shot at me."

There was a short pause in which I heard the crackle of papers being sorted. "We've done ballistics tests on the bullets in your mattress," she said. "They definitely came from the gun your attacker dropped in your bedroom. Your gun."

"Meaning what?" I said dangerously.

"Meaning only that. In any event, we'd like to question Mr. O'Brien, believe me, but we still can't find him."

Super. Just great. I thought of Ruth D'Allessio and wondered what it would be like to love the same person for fifty years. I felt numb.

"There's one more thing," Lichlyter said. "You said Mr. Turlough had gone to Los Angeles for the night?"

"Yes," I said huskily. My voice was deserting me.

"We checked. He wasn't on any of the L.A. flights. A highway patrolman did stop to help a tourist in a rental car with a flat tire early this morning, south of Mendocino. The tourist had a passenger, a heavyset, balding man about fifty years old —"

"What's this got to do with us?"

"The tourist had a Washington D.C. driver's license in the name of Bramwell Turlough. It's an unusual name. Unique, I'd say."

I felt a wrench that was like physical pain. And then realized she had stopped talking. Mendocino is only a hundred and fifty miles — about three hours' drive — north of San Francisco. Los Angeles is seven hundred miles to the south.

"He told me he was going to L.A.," I said. I tried frantically to think of a reason for Ben to lie. I needed some relief from the pain in my chest or I was going to die.

"I don't know if I have confederates falling out, one liar, or two," she snapped. "But be careful, Ms. Bogart. If you're telling the truth, then he's lying to you."

She hung up and my thoughts flew backward, like a vehicle veering into an unavoidable boulder. Ben had been alone in the living room.

I spun around to look at the firewood basket. The gym bag lay on the hearth, not safely hidden under the logs. I skidded over to it, grabbed it, and pulled open the zipper. The CD was gone. I dug around frantically in the bag. It had to be there. Had to be. The telephone chirped again as I stood stupidly in the living room, staring at the empty bag in my hands. I answered it like a robot.

"What is the matter with your voice?" Grandfather said as soon as I said hello.

"I'm coming down with a cold," I said, and sniffed miserably.

He made an impatient noise. "Tcha. Nonsense, Theophania. What is the matter? I assume you felt no ill effects from the earthquake?"

What earthquake? Oh, right. Probably because he didn't sound in the least sympathetic, I poured it all out about the gunshot and the cleaned-out garage. After an intake of breath and a second's silence, he only said: "You were lucky, Theophania. I have warned you not to be so impulsive."

I barely heard him. "He lied. He wasn't in L.A. He could have been here in San Francisco last night when my garage was cleaned out."

As I talked, I thought of something so damning that it took my breath away. I felt something go very still, deep inside me.

"Theophania?" Grandfather said sharply. "Are you still there?"

I felt physically ill. "I found a lapel pin in the garage," I whispered. "I didn't say it was a shamrock, but Ben knew. How would he know?"

Grandfather remained quiet until I had talked myself into silence. When I began to repeat myself, he said austerely: "I am seldom wrong about people. Men, anyway," he added, in a rare flash of insight. "The most direct solution to a difficulty is usually best. He might have had a good reason for changing his plans and not going to Los Angeles. It's possible that he has an explanation for all these things," he added with more compassion. "Ask him, m'dear."

Just because it was simple advice didn't mean it was a bad idea. But Ben wasn't at the shelter — where AnaZee told me they didn't have a computer — and he wasn't downstairs in the studio apartment.

Ben had disappeared.

CHAPTER TWENTY-SIX

I telephoned Ruth D'Allessio, still feeling like hell. Haruto answered their phone and told me that Ruth was at her husband's bedside at St. Francis. "I'm only here for a few minutes to pack her a bag and to field phone calls," he said. He sounded as if he'd been crying.

"Give her my love when you talk to her, and let me know when he can have visitors. Can you tell me what happened?"

"Ruth said he told her he'd be home for lunch — he said he was going to talk to someone about — about the compost pile." His voice cracked. "Ruth went out to find him when he was late for lunch. She thought he'd had a heart attack at first, until she noticed he was bleeding. The paramedics said he's lucky she found him so fast."

"He hasn't been able to say who did it?"

"I guess we won't know until he comes out of his coma. If he does."

"There's some doubt?"

"More than a little. It's serious, Theo."

I hung up feeling even worse than before.

The meeting almost immediately afterward with Inspector Lichlyter gave me no time to recoup. It took place in the presence of a surly Basque locksmith in a black wool beret, who worked stolidly to replace my back-door lock and install a safety chain. He insisted on being paid in cash. I had to borrow five dollars from the inspector. She handed over the five dollars with an exasperated smile, but the depressed-looking lines in her face returned when I gave her the torn gym bag. She punctiliously folded it into a see-through evidence pouch, but I could tell that the absence of the CD was a sore point.

"This CD you say you found —"

"I did find it. Ben Turlough and I found it together," I said through my teeth.

She took off her glasses and pinched the bridge of her nose between thumb and forefinger. She looked at me with those odd eyes and the skepticism in her expression was indisputable.

"And where is Mr. Turlough now?" She replaced her chic glasses and her eyes rested briefly on Lucy, curled up and fast asleep on Grandfather's Oriental rug.

"I don't know."

She drew her skirts aside, figuratively speaking, and left through the back door. I engaged the new door chain emphatically. And that was another thing — didn't anyone ever use front doors anymore? As if to prove that no, they didn't, there was a decisive knock on the back door. I opened the door the few inches the new chain allowed.

"Theo, let me in; it's me, Kurt." He looked nervously down the stairs to where the top of Lichlyter's head was disappearing. A lock of his pale hair fell over one eye. For Kurt, always conscious that his wealthy patients preferred a doctor with dignity, it was the height of dissipation.

"Sorry, Kurt," I said firmly, "I'm not in the mood for company."

He pushed against the door. It never even occurred to me to be concerned about a threat until he grabbed the edge of the door. The hand that curled around the edge of the door was heavily bandaged. I vividly remembered smashing down my heavy cane on the hand of my shooter and leaped away from the door as if it had suddenly sprouted cobras.

"What happened to your hand?" I shouted wildly.

He yelled back furiously: "To hell with

that! Nothing. I've been worried about you —"

"What do you mean? And what did you do to your hand?" He rattled the door again. "I swear, I'll slam your hand in the door. I'm counting to three. One —"

He hastily withdrew his fingers. "For Christ's sake, what's wrong with you women!"

"What women? For God's sake, Kurt, do you mean Sabina?"

"To hell with Sabina," he said furiously.

"Nice."

"I meant Helga — she's a problem I don't need."

"You're worried about someone having a little crush on you?" I said incredulously.

"It's more than a little crush, she's sending boxes of croissants to the office," he said sulkily.

"Poor you," I snapped. "With all that's been going on, *that's* what you're thinking about? What about Professor D'Allessio —"

"That miserable old bastard! What did he say? I told him this morning I'd —"

I felt cold. "What? Why?"

"I told him to keep quiet and mind his own goddam business or — nothing. I didn't tell him anything."

I slammed the door and shoved on the

dead bolt. After shouting my name a few times and rattling the doorknob ineffectively, he stamped down the stairs.

CHAPTER TWENTY-SEVEN

I fled through the front door and half ran up to Nat's. It was nearly four o'clock and I had to dodge around middle schoolers who were taking up the sidewalk in little clumps.

"Girl, you look as if you need a hug and a cup of tea. Which would you like first?" Nat greeted me, looking handsome and immaculate, the twin-rings pendant nestled against pale yellow cashmere.

"Neither," I growled. He took care of the first anyway, which must have been like hugging a telephone pole, and after giving me a searching look, took care of the second by putting on the kettle.

"You know you shouldn't drink, Theo. Gin ruins the complexion and puts bags under your eyes," he said kindly. I couldn't imagine what he was talking about — and then I remembered last night's binge. It felt like a long time ago.

"You're not looking so hot yourself," I

said, knowing it sounded bitchy and not caring. Besides, it was true. He looked as if he hadn't slept. He ignored me, which is what I deserved, and I sat moodily on a tall stool at the breakfast bar. Watching him fuss around the kitchen was oddly soothing, and as he flitted around putting things away and finding a tray to hold the cups, I started feeling better. My suspicions, which had been growing every moment, began to seem like the stuff of bad dreams.

And yet Tim Callahan and Nicole had been murdered and Professor D'Allessio was near death.

"How about that earthquake, hmmm? We lost a couple of wineglasses. How about you?" he said.

"What? Oh, nothing. I guess the new shear walls worked."

The big kitchen had a professional stove against one wall, and copper pans and exotic-looking cooking hardware dangling from an enormous pot rack. He and Derek shared cooking duty and were inclined to appear at potlucks with things like Thai spicy beef salads or Cajun peanut sauce with batter-fried catfish rolled in parsley for dipping. They showed up once with a gigantic lobster lasagna, using phyllo dough for the layers. Everyone fell on it like locusts.

He cleared away several bright and shiny pans and utensils from a drying rack. "Lamb brochette for lunch," he said, waving the stainless steel skewers like a picador. "Derek wanted to try out a recipe from *Gourmet.* Earl Grey okay?" he added, beginning to fuss with a milk jug and sugar bowl.

"You know you're a compulsive neat freak, right?"

"Like that's news," he muttered.

"And I love Earl Grey, you know that," I said, then added, a little shamefaced: "How do you stand me when I'm like this?"

"Because you never are like this," he said. "You know about Professor D'Allessio?"

I nodded glumly.

"I refuse to talk about it. Look," he said, waving a small white paper bag, "cookies from the patisserie on Union Street; somethin' to take our minds off our troubles. Don't tell Helga."

He tipped the contents of the paper sack out onto the tray. Each cookie was sheathed in its own little sealed paper bag. I knew from experience that they'd be fresh, spicy, and delicious. My stomach protested at the mere thought. I climbed off my stool to help him. The raw skin around my wrist stung. It was getting more painful as the hours passed and I grimaced to myself.

"Ooh! What's that?" he said, catching sight of the scrapes and the bracelet of torn skin as I reached to take the tray. He carefully lifted the edge of my cuff and looked up, appalled, as I winced.

"Jesus, Theo."

"Part of the long, sad story of my life — or at least the last few hours of it," I said. "Do you have any antiseptic cream? Real antiseptic cream," I added hastily, "not one of Derek's nostrums."

"In the bathroom. Second shelf in the medicine cabinet. Are you goin' to tell me what the hell happened?" He followed me down the hall and I found the antiseptic cream exactly where he said it would be. It was an almost new tube with Derek's name on the pharmacy label. "Is this the stuff?"

"Yeah. Those cuts from the broken mirror got red and swollen. Dr. Kurt told him the cream would take care of any infection."

I squeezed a little on the worst patches and cautiously spread it around, catching my breath as I did so. The stinging intensified. It wasn't just my wrist; my whole hand was black and blue. I wiped the excess cream off my fingers with a tissue and dropped it in the empty wastepaper basket. It reminded me of the soap wrapper I had put there only the night before. Time was telescoping lately; it seemed a week ago. The wrapper had gone. There wasn't so much as a dried water drop on the faucets.

"So Derek heads straight for Western medicine when he's hurting, huh?" I said as we got back to the kitchen.

"I was teasin' him about that earlier," Nat said. Then he blurted: "Damn, that looks painful."

"It's okay," I hastened to reassure him. "No permanent damage."

His eyes filled with tears. "God, I already felt terrible. I couldn't go back in to work this afternoon." He looked suddenly stricken and sniffed into a handkerchief. "I'm being self-centered again. I know it; don't try to spare my feelin's. What the hell happened to your poor hand?"

"Nat —"

"No, I mean it," he said staunchly. "I'm just depressed. And don't tell me I'm oversensitive; events around here lately would depress Mother Teresa. Tell me what's botherin' you first. And tea isn't what you need." He poured white wine into two glasses and added them to the tray. He carried them into the living room, where I settled into a corner of the couch and he sat in a plump, oatmeal-colored armchair.

"Let's see. Shall I start with being robbed,

coshed, handcuffed, shot at, or betrayed?" I said, sipping my wine and helping myself to a cookie, to please him.

He blinked. "All that since last night? What's this about bein' betrayed? It has a nasty, biblical sound."

I gave him an edited version of how Ben and I had spent the afternoon.

"Soooo," he drawled. "I hope you were a good girl and took advantage of my little gift. Fluorescent orange is so your color, and like I said, it's a dangerous time of year in the North Atlantic."

"Idiot," I snorted. I told him about the CD and Ben's disappearance.

"And I thought he'd be good for you!" he wailed. "God, I'm a worse picker of men than I thought. One good thing about havin' Ben in the flat this afternoon — you should pardon the pun — you can alibi each other over the attack on the professor for that miserable inspector. Fortunately Derek and I were cookin' lunch. At least I can explain to the police what I was doin'." I looked at him over my wineglass. His frivolity was covering some real disquiet. Before I could ask again, he went on: "What about the rest of your menu of woes?"

"Let's see. Nicole had some crates of rhinoceros horn that ended up in my garage and it was stolen last night. I interrupted the robbers and so did Haruto and they handcuffed us, which is where my wrist got mangled. I escaped and staggered up to bed, whereupon a gunman —"

"What?" he yelped. He had been listening with growing amazement and now his eyes were wide and horrified.

"Luckily I heard him coming and hid behind the door and managed to jam his hand in the door. He dropped the gun, thank God, and ran for it. That's it. Oh, not quite. The gun he used was my own gun. Pretty neat, eh? Lichlyter thinks I invented it all."

His facial expression ran arpeggio-like from incredulous to furious. "Someone shot at you?" He hesitated. "How did he get hold of your gun?"

"I have no idea!"

Of all the incidents, I expected the rhino horn, being the most surreal, to appeal to him the most. But the gunman staggered him even more.

"Tell me again how he shot at you," he said. He was wearing a slight frown.

"It was so dark — of course if there'd been more light, I probably wouldn't be here telling you about it."

"At least you got a few blows in. Was he

right- or left-handed?" he asked suddenly.

"Right-handed," I said without thinking. "Good for you, Nat; Lichlyter didn't ask me that."

"It's not much help. Just about everyone is right-handed," he said uneasily.

"It would have been better if he'd held the gun in his toes," I agreed gravely. "Now that's unusual."

Nat giggled and I joined in, until we were both chuckling feebly, less because we were amused, than to let off some steam.

"I think the crates of rhino horn are the strangest thing of all," I said as I wiped my eyes.

"I don't get it, Theo. What's the big deal with it?"

"Ben said the shipment was worth about a million."

"Dollars?" he blurted. Then he added: "Ben? How does he know about it?"

"We found the stuff together."

A small frown appeared on his lovely face and he stopped meeting my eyes. "We don't know much about him, and there's the CD or whatever . . ." His voice slowly trailed off and he sat looking at me like a scolded puppy.

"It's okay," I sighed. "I've already tried to fit him into things and the whole mess fits him like a glove. He sure showed up at the right time. Tim Callahan discovers the rhino horn, so he gets thrown from the window. Nicole and Ben argue about the profits or something, so he kills her. The professor sees him burying Nicole in the compost pile and so he has to be eliminated. And I swear there's some connection between him and Charlie O'Brien." I fell back on the couch, feeling about as miserable as I sounded.

He grimaced. "I guess I'm ignorant, but the rhino horn isn't illegal to own, right? I mean, why is it worth so much?"

"How do you know it's not illegal, you fluffy head?"

He looked confused. "I guess Mr. Choy must have told me when we were talkin' about Derek's medicines. Is he right?"

I nodded. "Apparently the big money comes in because it has to be smuggled into the port of entry. I assume that means bribing people and generally getting your hands dirty. Once it's in the country it's not illegal to have. Screwy, huh?"

"That's what he said," Nat said.

"Who?"

He hesitated. "Mr. Choy."

"No one's had a sudden big boost in income lately, have they?" I asked him abruptly. "At a million dollars a shipment, even with paying bribes and what all . . ."

"Kurt was talkin' about buying a Porsche," he said doubtfully.

"Great. Of course, he's a doctor," I added thoughtfully. "Although come to think of it, I guess a Western-trained doctor would be the last person to use a rhino horn medicine."

Nat looked ever more doubtful. "I don't know, Theo. Some of the new research has found good in alternative therapies. Look at Derek and his hair tonics."

"They're not working!"

"They might eventually," Nat said defensively.

I sat up straight suddenly. "I've been leaving out an obvious connection — how could I be so stupid! Mr. Choy!"

Nat rolled his eyes at me. "Can you truly see seventy-year-old Mr. Choy creepin' around breakin' into your place and shootin' you, or stabbin' Professor D'Allessio?"

"Er — no, I guess not. Too bad, it sounded great there for a minute," I said. "I've been trying to think of a reason Nicole was killed. Before all this rhino horn stuff came up, I thought it might be something personal. Suppose it still is?"

"What do you mean, personal?"

"The smuggling would be business —

thieves falling out or something. But if we leave the rhino horn out of it for a moment, what reason could someone have to kill Nicole? We know about the cocaine — I suppose a drug dealer could have done it, but if *Law and Order* is right, they usually make a public example of people, so he would have no reason to hide her body. He'd want it to be left in the open as an Awful Warning, right?"

"I guess that's right," he said slowly.

"So maybe it's not the cocaine, or the rhino horn. Maybe it's somebody who has a personal hatred." I shook my head impatiently. "That sounds sort of medieval. Do people hate like that anymore?"

"Honey, ask any gay boy who's been beaten up. Believe me, hatred exists."

I reached out and touched his hand. "So we try and think of anyone who has a reason to hate her — and Tim Callahan and Professor D'Allessio, let's not forget. We know Nicole and Tim were married once," I said.

"Which feels as if it should mean somethin', but what?"

"You know, there's something else. Why was Nicole buried? Tim was thrown onto the lawn like a gauntlet, and the professor was left bleeding out in the open —"

"Theo, have a heart," he said, looking sick.

341

"Sorry. But he was. So why was Nicole buried?"

We looked at each other in mutual puzzlement. Nat shook himself and stood up.

"This amateur sleuthin' isn't as easy as Miss Marple makes it seem. You know what? I think I have somethin' to take our minds off things for a minute. Derek finished a commission this mornin'. I'm going to show it to you — even though he'll probably skin me — because they're the most beautiful work he's ever done and I'm so proud of him, I could bust. Seein' them will make you feel better." He darted off into the back of the apartment and came back with something carefully wrapped in pale gray jeweler's cloth.

"Look," he said, carefully unwrapping it.

Resting on the cloth were a pair of earrings — wild roses of thin beaten gold, each vein in the petals clearly visible, with leaves of pavé diamonds. The delicacy of the work was astounding.

"They're beautiful," I said sincerely, touching one of them gently.

Nat looked pleased. "They're for Ruth D'Allessio. The professor wanted them finished by this week for their anniversary. They were a surprise. When I told him Derek trained at Tiffany, he couldn't wait to commission them. The old snob." He paused for a few seconds. "I talked to Haruto; he's pretty broken up."

"It's funny Haruto and the professor are such close friends," I said. "God, I hope he's okay."

"He's a gossipy old fraud. And I hope he's okay, too." After a pause, I said: "I saw Kurt an hour ago. He's got a splint and a huge bandage on his right hand. Do you have any idea what happened?"

"Sabina maybe? She's not exactly stable at the moment. They were havin' some sort of argument this mornin' — in which Nicole's name figured prominently accordin' to your Davie, who absorbed every round of the fight with great interest. I gather the professor showed up and joined in to defend his granddaughter's honor."

"How did he hear about it?"

Nat leaned forward, his eyes dancing. "Hear about it? Darlin', it happened practically on his doorstep. Kurt and Sabina screamin' like banshees. The professor wavin' his hoe around and yellin' about male whores. Quite the scene, according to Davie."

"Wow!"

"Wish I'd been there," Nat said a trifle wistfully.

"None of that sounds like Kurt," I observed.

"The professor called this mornin' after it was all over to talk to Derek about the earrings. But he couldn't wait to tell me about the fight. The old boy sounded ready to do murder."

"Whereas," I finished for him, "it was he who was nearly murdered."

Nat grimaced ruefully.

"What time did he call? It might be important," I asked.

"It was just before he was stabbed. Must have been around noon. I told Lichlyter and she had me giving her the conversation, word-for-word. Brrrr!" He shivered.

"But how could Sabina hurt Kurt's hand?" I said worriedly.

Nat looked troubled. "This is goin' to sound weird — but Sabina had your gun last night. I don't know what to think about someone takin' a potshot at you with it; I think you're the only person in the world Sabina likes."

"You think she shot at me?" I said blankly.

"She had a revolver like the one you were wavin' at me the night before. It's pretty distinctive. It was missin' today when Derek and I got up. I figured Sabina took it back once she cooled off."

"I remember putting it on the washing machine when you got to the flat. And I didn't see the gun after everyone left." I hesitated. "What were you and she arguing about in the bedroom last night?"

He looked uncomfortable. "She wasn't herself — she was furious with Kurt about somethin' and she was wavin' the gun around. I don't know what'll happen to the earrings now." He was almost mournful, and carefully wrapped them in their flannel veil.

I heard the front door of the apartment open and close. Derek dropped his briefcase on the dining room table.

"God, what a day," he said, and bent down to kiss the top of Nat's head. His face was etched with fatigue. He yawned and stretched. I've known him to spend ten straight hours hunched at his worktable, working with tools and techniques so fine they're almost invisible to the untrained eye.

"Hi, Derek," I said quietly from my corner.

He positively started. More evidence, if any were needed, of the emotional high-wire we were all on. He managed a rueful laugh.

"Hi, Theo," he said, coming over to take a cookie. "What are you two gossiping about?" He flopped heavily beside me on the couch and loosened his tie.

"The rose earrings," Nat said, a little shamefaced. "I was showin' them to Theo."

Derek's face went suddenly dark with anger. "For Christ's sake —" He snatched the jeweler's cloth from Nat's hands and the earrings skittered across the floor. He bent to scoop up the roses and stuffed them furiously in his pocket.

Nat looked wildly from Derek's furious face to my astonished expression.

The pendant around his neck swung like a pendulum and tinkled like a mini-sonata. The delicate, familiar sound suddenly was as shocking as a rifle shot. I remembered hearing it recently in some wildly improbable place.

The baffling fury died out of Derek's face as suddenly as it had arisen. He stuck his hands moodily in the pockets of his slacks. "Jeez, Theo, you must think I've lost my mind. I told you it's been a hell of a day. These are supposed to be a surprise and this decorative idiot lets the cat out of the bag before the client's even seen them." He laid a penitent hand lightly on Nat's shoulder. He was wearing a wrist brace and it gave me a nasty feeling of déjà vu. "Sorry, kitten," he said.

"It's okay," Nat sniffed. But he still looked

hurt. "I suppose with everythin' that's happened today it's no wonder we're all on edge."

Derek looked blank.

"You don't know," I said.

"Don't know what?" He looked from me to Nat, and back again. His expression changed from mild curiosity to dread as I hesitated. "What's happened?" he said warily.

"Professor D'Allessio has been stabbed."

He sat down again suddenly. "God. When?"

"About the time we were havin' lunch," Nat said hurriedly.

"Dead?" Derek said in a strangled voice.

"He can't speak yet. He's at St. Francis in intensive care."

"Jesus." He stared into space for many seconds and then roused himself. "And I thought I'd had a tough day. Carpal tunnel," he added to me. "My hand is killing me." He stretched it gingerly. "Sorry, both of you."

I said nothing, thinking hard. Two men with injured hands — only one with an explanation. But did I believe it? And where — where had I heard that faint tinkling sound?

"Hey," Derek said gently, leaning over to

me. "Am I forgiven?"

I shook off my mental fog. "Derek, what do you remember about Nicole and Tim Callahan from art school?"

"I didn't know them all that well," he said, not in the least bit thrown by the change in subject. "They were only kids. I do remember they couldn't keep their hands off each other."

"Were they involved in anything in particular?"

"What are you thinking?"

"Both of them killed within a week. It can't be a coincidence."

"And you think something from fifteen years ago might be the reason?" His skepticism made me more determined.

"It could be, couldn't it? What were they like?"

"They were both passionate people in a fairly simple way," Derek said slowly. "They were part of the student activist group — always supporting embargoes and going off to Berkeley to spit at cops. All the usual stuff. Their high-water mark — or low-water mark, depending on your point of view — was the mess at the Adelphi Club. Remember, kitten?" He turned to Nat, who nodded. "It went on for weeks — commando groups splashing red paint around and digging holes in the greens down at the golf club at night. It ended with busloads of activists screaming at rows of cops. Someone got injured or something and it cooled everything down. Still, give credit where it's due, Nicole presented the club with a list of demands and the color bar came down. They were probably the last institution in the city to fold. Just in time for the dawning of the twenty-first century."

"I've heard the story. But it seems like a good thing," I said.

"I guess it depends which side of the police cordon you're on," he said with a smile. "My guess is the club didn't see it that way. Hey, you know, you could ask Helga."

"Helga? Our Helga?"

"Her dad was a member or something to do with the club in those days. She used to kid with Nicole about it; she might remember something."

I tried to decide whether this was a trail worth following, or if the rhino horn connection was a more likely reason for Tim and Nicole's deaths. I said the first thing that came into my head. "I've always meant to ask you, Derek —" He looked at me expectantly. "What's your nickname? Professor D'Allessio calls me 'the soap one' —"

"— and I'm 'the furry one,' " Nat interrupted. "You know, because my body hair's so silky." I rolled my eyes. "It is! He used to call Derek 'the ugly one,' which was just mean, but now he calls him 'the earring one' because of the rose earrings. I think it's a step up myself."

Something about that nickname, Nat's pendant, and the rose earrings troubled me. What was it? Why was I worried about jewelry, of all things, when rhinos were dying?

What could rhinoceros horn possibly be good for? Ben had said arthritis, but he hadn't sounded all that certain. I hoped, somehow, that it wasn't for something trivial like flatulence, that at least the rhinos were dying to cure drug addiction or something. And there was another thing to add to my weird jewelry obsession. Ben had said something the other night, after he and Nat met for the first time. Haruto — no, "some character" was yelling at him about the compost. Professor D'Allessio had been muttering about the compost, too, and about "the earring one" arguing with someone. And Derek and Kurt both had injured hands.

I had to talk to Kurt. I looked up into their curious faces, suddenly aware that I had been silent for too long and that they were beginning to look at me strangely.

"I'll put this away," I said abruptly, and started to pick up the tea tray.

"It's okay, I'll do that," Nat said, obviously puzzled. "Are you leavin'?"

"I'm going to get back to my flat and figure out why Charlie O'Brien and the compost pile and Tim and the rhinoceros horn are rattling around in my brain together. Helga was asking why Nicole was buried, and I can't figure that out either." Derek went pale, which hurt me more than it should. "Or maybe I'll take a long nap," I went on. "Wake me up in a couple of weeks you two, okay?"

I waggled a hand at Nat in adieu and glanced back as I left.

Derek's eyes were closed as if he was in pain and Nat looked as if he were staring at the end of the world.

I took the long way home and when I climbed the back stairs to my flat, Derek was waiting for me. He was sitting on the roof next door, with his legs dangling out over the edge.

"I could see you were figuring things out," he said, giving me much more credit than I deserved. His face was ashen. Perhaps I should have been afraid, but he looked so defeated I felt almost sorry for him.

"It wasn't Haruto who argued with Ben 'Turlough over the compost pile. Professor D'Allessio saw you — the earring one," I said harshly.

He nodded. "Nat doesn't know I'm here. I want to explain."

"Go ahead," I replied, and sat on the top stair of my landing where I had broken the pot of oregano over Charlie O'Brien's head.

He wasn't looking at me. He was staring across the Gardens, his body rigid, his hands gripping the edge of the roof next to his thighs. "Nicole and I were partners over the rhino horn," he started quietly. I didn't say anything. "Yeah, I know. Disgusting." He shook his head. "I told her about some of the Asian remedies and we got talking one night about the rhino horn and how much money could be made with a little planning. We decided to try it to see if we could get away with it. The payoff was so huge and we felt the risk was minimal. It took a while to set up — we had to find the right people to include —"

"Bribe, you mean," I interrupted him.

His eyes flickered to me and back. "Yeah, okay. Anyway, we did it. We could hardly believe how easy it was. And we split two hundred thousand dollars. We learned a lot with that first shipment last year — and we decided to do a larger one. Nat had gotten wise that something was going on between us — we kept playing up our so-called flirtation as a beard for what we were doing. She came to the house that evening she was killed, but Nat threw a complete jealous fit and made her leave. It wasn't like him to make a scene like that. I thought he was still partly shaky from fainting at your place that morning."

"You broke the mirror when I told you the police were interested in the things being stored in the attic at number twenty-three."

"I damn near fainted myself. Shit. I had my hands full with Nat after Nicole left; it took me an hour to calm him down. I couldn't risk having her come back to the house. I settled Nat in the guest room with a sleeping pill, and Nicole and I met down in the garden late that night. We'd agreed to a fifty-fifty split, but she wanted a larger percentage — she said she was taking all the risks, but she wasn't. I made all the Hong Kong contacts."

"I'm sure you were doing your fair share," I said acidly.

"Right. I left Nat asleep in the guest room.

Nicole and I met downstairs and we argued and I left her down there."

"Alive?"

His heavy face stretched into a grimace and his mouth fell open in shock as his head snapped to look at me. "God, yes, alive! Did you think — ? I couldn't kill anyone, Theo. No, seriously, for God's sake!" He turned to face straight ahead again but now he was looking at me sideways as if to gauge the effect his tale was having. "When I got back, I checked in on Nat and he was gone. I had no idea where he was. I looked out into the garden and saw someone lying on the ground. My only thought was Nat — that somehow he'd had another episode and fainted. I ran out there and it was Nicole." His voice broke. "God, it was terrible. I was frantic, Theo. I got it into my head that Nat had seen us together and killed her."

I started to say something, but he raised a hand. "I know. But late at night, with the threat of losing everything hanging over me, and Nat not being at the house — you didn't see the scene with Nicole, Theo." His voice faltered. "He was irrationally jealous — I thought maybe he'd seen us together in the garden and — he knows that in the past, I've —" He hesitated. "Nat knows I've had a couple of — with women —"

"Right," I drawled. "So Nat thought he had reason."

"He didn't, Theo. I swear. There's been nothing like that since Nat and I have been together."

"Not me you need to convince."

"No. Shit, I panicked. I had to hide her until I could find Nat. I thought if she wasn't found right away it could confuse the time of death. It would have taken me too long to dig a hole, but we were right next to the compost pile, and — well, you know the rest. The professor must have seen me arguing with the new guy — whoeverthefuck, Turlough? — when he found me out there clearing up. I was nearly insane. I had no idea who the guy was, for all I knew he was the killer. I took the offensive, figuring whoever he was he'd want to avoid a scene. He left me to it."

"What about the machete?" I asked. "Where was that?"

"It was lying next to her, and I put it under the wire screen in the fish pond — I figured to get it out of sight so no one would know anything was wrong. All I knew at that point was that Nat was missing during the time Nicole had been killed, and I wanted to protect him."

"And yourself," I said with distaste.

"I swear, Theo, that wasn't it." But I thought it probably was. "I was a goddam mess by the time I got back home, covered in dirt and blood. And Nat still wasn't back. I cut my clothes up in small pieces and put them in gallon-size plastic bags in the freezer downstairs. Then I took a shower and waited for Nat to get back. And he said he'd been with you and he told me about the guy who broke into your flat, and I was so relieved, Theo." He put his head in his hands. "I was sure it must be the guy who killed Nicole. But I didn't want to tell anyone I'd buried her — and I sure as hell didn't want to be there when they discovered her at the Open Garden, so I stayed away and made sure Nat stayed away, too."

His callousness was appalling, and I don't know why I believed him when he said he hadn't killed Nicole, but I did.

He looked at me carefully and said in a changed tone: "What do you want me to do, Theo? I've watched *CSI*; I know they'll find plenty of blood evidence and compost scraps or whatever if they know where to look. Are you going to tell them?"

"Are your clothes still in the freezer?"

It didn't surprise me that he'd shown presence of mind about that, too. "I took the bags and distributed them among the

356

trash cans downtown on trash night," he said. "They're long gone."

Hardly able to process all he'd told me, and feeling I never wanted to look at him again, I still found myself thinking that no serious harm had been done; Nicole was already dead when he buried her. My thoughts slid to a stop when I realized what I was considering. I didn't give a rat's ass if Derek got caught up in all of this mess he'd created. But Nat was in love with Derek and I owed Nat my life; I'd often told myself I would do anything for him. Now I knew what that meant.

"I won't tell Lichlyter what you've told me about burying Nicole. You're on your own with the rhino horn though," I said. "Did you hit me and steal the crates from the garage?"

He looked shamefaced. "Yeah. I'm sorry, Theo. First you and then Haruto showing up —"

"You didn't move those crates by yourself."

"I'm not getting anyone else involved."

I had a good idea who it must have been. It was a very painful realization.

I left him sitting on the roof, legs still dangling over the edge, staring at nothing.

CHAPTER TWENTY-EIGHT

I needed time to absorb Derek's confession and figure out what it meant. I also wanted to hear Ben if he came back to the studio so I could call Lichlyter. I went downstairs to Aromas.

Darkness had fallen by the time I looked up and realized I needed to put on some lights. A light tap on the street-side door made me jump. I looked over and saw Kurt beckoning me through the glass door. I was very aware suddenly of being alone in the store.

"What do you want?" I said stiffly through the glass. I wanted to talk to him, but in daylight. With witnesses.

"Can I come in for a few minutes?" His earlier anger was gone and he was shivering in shirtsleeves, and for some stupid reason I took pity on him and unlocked the door. In a different mood, I might have enjoyed the sight of Kurt pared down to the inner man.

His disheveled blond hair and the patches of pink high on his cheeks made him look like a discarded doll.

"I don't have much time," I said when, in truth, I had nothing but time.

"I don't expect much," he said humbly.

I hesitated. "Come in," I said, and opened the door wide enough to admit him.

"I guess I haven't been here in a while," he said as he looked around, trying to make it seem casual. He was keeping his taped-up hand in his pocket. "Still wanted to check that you're doing okay. You've had a lot to deal with."

"Tell me something," I said as I casually walked over to stand behind the counter. Still watching him carefully, I ran my fingers over the assorted detritus down there.

"What?" he said cautiously.

"Someone tried to kill me last night and I injured their right hand. Tell me how you hurt yours." While I was speaking, I pulled a pistol-shaped soap out of its box under the counter and aimed it at him. It looked amazingly real. In the half-light it almost fooled me.

He goggled. "Theo, what the hell!"

"Keep your hands where I can see them. I don't have to kill you, I can shoot you in your other hand. You'll probably never operate again —" I narrowed my eyes and tried to look threatening and it must have worked because his pink cheeks turned faintly green.

"For God's sake! What do you want to know?" he said wildly.

"How did you hurt your hand?"

He ground his teeth. "Sabina slammed it in a car door."

I blinked in surprise and couldn't stop a grin from coming. "Go on."

"It's not so goddam funny. It broke two of my fingers and my hands are —"

"Important, I know. Not too many one-handed surgeons around. Why the fight?"

He scowled. "That's all we do, all the time," he said petulantly.

I suddenly remembered Sabina's visit to the medical building at 450 Sutter for collagen injections. Insight came in a flash. I almost groaned aloud, it was so clear. "Sabina's pregnant."

He made an involuntary move toward me and I raised the soap pistol a couple of inches even as I stepped back in alarm.

"Damn that interfering old sonofabitch! I knew he wouldn't keep quiet!" He slammed his fist into the palm of his injured hand. It must have hurt like hell, but he didn't even pause for breath. "Did he tell you it's not my baby?" he said in a fury.

"What? Who?" I said, mystified.

"Old man D'Allessio. He saw us fighting. Sabina was screaming at the top of her lungs; I knew he'd overheard everything. I told him to keep his mouth shut. I'm glad someone knifed him. The miserable old bastard."

"Nobody told me anything," I said roughly. But she'd given up hot whirlpools at the club, and she wasn't drinking alcohol or coffee. Her jeans weren't just fashionably tight; she was putting on weight. Nat believed the lie about those lip-enhancing collagen injections because he met her outside 450 Sutter. But in that expensive medical building, plastic surgeons practice side by side with other kinds of doctors. "It was a guess," I said more gently.

He looked at me, baffled and still furious as I used the barrel of the gun soap to count out the points on my fingertips. "So, let me see if I've got this right. Sabina started a baby. The father either ducked out, or she turned him down — maybe that fellow in the black limousine she was seeing until last month. You've been waiting for your chance with her but when the two of you started to get serious, she told you about the baby. I'd bet money you were clueless enough to suggest an abortion — no wonder she's been so pissed at you. She's Catholic, you idiot."

"I didn't know that!"

"You didn't want to get involved with the mother of some other man's baby because of what people would say about you . . ." I took a deep breath. What an oaf.

He made a quick movement in my direction and I raised the gun soap again. He stood still. He was breathing hard and the boyish charm was hidden underneath his rage. His eyes, the winter-cloud eyes, were like splinters of ice.

"Did you stab him to keep him quiet?" I asked calmly.

"What? What're you talking about?" He seemed genuinely surprised.

"Professor D'Allessio. He knew about the baby — you'd be a laughingstock if everyone knew about it."

He passed shaking fingers over his upper lip. "Don't be ridiculous. All I had to do was break things off with Sabina." He flushed. "I told her everyone would know! I told her I won't have anything to do with someone else's baby." He seemed suddenly to recollect himself and fell silent, breathing hard.

"I won't tell anyone," I said. He looked disbelieving and I shrugged. "You can't help being a jerk."

I caressed the neck of a gallon jug of shampoo and tamped down an almost physical need to hit him with it. Instead, I walked over to open the door, still struggling to be civilized.

"Sabina might still be prepared to take you back; I wouldn't push her too hard though," I said through my teeth. If Sabina had any sense she'd run a mile.

His face suddenly tightened. "I could have you arrested for — for threatening behavior! Sabina said you didn't have the gun anymore!" he said, darting a furious look at the gun soap.

I paused. "How did Sabina know that?"

"She said she took it from your place; God knows why. She says she gave it to someone. Haruto or Nat or someone."

"Which one of them?" I said, and held my breath.

"I don't know. Obviously, she was lying," he sneered. "Your inspector friend will be interested. There's no way you have a license for that thing. You always said you were afraid of guns."

I held it up and snapped the barrel off. Little chips of soap fell on the floor. "I won't tell if you don't," I said. And then, because I couldn't help it, I chuckled at the expression on his face.

He hesitated, clenched his unwrapped hand into a fist at his side, and stalked out. I watched him go. Jackass. But unfortunately I believed him. And I could always check with Sabina about the car door. I bit my lip to stop another smile coming. That had to hurt.

I looked around the store and sighed heavily, amusement gone. All hell was quietly breaking out all around me. Did everyone I knew have secrets? And I'd thought it was just me.

I started lining up stacks of soaps and bottles of lotions on the shelves, giving myself time to think. I ran through the facts I had, but the conclusions I came to were so confusing I couldn't decide for certain what I believed. I thought Derek was telling the truth, as far as it went. So was it possible that the rhino horn wasn't involved in Nicole's death, that there was some other, more personal reason for her to be killed after all? But how did Tim Callahan's death fit into all of this? He'd been the first one killed, practically in the act of breaking into one of the crates, which brought the rhino horn back into focus again. Shit! And why was Professor D'Allessio attacked? Had he seen something dangerous to the killer?

364

And where the hell did Charlie O'Brien fit in?

CHAPTER TWENTY-NINE

I climbed the stairs to my flat and kicked the door behind me savagely. Lucy greeted me, and I scratched her ears. She wandered off, duty done, and I went into the bedroom, forgetting that my mattress was riddled with bullets and my pillows trashed. I sat on the floor with my laptop and thought about friendship and betrayals and the evil consequences of good intentions.

I knew Derek had buried Nicole, and why. I'd also remembered why the gentle sound of Nat's pendant had been bothering me: I had heard it in the garage last night, before Haruto and I had been coshed and tied up. I thought suddenly about Derek and Tim Callahan and Nicole all knowing one another fifteen years ago. They were together in school — but there might be another connection.

I tapped Professor D'Allessio's name into Google and came up with hits about Renaissance drama and a lot of articles in Italian, which, when I put some phrases into the translate program, were even less helpful than the originals.

Nicole's name brought up a photo of her at an art show, which brought tears to my eyes because — well, just because.

Tim Callahan's name produced a small article about the riot at the Adelphi Club and when I dug a little deeper more familiar names popped up. Including the name of the Adelphi Club president who was mishandling the protests and who had fallen from grace with a resounding thud. Omigod. I started to hyperventilate — if I could find connections on the Internet, anyone could! And if they *began* their search with the Adelphi Club, it wouldn't take long for the same familiar names to surface.

Lucy had been pestering me for most of the time I'd been upstairs. She needed dinner and she needed to go outside. When she abandoned me I knew she was minutes away from destroying something as payback for my neglect, so I snapped shut the laptop, called Lucy, and hurriedly opened a tin of her favorite beef and bacon food. I mushed the vile stuff around in her bowl with some dog biscuits and put the dish down, expecting to hear her nails on the floor as she charged down the hall. When I didn't hear her, I called her name again, surprised that I should have to. Perhaps my inner turmoil was affecting her. Maybe she didn't feel much like eating, either.

I returned to the bedroom. "Lucy, where are you? Dinner's on."

But there was no answering patter of footsteps. At least, not in the house. I went back through the kitchen and into the utility room. The door was ajar and I heard her flopping down the stairs. I remembered the backward kick I'd intended should close the door but obviously hadn't. I called her again, but she ignored me. I locked the back door (lesson learned, finally) and started down the stairs.

I followed her into the garden. Nothing was going to happen, I told myself nervously. There were too many lights on — too many people on the other side of their windows and doors. Kurt. Sabina. Helga. Davie. Haruto. And my best friend, Nat.

I'd have to flip the start and end points of my Internet search to be certain; I'd have to double-check, but somehow I knew.

"Lucy!" I hissed. "Lucy! Where are you?"

I searched in a random pattern across the darkened garden, calling her name and checking under her favorite shrubs until I found her. She gave me a welcoming lick in the eye when I snatched her up, and then wriggled in her eloquent way to tell me business had not been taken care of.

"Hurry up," I muttered at her, looking around anxiously. There were moon shadows in the garden and Lucy's white fur was dim in the gloom under an azalea bush. She was a small, humpback oval, like a guinea pig or a molded cream cheese salad. She rustled furtively and I looked away into the darkness to spare her embarrassment, and check once more that we were alone. The garden melted into a series of shapes, each blacker than the last, like hills rolling into the distance. I could see the shape of the toolshed near the vegetable garden. To my left, the frame of the children's swings looked like a gibbet, and the lights in the buildings were like holes in black velvet. I heard the occasional snatch of laughter, saw the shadows as people passed behind their lighted drapes. Lucy's steps crunched lightly on the path. I looked toward the sound and called her name. "Lucy! Stay close!" She looked back at me suspiciously, her cataracts glittering in the moonlight like opals.

I don't know when I realized someone was there, or how long he had been standing in the dark, waiting for me to turn my back.

Suddenly he was there, a few feet from where I had been staring into the shadows. In my highly sensitized emotional state, the silhouette looked terrifying; shapeless and malevolent. I took a step backward. The intense black shadow stepped toward me.

"Who's that?" My voice cracked. Terror and misery closed my throat in a helpless squeak.

The shadow flew at me in a flying tackle like a headlong dive. I turned to run, tripped, and flung myself into someone else. I automatically raised my fist at the second attacker's head and lashed out. The keys arrayed around my knuckles connected, and I heard a heavy grunt. I aimed low with a furious piston-action kick and felt it connect. He bellowed like an animal and leaped at me. I raised jerky arms to ward him off and his partner cannonballed into me from behind, lifting me and flinging me to the side. I fell like a stone and heard something in me crack. For a suspended, fluid moment I thought I was dead — except surely death didn't hurt so much. And then, outlined above me in the moonlight, I saw Nat vault over me.

There was a bewildering, fierce, piglike grunting and the ugly, squelching slaps of bone hitting flesh, and two voices snorting incoherent threats. A voice snarling "Fuck you!" And then the sound of a scream and staggering footsteps and someone crashing heavily through the shrubs. Nat, panting and heaving deep, tattered breaths, was leaning over me. The moonlight glinted on a blade.

"Theo?" Nat said faintly. Still fearful and not quite comprehending what had happened, I struggled to shimmy backward along the ground. The torn sleeve of my sweater hung loose around my elbow. In the light from the moon, blood ran down my bare arm. I looked up at his terrified face, heard the soft, feathery fall of the knife from his hand. I couldn't breathe. Shallow gasps were absurdly painful. Ribs. He'd cracked my ribs when he threw me sideways; knocked me out of harm's way, out of the killer's path.

Familiar voices shouted, "What's going on out there?" "What's happening?" Footsteps pounded toward us. Nat's eyes fluttered, then rolled, and he fell on top of me.

Caught between relief and agony, I almost laughed. He'd seen the blood in the moonlight and fainted. I pushed him aside, took an experimental, painful breath, and rolled him over. He flopped inelegantly, still out cold and damn near breaking my legs with his weight. I checked myself for wounds, but couldn't tell where the blood had come from.

"Theo! Thank God! What the hell's happening?" Haruto's voice was shrill, his face taut with agitation. He knelt down beside me on the grass. "Are you okay?"

"I'm fine," I gasped.

"Hey! Somebody — a little help!" Astoundingly, Ben's voice came from the lower reaches of the garden. I now realized I'd been hearing disjointed swearing and more slaps and squelchy thumps.

Haruto leaped to his feet. He shouted something and disappeared. I sighed, winced painfully, and gave Nat a nudge.

"C'mon, Nat. Rise and shine." But he made no sound and didn't move. I looked at his face again, and leaned over him in alarm. He looked like a ghost.

"Nat!" Every move I made was excruciating, but I tried to shake him anyway. In my own body the action set off a series of inner crackings and grindings and agonizing catches of breath, but it didn't rouse him. I dragged my legs painfully out from underneath him and lifted his head into the crook of my arm.

"Nat, can you hear me?"

His eyes fluttered slightly and a faint smile

came to his lips.

"What's wrong? Are you hurt?" He'd seemed okay; winded, I thought. And he always fainted when he saw blood. It had been that, at the last, which persuaded me of his innocence.

Nicole's killer had no fear of blood.

He half opened his eyes. He looked almost sleepy. I saw his eyes shift, and he made a weak, uncoordinated gesture with one hand. I followed it and unzipped his black Windbreaker. It was warm and damp. My head swam as I pulled the jacket aside. There was barely enough light for me to see the big seeping dark patch nearly covering the front of his yellow cashmere sweater. The sweater I liked. The one that made him look so handsome. Dear God.

I looked up frantically and shouted at random. "Somebody! Somebody call 911!"

"They're already on their way," Sabina's voice said from somewhere in the gloom. And suddenly, the electric lights in the trees sprang on looking horribly festive and giving me enough light to see everyone, looking like a chorus in a semicircle around the pietà at center stage.

"Call them again! For God's sake, he's dying!" My voice cracked. She came over cautiously, took one look, and her eyes met mine in horror.

"I'll call again. Put pressure on the wound." She wriggled out of her own jacket, bundled it into a makeshift pad, and pressed it more or less in the middle of the seeping, expanding red stain. "I'll tell them to hurry." She got off her knees and turned away with her phone already at her ear.

"It's okay, Nat. It'll be okay," I whispered. He smiled at me faintly and said something I couldn't hear. I bent my head lower.

"Love you," he said faintly.

"I love you, too. Don't die, Nat, please don't die."

"No." He looked thoughtful, as if he was deciding whether further speech was worth the effort. "Nicole and Derek . . . partners. Yes?" He paused for my nod of understanding. "Rhino horn . . . for medicine . . . help people . . . make a fortune. I didn't know."

"I understand. Don't talk, okay?"

His eyes slowly closed and he was quiet for more than half a minute. I looked around anxiously, and was startled to see Helga, drooping and apparently unconscious, being held up between Ben and Haruto. I started to ask them what the hell had happened to her, but I turned back when Nat groaned softly. He licked his lips. "Thirsty," he said.

My eyes filled with tears. "Don't talk, Nat. Don't say any more."

He moved his head from side to side and his unfocussed eyes wandered, perhaps searching for something. "Sabina stole your gun . . . I took it from her." Another long pause. "When it disappeared . . . I thought it was Derek. He thought I . . . killed Nicole in a jealous fit." He made a wheezy laugh, which turned into a painful cough and he was silent for a moment.

"Derek said maybe drug dealers killed Nicole. Told me about the horn . . . Not illegal he said . . . p-politically incorrect . . . I helped him move it." He closed his eyes again and lay quiet.

"I heard you," I said brokenly. I couldn't finish. Couldn't tell him I'd heard the faint musical tinkle of his pendant in my garage, just before he — or someone — knocked me unconscious.

I heard a siren coming closer, and red flashing lights bounced off the shapes in the garden. Nat opened his eyes again. "It sucks," he said clearly. He closed his eyes. I angrily shook him. His head jerked flaccidly. I called his name. "Nat! Nat! Don't go!"

Hurried footsteps, and then a stranger's hand reached for the pulse point in his neck and rested listening fingers there for the space of a few long seconds. Someone unlocked my rigid arm from around his head. Derek came running out of the darkness, shoved aside someone who grabbed at his arm, and skidded to his knees at Nat's side.

I was helped to a bench and I sat numbly and tried to breathe while competent hands felt me all over impersonally, pressed a couple of ribs, which yielded in a curiously inappropriate way, and fixed an oxygen mask around my face. I was aware of a jumble of voices explaining the general carnage to a mixed crowd of police and firefighters and paramedics. More police were on their way. Inspector Lichlyter. And the coroner. I looked over to where Nat lay with his face half in shadow and his eyes closed. He was so handsome. And I loved him.

I heard a snarl and looked toward the sound. Helga was now tied at the wrists and ankles with straps of some kind. Belts, I thought wisely, and felt dissociated from everything. She was still groggy, fighting against the restraints, glaring around her with hatred. She shouted at me, her mouth uncontrolled, lips flecked with saliva. "I hate you!" I shrank from her frenzy and the lack of reason in her eyes.

I sought out the comfort of familiar faces in the crowd. Staring with open mouths at Helga. At me. I could see the questions, the accusations, forming in their eyes. Ben stood off to one side. He didn't look as if he had any questions at all.

"Not Nat, not Derek," I said brokenly.

He shook his head.

Not Nat, I thought with relief. Before I came down to the garden I'd almost worked everything out. Derek was the man Professor D'Allessio meant he'd seen at the compost pile the night Nicole was buried; it was Derek he had telephoned to demand an explanation. It was Derek who had taken the offensive and shouted at Ben when he, too, stumbled across his desperate attempt to hide Nicole's body. Because, love apparently being stupid *and* blind, he thought Nat had killed Nicole. And Nat thought Derek had shot at me with my gun. Their attempts to protect each other had caused most of the subsequent confusion.

But my on-line search had finally given me the key. It was Helga who had pushed Tim Callahan from a window; cut Nicole's throat with the lost machete; who had stabbed Professor D'Allessio; and tried to kill me.

A sob forced its way out of my throat. I

had been afraid, so afraid it was Nat. Helga's guilt came as a terrible relief, mixed with a sort of stunned incredulity that so many of us were apparently the objects of her hatred. What the hell had I ever done?

Inspector Lichlyter's red jacket appeared in front of me. I heard her say: "How is she?"

I didn't look up.

She crouched in front of me. "Okay?" she said gently. My eyes filled involuntarily with tears. I nodded. She stood up and squeezed my shoulder then dug around in her shoulder bag and closed my fingers around a lace-trimmed handkerchief. Time passed. I heard Sabina telling how she had heard me scream and come running out. I didn't remember screaming. And Ben was explaining to someone that he was too far away to stop the attack. He had heard it, and tackled Helga as she ran away.

"And I helped him," Haruto said, "and we managed to knock her out — my God, she fought like a tiger — and, well, I guess that's it."

"You'll feel better out of that crowd," one of the paramedics said as he helped me over to a pull-down seat at the back of the fire truck that had arrived, somehow, without me noticing. The paramedic had bright blue eyes. I concentrated on breathing, and the oxygen did help. But it didn't help everything. I couldn't help crying for the man I had been afraid would be my murderer. My best friend. My rescuer. And then I noticed paramedics still working urgently over Nat. Very urgently. They wouldn't do that if he was dead — I stood up and saw them shift him onto a stretcher and put him in the back of the ambulance.

Okay then.

CHAPTER THIRTY

I spent two weeks at Grandfather's home on a secretive lane on Telegraph Hill. I slept for most of three days under the influence of serious painkillers. Late one night I opened my eyes groggily and thought I saw Ben sitting in a pool of light on the other side of the room. He put a book down and came round the bed, and I fell asleep again, dreaming I felt his hand on my face.

As soon as I was able, I telephoned Haruto and Davie to let them know I was again among the living. I asked Haruto to reopen Aromas. He laughed and told me he couldn't wait to get back to work; he didn't even mention his Japanese gardens. I asked him why he and Nicole had been at each other's throats.

"She owed me money, Theo."

"I'm sorry," I said helplessly. "When I've had the accounts audited, I'll try to pay you back."

"Thanks," he said gruffly. "It can wait."

Davie asked me when I was coming back. A week or two, I told him.

"Don't worry about the butterflies," he said, as if I'd asked. "Your grandad came over with the keys and gave them to Ben and he lets me in to feed them."

"Good," I said faintly. "Is — er — everyone else okay?"

"Oh, sure. Everyone's fine. Sabina and Kurt are having a baby and getting married next month, I think. Professor D'Allessio is going to a nursing home for a while, but he's gonna be okay. Nat's still in the hospital. Ben's fine. I'm helping out at the shelter."

"Good," I repeated feebly. "Take care of yourself and I'll see you in a few days, okay?"

"Okay. Bye," he said cheerfully.

Inspector Lichlyter visited one morning. She sat in an armchair at the side of my bed and didn't take off the red jacket. My grandfather's housekeeper brought her a cup of tea. She drank it thirstily. I said I couldn't talk much because I was having difficulty breathing.

"Ribs are like that," she said, as if she knew from personal experience. "Your official statement can wait a few days. Helga

Lindstrom's made a full confession."

"It was somehow connected to her history with the Adelphi Club," I said simply. "I've had plenty of time to think," I added at her startled expression.

She nodded. "It goes back a long time. Tim Callahan, Nicole Bartholomew, and Damiano D'Allessio were all involved in a student demonstration fifteen years ago. A busload of students and professors drove over to the Adelphi Club golf course and held a sort of sit-in — a throwback to the sixties — to demand that the club open their membership to people of color. The club had fended off legal challenges to its policies for years and wasn't about to bend to a crowd of riffraff. The president of the board mishandled it. There was destruction to some of the club's property, the police were called, and it made a huge splash in the local news. The news coverage went on for weeks and shone a spotlight on the club's policies and its members —"

"I Googled the riot —"

She gave me a repressive look. "It gets better. Several members were asked to resign in the wake of the mess, including the board president, who also lost his hedge fund investors because of the publicity and declared bankruptcy within a year. His business was skating on pretty thin ice anyway, but as long as no one looked too closely or stopped the merry-go-round, he hoped to come out of it okay. When the publicity put him under a spotlight, he and his family went from a highly leveraged mansion in Pacific Heights to near-homeless paupers almost overnight. Their kids — a son and a daughter — went from ski weekends in Tahoe with a personal chef to lunches at McDonald's. The parents divorced. They all struggled from then on. The boy turned to drugs eventually and died on the streets. It's an ugly story."

"The club president was Helga's father."

"Mmmm. He died a couple of weeks ago in an SRO a few blocks from Fabian Gardens and Helga snapped. She knew Nicole had been involved in the demonstration, but she found out she wasn't the only one — the Internet search is still on her home computer. The combination of her old enemies being here, and hearing the story of her father's ruin over and over as a sort of cocktail party joke, apparently tipped her over the edge."

"But why me? Why did she hate me?"

"She's in love with Kurt Talbot. You and he had been lovers; it was enough. She'd already made an attempt on Sabina

D'Allessio and planned to try again."

"How? When?" I said stupidly.

"She said something about a skateboard. She tore it off some kind of artwork in her coffee shop — that doesn't sound right," she said, referring to her notes with a frown.

"I know what she meant," I said. "There are some big art pieces in the coffee shop with skateboards on them."

"Huh." Lichlyter looked genuinely non-plussed. "That's what she said. Apparently she put the thing on Sabina's stairway. That was her first attempt to right the wrongs she felt she'd been dealt and she was determined to rid herself of everyone who ever hurt her. She was actually very careless — she didn't care if she was caught. She pushed the painter, Tim Callahan, out of the window after following him into the building early one morning. It was sheer good fortune the building was empty and no one saw her enter or leave. She interrupted Callahan breaking into one of the crates of rhino horn, but that had nothing to do with his death." She frowned again. "I was too close to that to see things clearly.

"Nicole Bartholomew was in partnership with Derek Linton over the rhino horn shipments," she went on. "She went to see him and they went out into the garden when his lover was absent for an hour on Friday night. They argued, and he left her there. Ms. Lindstrom was in the garden. She took advantage of the proximity of the toolshed with the machete and the sudden appearance of her old enemy and slit Nicole's throat."

I took a painful breath and spoke rapidly before I had to take another. "Nat came to see me that night, after Charlie O'Brien broke into my flat," I managed to explain. I could still see him dabbing at his sweater with a sponge and laughing; could still feel the comfort his visit had given me. Hateful to think that Nicole was dying then.

"She stabbed Professor D'Allessio with that meat skewer when they met in the garden to discuss planting a memorial tree in her father's memory. Apparently the skewer belonged to Nat and Derek — it sounds as if it had been left behind after some sort of neighborhood picnic." I thought of the stainless steel skewers Nat had been fooling with and the lamb brochette recipe from *Gourmet* magazine and felt slightly sick.

"She seems to have had nothing but luck on her side; she wasn't trying to hide anything. She said she didn't bury Nicole — I'm not sure what to make of that." She scowled at me and I returned the look blandly. A promise is a promise. She went on: "Professor D'Allessio was able to identify Helga as his assailant when he regained consciousness yesterday. She's totally collapsed —" She sounded pleased, and I couldn't blame her exactly. It wasn't her fault that her triumph was my life in pieces.

"We're still trying to put all this together, but apparently Helga stole your gun from Nat the same night she tried to kill you. You and Sabina weren't the last of those she saw as her enemies —"

"I wasn't her enemy! I tried to help her when her father died!"

She shook her head. "She knew about your history with our doctor friend; she saw the two of you together that evening in your store and it tripped her trigger. Don't try to make sense of it. The short form is: you had to be disposed of, too. She apparently saw the gun in Nat's bedroom through the open door. She walked in and took it, with no particular victim in mind; she just thought it would be useful. As I said, luck was definitely on her side."

"My God," I said blankly.

"Derek Linton will find himself in court potentially for bribing customs officials, and if you want to press charges they'll both find themselves up for battery for the episode in your garage. He's also on the hook for knocking our officer unconscious and stealing her handcuffs. But his attorney is already insisting that Nicole handled the smuggling. To hear him tell it, Derek was an innocent trying to make a more-or-less honest buck." She puffed out a breath. "A two-year-long investigation up in smoke."

"What about Charlie O'Brien?" I asked after a couple of minutes, because she hadn't mentioned him.

"Oh, he's helping us quite a bit," she said dryly. I assumed she meant that he had at last been apprehended. I felt tired suddenly. As long as he was finally in jail, Charlie O'Brien could wait.

Two afternoons later I lay on a sofa with Lucy at my feet, overlooking a view so green and leafy I could imagine myself in the English countryside except for the looming presence of Coit Tower above the trees. Lucy growled happily in her sleep and rolled over, totally at ease with the new regime. Burnished mahogany and polished silver twinkled inside the room. There was a silver tea service — with the Crown Derby cups — on a low table next to my sofa. My grandfather's cook-housekeeper had made a Victoria sponge cake and provided delicate edibles of the invalid-tempting variety. I felt like Elizabeth Barrett Browning. I also felt distinctly better, even if breathing was still a problem. I had, Grandfather informed me, broken two ribs, cracked another, and torn several muscles that were critical to the breathing process.

"I never trusted them," Grandfather said. We were discussing Derek and Nat. It still clutched at my heart to think of Nat.

"Because they were gay," I said resignedly.

He pursed his lips and shook his head as he poured tea and handed me a cup. "Plenty of homosexuals in the military, m'dear. Good soldiers, most of 'em." I spluttered in my tea, and he wordlessly handed me a linen napkin before continuing. "No, I didn't trust those two. Saw you were fond of 'em, so kept my own counsel, but never felt quite comfortable. Weak, that Nat. Weak. A follower if ever I saw one. But I know I owe him a debt too large to pay," he added in a different tone, and patted my hand. "And the jeweler chap," he went on. "An ambitious type. Willing to do anything, I thought. I was right, too. How're you feeling now? Any better?"

"Hungry," I admitted.

"Here. Have one of these." He efficiently shoveled two or three miniature pastries onto a plate for me. "Didn't think you'd want anything heavy, but had Mrs. Warner make plenty of these little things."

The little things — whatever they were — were delicious. I ate five.

Lucid thought continued to elude me much of the time; several friends telephoned, but I didn't want to speak to them. Grandfather took messages and told them I'd be home soon. Ben didn't call.

"This looks like the view outside your house in Kent," I said on another morning when I'd woken from a nap. I couldn't seem to stay awake for long.

"I thought so, too. Always liked that house. Sorry to leave it," he said. "Leased it to an M.P."

"Why did you leave?" I'd often wondered, and never felt comfortable asking, why he'd moved lock, stock, and barrel from his comfortable *Town and Country* kind of life to the slightly bizarre and unfamiliar social milieu of San Francisco.

"Moved here to help you after that goon attacked you, Theophania. Wanted to be near you anyway, my only decent relation. But when I got here, I could see you'd frozen solid, so thought I'd hang around and help you if I could. Couldn't much, not enough practice. Meant well though."

"You moved all this way to —" I gulped. My emotions were pretty close to the surface and I cleared my throat before a tear could fall on my cheek and horrify him. "You did help me," I said. "I just didn't realize it."

He cleared his throat in turn, and avoided my eye by looking around his living room. "I, er, thought of giving you some furniture, Theophania. Didn't want to send it over without warning, might not be welcome. How does the rug look? Thought it would be right for that big front room of yours."

Poignantly, he seemed to want reassurance. "It looks beautiful."

He nodded, apparently satisfied. "Know you don't especially like fine antiques" — he snorted — "but I have some nice late-eighteenth-century pine in storage. A couple of the chests of drawers might do you for the bedroom."

I knew the pieces he meant. They were perfect. I swallowed the lump in my throat. He went on without giving me a chance to thank him: "And I have some more Oriental rugs; don't know if you want them. Do you like patchwork quilts?"

I nodded.

"There's a couple your grandmother always thought she'd give to you one day.

Didn't know if you . . . being a modern-ist . . . and . . . well, about thirty yards of old lace. Thought of having curtains made but never got around to it. Don't care for lace m'self." I smothered a smile.

"It's too good for curtains," I said, in a sort of wonder at the conversation and remembering the lace he meant. "Plain muslin curtains would be lovely with the pine."

"Muslin!" he snorted. "Ah-hem, perhaps you're right." I looked down at the floral linen of the sofa to hide another smile.

I could have a platform bed made, I thought, and use the patchwork quilt on it. It was unaccountable and strange to think of feathering my nest in the midst of chaos; stranger still to be feeling secure about it, even though the branches holding it had felt a little shaky lately.

"Nicole's sister said I could have anything I wanted from her apartment," I said. "There's a gold-leaf coffee table —" He snorted again, too loudly to be ignored. "It will look perfect in that living room when the sun shines," I protested.

He laughed, short barks of laughter, like a seal, and I joined him, although the pain in my chest cut me off in mid-chuckle.

After two weeks' absence, I limped up my

front steps on Grandfather's arm, and followed Lucy through my front door with a feeling of coming home and no feeling at all of apprehension or fear. I had glanced into Aromas on the way past, and everything looked the way it should on a Wednesday evening, except that a small pink-shaded lamp was burning in the window. As I peered in, two passersby stopped to look. Bravo to someone for thinking of the light, I thought.

Business was good, according to Haruto's daily telephone reports. Probably boosted by curiosity seekers, he'd said disapprovingly. I told him to take advantage of it while it lasted; we needed the money. It wasn't true of course; I didn't need the money. Or the store for that matter. Perhaps Haruto would like to take it on as part-owner. First, I'd have to tell him about my past. I was sick of secrets.

I went to the bedroom to leave my jacket and Grandfather followed with my small suitcase. Lucy's nails didn't click on the floor because there was an Oriental runner in the hallway glowing with dark reds and gold. She ran ahead of me into the bedroom and I heard her jump onto the bed. I stopped in the doorway and looked in at a room vastly changed from the bare place it had been. The pine chests of drawers were against one wall; a patchwork quilt was folded at the foot of a new bed. I had new feather pillows. There was a large vase of red tulips on one of the chests.

"It's beautiful," I said, almost overwhelmed, and kissed his cheek.

"I, er, had help," he said. I watched him secretly as I put my jacket away. His long nose quivered with amusement and he looked pleased with the success of his surprise. He was dressed in what he would no doubt consider casual clothes, which included the navy blue cashmere blazer and a regimental silk tie. His face looked less forbidding, as if he had given himself permission to relax. Or perhaps, I thought with unexpected insight, I had.

He made his way to the front of the flat saying something about tea and left me alone. I glanced down at the garden. The police barrier tapes had been removed; the broken roses had been pruned and repaired, with freshly turned soil heaped around their roots; a young woman was pushing a child on a swing. Professor D'Allessio crossed the garden at a slow walk using his hoe as a cane and as I watched, swiped at a weed daring to sprout in his path. He looked up, saw me, and raised the hoe in salute. I smiled and waved. There had been a lot of healing done while I was away, I reflected.

A white phalaenopsis orchid sat on the bathroom counter in a basket of moss. I ran a comb through my hair at the mirror. It was longer, and showing a tendency to break into waves at the sides. My face was thinner and there were shadows under my eyes. My ribs still hurt, but I wasn't convinced that the pain was making me so pale. I wished Ben had tried to contact me. Not that I would have talked to him anyway, I reminded myself. I could still almost taste my disillusionment. It was not sweet. And I still had no idea what was on that damn computer disk.

I pinched my cheeks to give them some color. "Did Davie help with the furniture?" I said to Grandfather as I passed the kitchen.

"And me," Ben said, unfolding himself from his perch on a pine trunk in the living room.

I stopped dead and caught my breath. My confusion was magnified by his dark striped suit, white shirt, and dark tie. For a moment, he was an intricate piece of parquetry — the theft of the computer disk notched into his inexplicable reappearance the night he helped apprehend Helga, which fitted into a clear vision of him naked in my living room. And which was he? A social worker in black leather? Or a lawyer in pinstripes? The scar over his eyebrow still produced a permanent frown. He moved his head and a flash of light glinted in his ear from the pirate earring.

"I don't believe you two were ever formally introduced," he said. His expression was guarded as he turned to someone in the shadows at the far end of the room. "Charlie, this is Ms. Theophania Bogart. Theo, meet Charlie O'Brien."

And sure enough, there, absurdly, was Charlie O'Brien: mild-mannered accountant; the man on the washing machine; Nicole's uncle and partner in crime. He shyly bobbed his head. I stared at him wordlessly, too staggered to do anything else.

CHAPTER THIRTY-ONE

Charlie O'Brien wiped his hands on the knees of his slacks and said nervously: "I guess I'd better fill you in."

"I don't think so!" I said angrily. "What the hell are you even doing here?"

He looked over at Ben, who simply said to me, "Trust me. Listen for a few minutes."

"Trust you!" I said incredulously, and then threw up my hands. "Fine! Why the hell not?"

Grandfather came to roost on the hearth; Ben was on the pine trunk, his hands linked around one knee; Charlie O'Brien was cross-legged on the carpet; Lucy lay on her back next to him wearing a blissful expression as he rhythmically rubbed her tummy. I sat on one of the folding chairs brought in from the dining room. Like story time in the seraglio, I thought.

"Go on, Charlie," Ben said.

The gentle tone of his voice was a minor

shock. How the hell had they gotten so chummy?

Charlie nodded and then looked at Grandfather and me. "Me and Nicole and Derek and Tim Callahan knew each other from years ago. I never liked Derek much but Nicole thought he was okay. He was always into this Oriental medicine and cures for this and that, and he and Nicole got to talking about how much it all cost and anyway, he somehow arranged to get the stuff smuggled out of Africa and in through Hong Kong and then to San Francisco.

"Nicole picked the stuff up from customs, stored it, and delivered it to the local buyers. She even shipped it on from here to buyers in New York. Everyone was used to seeing her with shipping packages and cartons from your store so it was good camouflage."

Which explained why Nicole had been so protective about filling out the orders for Aromas and overseeing the inventory, I thought.

"Anyway, this was their second shipment, I guess —" Charlie's eyes flickered. "— and Nicole decided she wanted a bigger share. She put everything on a computer disk — the African brokers; customs guys who could be relied on to turn a blind eye for a price; the customers' names. Everything. She asked me to take care of the disk for her. I was sort of her insurance policy. She was gonna tell Derek about the disk, but she never got to it. I tried to tell her an insurance policy's no good unless he knew, but she kept saying she wasn't ready to tell him yet; she'd tell him if he got ugly." He sighed. "Anyway, she'd been slipping me a few bucks to do your books —"

"My books?" I said, and then remembered seeing Aromas on the list of references he had given me.

He frowned at the interruption. "Yeah. Like I said, we go way back and I'd been helping her and we'd got to talking, so I knew something about what was on the disk. Jesus." He ran a hand across his mouth. "I talked to a friend of mine who sells these Chinese herbs, see? And he told me how much this stuff was worth and I got scared. I could see all the workmen around this place here, so I came over and hid the disk in the chimney 'til I could figure out something more permanent. I didn't know it was your place; Nicole never said."

"How did you get in?"

"It wasn't hard. Came over the roofs from Nicole's building. The construction guys thought I was an inspector or something; nobody ever asks on a job site. They all figure someone else knows who you are. Anyway, the day Nicole told me she was giving Derek an ultimatum, I had to get it back for her but I never saw her again. Honest to God, I thought Derek had killed her. I didn't know what the hell to do."

We sat in silence while I, at least, absorbed the new elements of his story.

"There's something Theophania would like to know, Ben," Grandfather said suddenly. "How did you know about the shamrock lapel pin?"

Ben turned to answer him. He didn't look at me. "Charlie told me Derek came to him that night and asked him for a favor. He, Derek, and Nat took the crates from your garage. Charlie wasn't too happy, the chump —"

"Jesus, they said it wasn't illegal to have the stuff," Charlie erupted.

"Which is true enough," Ben conceded.

"And I was afraid to refuse — what reason could I give? I felt as if my balls were in a vise. Jesus. I thought Derek had killed Nicole and I was terrified. He kept saying Nicole owed money for drugs and dealers probably killed her. He said if the cops found the crates of stuff they'd want to know where it came from and it would put him in a spot and would I help him out? I pretended to believe him; I was afraid not to do what he said. He says you're passed out drunk at his place, so we've got a clear field. Of course then you and that other guy show up and he takes care of you both. Anyway, the next day I notice the damn shamrock's disappeared and I figure with my luck it's in your garage. So I told him." He jerked his head at Ben.

"If ever a guy wasn't cut out for a life of crime . . ." Ben shook his head in mingled affection and exasperation, both of which emotions were completely bewildering. For the first time I felt a twinge of doubt, but my defenses almost instantly sprang back intact. I couldn't and wouldn't believe in him again.

Ben took up the tale, his voice uninflected. "I was walking through the garden from the shelter after midnight the night Derek buried your partner. When I came past he was scraping the spilled compost back into shape and laced into me for disturbing it. You assumed it was Haruto and it was too dark for me to be sure. I might have recognized Derek if I met him in daylight, but it didn't happen."

"I wish I had realized," I said to Grandfather. "I feel responsible. It's all so stupid. Professor D'Allessio was muttering about where 'the earring one' was, that 'the earring one' had been messing with the compost pile. When Nat showed me the new earrings Derek had made it made me think. They had an important anniversary coming up, and jewelry would be the kind of gift the professor would think of. And I realized Derek was keeping out of Ben's way; he was never around where Ben was likely to be.

"I was completely confused. So much of the evidence pointed to Derek, or he and Nat together, and there was Kurt with his bandaged hand — I didn't, honestly, think of Helga at all until it was almost too late. She always wore heatproof gloves so even if I'd seen her I wouldn't have noticed anything unusual. I even saw her as a potential victim.

"What happened to the rhinoceros horn?" I asked Charlie.

"Nat and Derek drove it to a storage place in Daly City. I guess that's when Helga took that shot at you. I didn't know about that."

"Trying to fit you" — I nodded at him — "into things wasn't easy. I never got past figuring out that your nickname was Cob."

Ben said: "Um — about that —"

Charlie looked slightly puzzled. "I don't

have a nickname."

I looked from one to the other. "But Sabina said Nicole's uncle's nickname reminded her of horses. And you're —"

Charlie's blank expression told me this was all news to him.

"You're not Nicole's uncle," I said weakly.

"No," he said indignantly. "I'm her ex-husband. We've been divorced for fifteen years, but we always kept in touch, you know? Her uncle lives down the peninsula in Redwood City."

"What's his name?" I had to know.

"Haywood."

I buried my head in my hands. "Is his nickname Hay?"

"You know him?"

I shook my head helplessly. Grandfather's lips twitched. "I'll get tea," he said.

I heard smothered, seal-like barks of laughter coming from the kitchen.

"How do you two know each other?" I asked Charlie when the silence in the room got too much to bear. Ben got up and stood at the window with his back to us. Charlie O'Brien looked at Ben's back with a sort of pride. "He's like the kid brother I never had, you know?" he said. "His parents died and mine sort of took him on. And later he wanted to go to law school and, well . . ."

"Charlie put me through school by giving up his own plans to be a CPA," Ben said from the window.

"It wasn't like that," Charlie said seriously. "I mean, Ben here is smart and I figured he'd do better."

"Charlie called me and said he needed my help. He said something about Nicole, but he was so damn vague, I didn't know how serious it was. I come out every couple of months for a few days, but this time I was planning a longer visit to get the group home set up. Nicole arranged for me to rent your studio and he told me that would be time enough but —" Ben shook his head impatiently. "I was playing catch-up from the minute I arrived. I'd never met Nicole but of course I recognized the name. When Lichlyter caught up with me, Charlie had just told me he'd been in on moving the rhino horn, and I denied everything, hoping it could be sorted out later. I'd driven him up to Mendocino, where some friends of mine have a house, and hidden him away up there. I figured if no one knew where he was, he couldn't come to any harm." He ran a harried hand through his hair. "When you and I found that damn disk the next day, all I could think of was grabbing it in case it implicated Charlie. It was a locked file with a secret password and I couldn't reach him by phone so I went back for Charlie, found a computer to read the disk, realized it was dynamite, and came rushing home right away to protect you, if I could. I was almost too late — again."

The front doorbell rang and when I answered it there was a uniformed police officer with a patrol car to take Charlie O'Brien downtown. Not, it appeared, as a suspect, but as a valued, cooperative informant.

"Stop looking so worried," Ben was telling Charlie dryly when I went back upstairs. "You haven't broken any laws — not serious ones, anyway. They want you to verify again what you know about the information on that disk and that it's the one Nicole gave you. I told you I'd come with."

But Charlie shook his head. "I'll call you later, okay?" He hesitated and turned to me. "He says you've got her locket. Can I have it? I don't have anything of hers."

I felt sorry for him. I could understand Ben's exasperation, but he was difficult to dislike. "The police have it for now. You dropped it here?" He nodded. "How did you happen to have it?"

"She told me she was giving up the junk. She laughed. Said I could have it as a souvenir, you know?" He sniffed and rubbed his nose vigorously.

"Her sister asked me to dispose of her things; if you'd like anything else —"

His eyes lit up. "Yeah. Okay. I'll call you, okay?" He held out his hand and after a hesitation I shook it.

Before he and his escort had cleared the end of the steps, I heard footsteps on the back stairs that could only belong to Davie.

"Hi, Mr. Pryce-Fitton," I heard him say. "Ben here? I was gonna ask if he'd let me in to feed the butterflies."

Ben handed me a key ring. "These are yours; I meant to return them."

"Why don't I let the boy into the shop?" Grandfather said, appearing suddenly and taking the keys before my fingers had time to close around them. "And then I think I'll be going, Theophania." He bent down for me to kiss his cheek. "I'll — er — telephone tomorrow, eh?"

Davie shambled over to me. "Hi, Theo," he said casually. "Do your ribs still hurt?"

I nodded. "Okay," he said, and gave me a tentative hug. I threw both arms around him and squeezed him tight, and then grunted as he responded enthusiastically, lifting me until my toes dangled off the floor.

"I've got a new design — look." He put me down and turned around to show me that the lightning bolt had been replaced with two interlocking triangles shaved into his short hair. He was wearing a gold stud in his nose instead of the amethyst. "Ben gave it to me," he said, seeing the direction of my glance. "He had two like it," he explained kindly.

"Nice," I said.

He nodded. "Yup. Are you coming in to the store tomorrow? Some little travel bag things arrived today. Haruto says they're pretty good quality for the price and maybe we can get more than the usual markup."

"That sounds good. Um — I guess I'll be in tomorrow all right. Do we still open at ten?"

He laughed his asthmatic's laugh. "Heh-heh-heh. Yeah. See you tomorrow."

He and Grandfather left together. I could hear Grandfather asking him about the butterflies as their voices receded down the stairs.

Ben and I faced each other across several feet of Oriental rug. It felt as wide as the Pacific.

Ben said: "I had to protect Charlie and I was afraid you'd have the law on him if you knew where he was."

"I tried, believe me. He scared the wits out of me."

"Ever since I first saw you in that bar on the corner . . ." He frowned.

I took a deep, painful breath. "You knew Charlie wasn't the killer. Why didn't you suspect me?"

"I knew it wasn't you," he said simply.

That kind of faith was worth almost anything. I still hesitated, and then I almost heard Grandfather's voice: "It might be a risk, Theophania, but impulsive doesn't necessarily mean imprudent."

I would have to tell Ben the truth. Tell him my real name, my family's history, the reason I was in San Francisco. I wasn't sure if I was ready to give up all my secrets. But a first step would be crossing the carpet. I watched his face as I took one step, then another, and then a third. I stood in front of him and waited, my heart hammering in my chest. I'd gone as far as I could. The next step was up to him.

ABOUT THE AUTHOR

Susan Cox is a former journalist. She has also been marketing and public relations director for a safari park, a fundraiser for non-profit organizations, and the president of the Palm Beach County (Fla.) Attractions Association. She considers herself transcontinental and transatlantic, equally at home in San Francisco and Florida and with a large and boisterous extended family in England. She frequently wears a Starfleet communicator pin, just in case. Her first novel, *The Man on the Washing Machine,* won the 2014 Minotaur Books/Mystery Writers of America First Crime Novel Competition.